OBSESSED

SERENA AKEROYD

Photographer: Michelle Lancaster

Instagram: @lanefotograf

Website: www.michellelancaster.com

TRIGGER WARNINGS

OBSESSED DEALS with some tough subjects. <3
> Stalking
> Dub con
> Infant death by SIDS
> Death of a parental figure
> Alcohol abuse
> Child neglect

NICHOLAS

The beat on the dance floor was sultry, and though it was warm out, inside, the air conditioning kept things at a delicious temperature that made it comfortable for me to sit here and watch.

My seat was on the cusp of the mezzanine that overlooked the rest of the club. In the VIP area, I could see everything up here. Everything—

"Would you like to dance?"

I scowled at the intrusion. "No." When the woman pouted, her over made-up eyes flaring wide in surprise that anyone would refuse her, I lied, "Thank you, but no. I'm waiting for someone."

She huffed and tossed her wavy black hair over her shoulder, but the lie seemed to work, and she flounced off with enough drama that I actually watched her go.

Not that I was interested in her.

I wasn't.

Sure, she may have had an ass I could bounce quarters on, and her tits were round and pert in the bustier-style top that narrowed into a sleek tube skirt, but she might as well have been a man to me, that was how little attention she merited.

I had eyes for one woman and one woman alone, and she worked the bar. When I sat here, she was whom I watched. She was more entertaining than a stripper, even if she didn't mean to be.

In her work uniform of a denim skirt, sneakers, and a simple tee, she outclassed every other woman in this place.

Phoebe Whitehouse made the one who'd just tried to dance with me look cheap, even though she'd been wearing designer gear and had two matching rocks in her ears I recognized as diamonds.

The trouble was, I knew it wasn't just me.

Phoebe lit up the room, illuminated it in ways that made the shadows recede. But I wasn't the only one affected. She had men swarming around her, men who wanted to hurt her. Some might say I wanted to hurt her too. Some might say that I meant her harm, but I didn't.

If anything, she meant *me* harm.

She tormented me with her beauty, reminded me of everything I couldn't have anymore. She tortured me with her friendly smiles, and made me miserable when I thought about how similar she was to another woman who'd made me suffer along the way.

Still, she needed protection.

There were too many eyes on her at all times, and the only way I could rest was if I knew she wasn't in danger, and in this city, danger was always around the corner.

Here, she was relatively safe. I didn't like the number of gazes trained on her, but I felt like I could protect her from my booth.

This was my spot.

I'd paid for it a long time ago when I'd put up the money for the club, and though he rolled his eyes at my dictates, Jay, my cousin, usually let me get away with murder because this sick club was only *sick* because of me. Without my funding, he'd never have gotten it off the ground, and I wasn't averse to taking advantage of that fact.

Not where she was concerned.

In class, I'd heard her on the phone one day. She'd been upset as I walked in, and because my radar always flickered to life around her, I heard her over all the other idiots in my classroom. They were talking about parties and who was fucking whom. Phoebe? She was worrying about making rent, about paying her bills.

She'd needed a job.

So, I'd gotten her this one at *Crow*.

Of course, she didn't know. She never would either. I didn't intend on ever revealing what she was to me, but some nights, like tonight, when I saw the way men hung on her every word, when she looked tired from a full day's work, I wished I had the right to make her life better.

I didn't.

Even though she was my everything.

But to her, I was and always would be nothing.

Someone in the shadows her light couldn't touch. Someone too dark, too hideous to ever be loved by someone like her.

It hurt, sure, being so close to heaven. It was like hovering my hand over a naked flame on a candle and expecting it not to burn, but I'd deal with it, would endure it, because she needed me.

She didn't know she did, of course. But everyone needed a savior. Even if that savior was a monster.

Sometimes, monsters could be heroes too.

I ran my thumb along my bottom lip when she reached up on her tiptoes to grab some of the expensive liquor from the top shelf. Her skirt rode up, revealing strong, sleek legs, and her breasts jiggled as she moved—I wasn't the only one to notice.

Running a hand through my hair to still my agitation, fighting the desire to touch and not just look, instead, I stared down at my phone and the notes I'd been making for tomorrow's class.

She'd be in it, and I always made sure that she knew she had my attention. It was the only time I could ever truly look at her without reprimand, and I took full advantage of it.

Maybe I was hard on her, maybe I was bitter—even monsters had feelings.

Eying the lesson plan, I thought about what we'd discuss, and then thought about how early I'd have to be up too.

Stalking wasn't easy.

People didn't give credit to stalkers, and they should. That level of dedication couldn't be bought.

Of course, Phoebe had it worse since she had to work throughout those hours, whereas I just hung out. But still, we'd be going home shortly before she had to wake up at four for her shift at the coffee shop.

I had papers to grade so I'd stay busy from my little corner where she never saw me, where I always sat so I could see her reflection in the glass opposite me. It was hit and miss, but it was better than nothing. I could watch her, know she was safe in the mom-and-pop joint that really needed more staff at four AM.

How could I rest knowing she was in danger?

How could I sleep in my warm bed knowing she was not only working, but that she was in peril?

The answer was, I couldn't.

And I stayed with her.

Kept her safe.

Last month, only my presence had averted a mugging, and she didn't even know. She'd been in the back when a guy had come in and started ransacking the register. Had she left the kitchen, he'd have blown her brains out.

Instead, with the skills that enabled me to stalk her, I edged out of my booth, shoved my own gun behind his head, and told him to back off.

Politeness worked sometimes.

My lips curved down at the memory.

Phoebe was in constant danger, and with it, I was constantly stressed.

When the lights flashed as a particularly irritating song was blared over the speaker, I took advantage and hungrily ate up the sight of her.

She was as pale as white silk, and her mass of curls made me wish I had the right to grab those waves in my fist so I could urge her closer to me. She had the brightest green eyes, and the softest lips.

She was a woman, all woman.

My woman.

She just didn't know it, and she never would either.

PART 1

THE END

1

PHOEBE

SQUINTING at the red lights of my alarm clock, I winced when I saw the time.

"How can it be four AM already?" I muttered to myself, then immediately yawned.

I'd been asleep for four hours. I'd arrived home at ten after a six-hour shift at *Crow*, the bar where I worked, but my mom being my mom, had left the place a sty.

I wouldn't care for myself or for her, but Scottie lived here too, and I wouldn't have him living in the filth our mother could subsist in.

Not only had I cleaned the place as much as I could, I'd cleaned *him* up too. His butt had been bright pink from the diaper she never changed from the last time I had cleaned him, and once again, I'd been tempted to call CPS.

Tempted, so badly, to let him go just to make sure he was safe, but this wasn't a perfect world. I'd spent too many years of my own child-hood in Child Protective Services' custody, and I wouldn't wish that on anyone, certainly not the baby brother I adored.

I had three months left of my last year at college. I had to pray that when the time came, I'd be able to get a semi-decent job and I'd be able to take care of my family better. Hopefully, I would also be able to be around Scottie more and get him away from our hag of a mother.

He was my brother, but he was almost my son. On yet another of her sessions, she'd managed to get knocked up by some lowlife I was half-certain was a regular client of hers, and I'd been graced with a newborn baby brother when I was twenty.

I could never resent him, but her?

Hell yeah, I could.

Especially when every aspect of his care fell to me.

The alarm I'd snoozed began blaring again, and another yawn escaped me until my eyes flared wide.

It was Wednesday.

God, I hated Wednesdays. And Mondays and Fridays.

I had Creative Writing those days, and though I loved that class, I hated the professor. He was a jerk and way too mean to be that hot.

Seriously, the guy looked like he belonged on the book cover of the novel he was making us finish for our final project.

Professor Maclean was the definition of hunky, but he was meaner than a rattlesnake.

Whenever I thought of him, I thought of that old adage, "Those who can't do, teach."

It wasn't a nice phrase, and to be honest, I was belittling myself since I was aiming to be a teacher, but I didn't care. Maclean deserved it.

With a huff that belied the dread dawning in my stomach at the prospect of a two-hour class with him, I hauled myself out of bed and began to shuffle out of my crappy bedroom and into the hall.

From this angle, I saw my mother slouched on the recliner she slept in, and eyed the disaster she'd made of the room I'd cleaned a few hours before.

For a second, my heart fell and my eyes burned with the futility of trying to keep this place up. Then, even that misery was forgotten when I saw the lit cigarette in her left hand lolling over the armrest where two empty containers of bottled liver cirrhosis spilled vodka onto the carpet. Fear immediately flushed through me.

It wouldn't be the first time she'd set fire to something while she was drunk. It had happened twice already, and the sofa and the carpet bore the burns to prove it.

Hustling over, I snatched the cigarette from her hand and stubbed it out in the overflowing ashtray I'd emptied last night.

When she didn't stir, I shook my head as disgust flowed through me.

She'd once been a pretty woman, but my dad's death had hit her hard.

She was sick, I knew that, and tried to repeat it to myself over and over when I came home to Scottie sobbing because he was hungry, when she almost set fire to our damn sofa, and spent half her time lying around in a puddle of her own piss. Those instances made it harder to remember she was sick, though, and not just a noose around my neck.

Sucking in a calming breath, I tried not to think about the woman she'd once been. When her cheeks hadn't been tunneled in, when her skin hadn't been like paper, and her eyes didn't look constantly bruised. Her nose was becoming bulbous and had red broken veins all along the tip.

Was it horrible that I was hoping she'd just drink herself into a coma and die?

I rubbed my eyes, trying to disperse the thought, because, of course, it was horrible, but it didn't take the hope away. She was my mom, and I didn't want anything to hurt her, but she lived in a perpetual state of misery, and that misery diffused itself onto Scottie and me.

Because the hatred spilling through me was enough to make me cry, and twice in one morning was excessive for anyone, I turned on my heel and headed toward the second bedroom.

It was too much to expect that she'd have checked on Scottie before she passed out, so I hustled in and had to smile. His diapered butt was in the air, his face smooshed into the blankie I'd saved up over a month for. Unicorns were his favorite, and though we didn't have much, I'd wanted him to have something.

Because he was okay for the minute, I didn't step inside, not wanting to disturb his sleep.

Shuffling into the bathroom, I quickly showered and dressed in the uniform the café where I worked the early morning shift insisted I wear.

It wasn't fresh, and tomorrow I'd need to do laundry, so I sprayed a crap ton of deodorant over myself in the hope it would veil that slightly sour smell that came from clothes that had been worn just a little too long.

Crinkling my nose in disgust, I wished, and not for the first time, that I could afford a second uniform, but my money was better spent elsewhere.

As I tugged my curly brown hair into a messy bun, I didn't even glance at my face other than to note it was clean, and rushed back into Scottie's bedroom. I found him awake, peering at me through the bars on his crib as though he were in a jail cell.

I had to admit, it was. The entire building was.

And I hated that for him.

It was worse, though, that he couldn't roam around the floors in his own home, couldn't crawl around to his heart's content. Couldn't explore things like regular kids could. He was either stuck in his crib, the car seat Mrs. Linden had given us, or his bouncer seat.

Why?

Because I couldn't allow him on the carpet.

I'd cleaned the place last night and my mother had already dumped ash onto it. There were bottles there, and I had no way of knowing if there was broken glass hidden within the fibers. Even in here, the carpet wasn't safe from her unless I vacuumed before I let him go exploring.

I picked him up, laughing when he giggled at me in delight. Patting his bottom, I pressed a kiss to his hair and smiled. This kid was the only joyful part of my day, even if he was my biggest worry.

If it weren't for him, I'd have left, been out of this dive a long time ago. But almost like she'd known I was close to running out on her, Mom had gotten pregnant and she'd needed me. Had promised she'd turn over a new leaf.

To be fair, she kind of had.

I hadn't seen her get drunk once during her pregnancy. She'd smoked though, and despite how often I'd complained, she hadn't quit. The second Scottie was born, she'd made up for the months of staying sober, and had been worse ever since.

"I love you, baby bro," I whispered into his hair. "I hope I'm doing right by you."

If I hadn't experienced CPS myself, I'd say I wasn't, but I knew the creeps that existed in the foster system, and I didn't want my innocent baby brother anywhere near it.

Three months.

That was all I had to wait.

It wasn't long.

We could survive until then, right?

I wrestled him onto his changing pad and quickly sorted him out. I didn't have time to bathe him, which would have to wait until tonight, so I baby wiped him all over, changed him, and got him ready to take downstairs for the morning.

With him tucked on my hip, a plastic carrier of fresh diapers and a couple of bottles of formula I grabbed from the fridge in my hand, and my school stuff on my back, I headed out the door without a backward glance at my mom.

Rushing downstairs, because I didn't trust the elevator in my building, I aimed for Mrs. Linden's flat. She was nearly ninety, wasn't as spry as she'd been just a year ago, but she was my best friend, and looked after Scottie until I got home from school—she was my godsend. I really didn't know what I'd do without her.

Knocking on her door, I pressed a kiss to Scottie's head and started my farewell song, but when nobody answered, I started to worry.

Another knock on the door had the neighbor across the hall opening hers.

When she saw me, she winced. "Mrs. Linden was taken to the hospital last night."

And even as my heart sank for Mrs. Linden, that was just the beginning of my day turning to shit.

2

PHOEBE

No one was in there except for a guy who'd been sitting in a corner booth since before my shift had started.

This place was a twenty-four-hour, privately-owned coffee shop, and some nuts came in at three AM and stayed for hours. I wasn't sure why they weren't asleep, because I sure as hell would be in their shoes, but frankly, I was grateful they were weird as it meant I had a job. So, *yay* for insomnia!

Still, the man hadn't moved from his position since I'd arrived, and the cash register was calling to me.

I knew it was stupid.

Knew I'd lose my job and maybe end up in jail if I was discovered, but who'd miss ten bucks?

And from the tip jar—who'd miss a twenty?

I needed thirty dollars, but thirty goddamn dollars might as well have been thirty thousand.

I'd already taken the twenty from the tips, but I knew I'd have more chance of being found out since the staff were pretty vigilant about counting them before the start of a shift. The cash register was even more dicey, but what choice did I have?

My bosses wouldn't pay me early—that would be like finding one of the unicorns on Scottie's blankie had come to life. They paid every second Thursday, and unfortunately, that was next week.

I didn't know anyone who'd loan me thirty dollars, because if I had, I'd have asked them already.

I wasn't a thief.

I wasn't.

But this morning, I had no choice.

Cheryl, Mrs. Linden's neighbor, said she'd look after Scottie for thirty bucks, and knowing it was either that or leave him alone for fourteen hours with my mother, I'd had no other option.

I should have expected this. Mrs. Linden was old and ill. I should have budgeted better, should have allotted money for a time when I'd have to pay for childcare, but I didn't have the luxury of savings.

Hell, my last luxury had been Scottie's blankie eight months ago.

There was no budgeting when there was nothing to budget with.

Nausea swirled through me as I stared at the register which had over a hundred bucks in there since I'd had a pretty busy morning so far, and though I was desperate, I wasn't a fool.

Closing my eyes, I keyed in the cash register and let the drawer open with a snick.

Sucking down a breath, I told myself I'd pay it back the second I got my paycheck, and slipped my hand into the old-fashioned register. If it was one of the new ones, I'd have been screwed, but it literally added up what we entered.

Grabbing the ten I'd put in there twenty minutes ago when my last customer had paid and I'd had the idea, I slipped it into my pocket.

God, the hole it burned there was as damning as anything. Dread filled me the instant I did it, and the nausea—how did people steal for fun? How was *this* fun?

"Phoebe?"

Heart sinking at the sound of my name, I turned and expected to see my boss. It wasn't unheard of for Lorenzo to come in this early to get ahead on the day, but when my gaze clashed with Professor Maclean's, my pulse spiked, and the nausea that had made me want to puke over the freshly-baked muffins I'd just plunked onto the counter doubled.

"Professor, I didn't realize you were here," I squeaked, darting a glance at the corner booth that had contained the café's sole occupant.

Had he been here all along?

"No, I'll bet you didn't." He frowned at me, stared at the cash register, then stated, "I expect to see you in my office after class ends."

My eyes widened. "Sir?"

His narrowed. "Don't you understand English now? Your last paper was certainly reminiscent of someone who doesn't have a full command over the language, but it appeared you could at least understand the basics."

My cheeks burned and my fingers curled into fists that had my nails pricking my palms. I'd worked damn hard on that paper, damn hard, and he'd graded it a C.

One of the best things I'd ever written, and he'd given it a goddamn C.

But reasoning with him was futile—I knew from other students who'd tried and failed. Plus, Maclean had a rep around campus. There were professors who got off on looking at their students' asses and tits, some who might be flirted into an upgrade on their final grades, but Maclean?

Nope.

He was squeaky clean that way.

Rather than snap at him, not when he had to have seen what I'd just done, I whispered, "I'll be in your office after class, sir."

That beautiful mouth of his curved in a snarl, but his tone was quiet as he simply said, "Good."

When he walked out, I staggered back into the counter, jostling some of the silver mugs and canisters awaiting their next use. As they tumbled to the ground with a clattering sound that had my ears ringing, I had to liken the cacophony to the shit storm that was heading my way.

Maclean was going to report me to my boss, hell, maybe even the police…

My mouth quivered and tears burned my eyes, because I knew no amount of reasoning would make him understand or empathize.

Three months to go, three months until I had something to offer the job market with my degree, and I'd blown it.

All for thirty damn dollars.

3

PHOEBE

HAVING CHANGED out of my uniform, and into a pair of jeans that had been laundered so many times they were close to falling apart at the seams and a simple white tee, I left the coffee shop with a heavy heart.

Lorenzo wasn't the best boss I'd ever had, but Maria, his wife, was a sweetie. She'd often give me leftovers to take home and had even bought Scottie a few cuddly toys over the past year.

I'd hated stealing from them, but Lorenzo would never have given me the thirty dollars, and if I let Mrs. Linden's neighbor down, if I didn't have the money to pay her, maybe she'd never babysit for me ever again.

Mrs. Linden had taken care of Scottie for free. I knew it was because she was bored and lonely. She'd said she enjoyed his energy, even though I knew he had to tire her out. Mostly, I thought she did it for me.

I was, this morning aside, a good girl.

Sometimes, there was no evading what you were. I was born to be walked on—be it by a parent or a boyfriend. I could only thank God that I was too busy for a partner, because if I had one, I knew he'd dump on me too.

As it was, dealing with my mom, Scottie, and Mrs. Linden was enough to handle.

But, as a child, when I'd seen Mrs. Linden struggling up the stairs with her shopping bags, I'd helped when I could.

The day her dog, Charlie, had been put down, I'd been with her.

And these past eight or so years, when I was too young to be doing my own grocery shopping, never mind someone else's, I'd even grabbed her food for her because the elevator was continuously broken, and the stairs were too much for her.

She was my only friend, and that friend was nearly ninety and in a hospital I didn't know the name of.

If I wasn't terrified for Scottie, I was terrified for Mrs. Linden. And where those two terrors dueled, there was the fear over what I'd done and what Maclean was going to say to me to worry about.

I spent most of his class avoiding those beautiful brown eyes of his. They were, I swore, as dark as molten chocolate and set in a face that would make the angels sigh. But those angels didn't know what he was capable of.

Cutting words.

Menacing looks.

Disgusted sneers.

I wasn't sure what I'd done to him, but ever since I'd plunked my ass in the seat in his class that first day, he'd hated me on sight.

Not only was I barely passing because his grading was impossible to predict, but because attending his classes was torture. And I knew what torture was.

Being tied to a mother who trapped you with a child she didn't want, who delved the depths of degradation to get her fix, was misery.

Yeah, I knew what suffering was, but for three hundred and sixty minutes a week, this torment was worse.

"A story isn't just words on a paper. If you approach any project with that in mind, you'll get nowhere. People don't want to read words; they need a visual representation of a world they wish they could dive into, but one they're glad they're safe from—"

His eyes cut to mine again, as they often did, catching the gaze I forgot to evade while I was mesmerized by his beauty. More often than not, he watched me. Like he thought I'd steal something. As if this morning was what he'd expected of me, and that I'd fulfilled his dire prediction of my character.

I ducked my head, letting his words spill over me like water.

He didn't know me.

He didn't understand what my situation was.

To him, I may have been a filthy thief, but I wasn't.

I was a good person in a desperate situation.

My palms grew slick as I stared at the clock above the whiteboards behind Maclean.

As the minute hand approached twelve, my nausea grew to the point where I wanted to puke in my book bag.

Only knowing that my uniform for tonight was in there stopped me.

God, I'd never felt so sick in my entire life. This was worse than when my mom had undercooked the chicken at Thanksgiving one year and I'd had salmonella—I'd thought I was dying back then. *That* was how bad I felt right now.

When Maclean gave us our homework, I felt the sweat beading on my face as my terror manifested itself. With shaky hands, I wrote down what I needed to read before the next class, and as the rows of seats slowly emptied, I slunk down into the chair and waited.

And waited.

And waited for everyone to leave.

Of course, Maclean didn't.

Did he think I'd run off? That I was going to avoid him?

I saw the bastard three times a week, and apparently, he visited the coffee shop where I worked—how had I only just realized that? But, with him at school and potentially at work too, how was I supposed to avoid him?

"My office," he ordered grimly, that steel-like jaw clenching as he stared at me like he hated me.

As if I were his worst enemy.

But I was a nobody.

I was just some girl who'd barely made it into this college, who'd only done so by working her ass off at high school, and who was in this place from a scholarship.

I didn't deserve to be loathed.

I really, truly didn't.

And it wasn't even related to this morning. That was the kicker. He'd judged me that first morning I'd come to class, and had condemned me ever since.

Inhaling a shaky breath, I got to my feet and hauled my book bag over my shoulders. It bulged with all the clothes inside it, and wouldn't you know? That split seam I'd been worrying over for a month just happened to burst open right at the moment I made it to the stairs.

As my uniforms dropped to the ground, my books too, eliciting echoing thuds, a deep, resonant silence filled the lecture hall.

I stared down at the ground and wanted to bawl my eyes out. Seriously, I'd never wanted to cry so damn hard in my life, and this was a day for tears. A day for misery.

My bottom lip trembled as I got to my knees and began collecting things. When I heard footsteps, I shuddered and, keeping my head bowed, carried on methodically folding clothes and gathering books together.

When brown Oxfords peeped into my line of sight, I gnawed my bottom lip and huskily whispered, "Sorry."

He didn't say, 'Don't be. It's not your mistake.'

Didn't tell me I had nothing to apologize for—it wasn't like I'd wanted my damn bag to break at that moment, was it?

Instead, he just stood there. Looming over me.

I could feel his eyes on me, crawling over my body and finding me wanting.

I'd never felt so small in all my life. So humiliated and mortified to be at this man's feet, picking up my crappy clothes, stuffing them into a crappier book bag, and smelling of the cinnamon and coffee from the café.

I was everything he wasn't, and I'd never felt that more keenly than I did now.

The only thing that could have made this more unbearable was if I allowed my rumbling stomach free rein. Puking over his three hundred-dollar shoes would really set the tone for our meeting that was for sure.

With my shit stuffed into the open sack, I tipped it so the weight rested against the sturdier half of the bag, and hugged it to me to keep it upright. When I got to my feet, I staggered as all the blood rushed to my head.

Dizziness hit me, but any color that came into my cheeks disappeared when I saw the look in his eyes.

"Why do you hate me?" The words were whispered, stolen from me by circumstance rather than intention.

"I don't care enough about you to hate you, Phoebe," he replied calmly, as though his words weren't like a knife to the belly.

If anyone knew the power of words, it was him.

How such a beautiful mouth could say such mean things, I didn't know.

"If you're done making a spectacle of yourself—my office. Now."

He didn't wait for me to respond, instead he turned on his heel and began his descent to the classroom desk. After he gathered his things together in an elegant attaché case, he moved toward the door and I, like the beetle I was to him, scurried in his wake.

The door almost banged in my face, and I gritted my teeth, refusing to let his lack of politesse affect me.

He was a jerk.

I knew that. This wasn't breaking news.

Leaving behind the fluorescent-lit classroom, with its uncomfortable wooden seats, and the glare that made my tired eyes ache all the more, I was relieved to find myself in the dimmer corridor.

Traipsing after him wasn't how I wanted to spend the short break I had between now and my next class, but what choice did I have?

No choice, that's what.

Hot and cold flashed in alternate waves over my body, and in the end, I was relieved when we made it to his office—at least I'd get to sit down before I fell over.

That was my thinking, at any rate.

As he opened the door to his own personal kingdom, I slipped in behind him and headed to the chairs in front of his desk.

It was a surprising office for a professor. It was neither modern nor old fashioned, and yet wasn't anonymous either. He'd made it look this way.

Unlike the other offices I'd been in, he hadn't painted the walls. These were a bland magnolia, a standard hue, which somehow brought how expensive everything was into sharp relief.

His desk was formed from a rich-hued oak and the grains were visible, darkened even, making the black leather chair with chrome accents stand out. To his left, there was a matching oak bookcase that didn't actually house books, but stones. Though I didn't get much opportunity to look, I realized quickly they were carved jade figurines.

I'd done my best not to be called into this office, because Maclean scared the bejeezus out of me with those eyes of his that should have made me burn, but instead froze me out worse than a cruise to the Antarctic. It sucked that his focus was now one-hundred-percent on me, and there wasn't a damn thing I could do about it.

"Take a seat," he directed, his tone allowing for no disobedience.

Not that I had it in me to argue—something about him made me jump before he even asked, and I never thought to question how high.

I plunked myself down, grateful to be off my shaky legs. The chairs in front of his desk matched his black leather and chrome one, but were smaller and, I recognized, lower to the ground.

Because I needed to feel more inferior than I already did.

With my book bag on my lap, I hid my fidgeting hands beneath the weight as I stared at him, watching as he unfastened his sports jacket, and hung it on a rack that was screwed to the door. As he did, he revealed a broad back, and the linen of his shirt was so fine, I saw the play of muscles beneath it.

There was speculation that he'd once played football for a big team over in Missouri, but I had no idea if that was true or not. Until now, I'd had no interest either.

Suddenly, that seemed stupid.

In this world, the only way to survive was to know your enemies, and I'd failed at that.

Maybe if I'd known his weaknesses, I could have played on them? Used them to my advantage?

Instead, I was in the dark. But, hell, who was I kidding?

To a man like Maclean, I was a bug and he could swat me away with his hand anytime he wanted.

When, finally, he took a seat, I tried not to notice that I could see his nipples through the fine lawn of his shirt thanks to the shadows offset by the overhead light, but the very fact I could see something so private had my cheeks burning as I stared down at my bag, just waiting for him to start speaking.

"What did I see this morning, Phoebe?"

The bastard clearly wanted blood.

I wanted to stare him straight in the eye and call him out, but I didn't. Couldn't. I needed to be nice. Needed to make this go away if I could—if he'd let me.

On a soft exhalation, I tried to implore, "You saw a girl who needed thirty dollars to pay for—"

He sneered at me. "*Need*? You needed to steal?"

My throat closed. "No. I needed the money. My babysitter..." Mouth working, I finally got out, "She's in the hospital, and the emergency childcare was more than I could afford."

"You're a mother?" he barked, and I stared at him, wondering at his sudden surge of temper.

His usual 'deep freeze' insouciance caved in as the lava-hot rage surged around me like a tsunami.

Uncertainly, I whipped my head from side to side. "I look after my brother."

His eyes narrowed. "How old is he?"

God, was he going to try to take Scottie away from me? No. He couldn't do that. Could he? Maybe he could send CPS around—oh, God, one look at my mom, and they'd haul him out of my apartment as fast as it took her to fall asleep after an all-night booze fest.

My lips began trembling, making it hard to speak clearly. "He needs me."

Maclean gritted his teeth for a second as he stared at me with those beautiful eyes that weren't made for such ugly glowers.

His fingers began to drum on the polished desk in front of him. The noise seemed to sync with my heartbeat, and the faster he drummed, the harder my heart pounded until I felt winded, desperate for air, desperate for respite.

"What am I going to do with you, Phoebe?"

I squeaked, "I only did it the once."

"That's what they all say," he sneered, suddenly looming forward and making me slam my back into the seat in response. "It starts with one time, until it becomes easier and easier to just steal when you 'need' something."

"You don't know me," I rasped, surprising myself with the balls it took to make that assertion. "You don't know my situation or my circumstances."

His mouth tightened. "I think it's time we rectified that."

I frowned. "What do you mean?"

"I mean, Phoebe," he mocked, "that I hold your pathetic little life in my hands."

Oh, God. He did. To many, it was thirty bucks, but in this place? To my bosses? It might as well have been grand larceny instead of petty theft.

Reputation was everything. I knew that, and it terrified me. With a few simple words, he could have my pathetic existence toppling to the ground.

Losing the job at the café when I needed every cent wasn't something I could afford. Hell, I barely made ends meet *with* the job, but without it? And now with Mrs. Linden unable to look after Scottie for only God knew how long?

Fucked.

That was what I was.

Royally fucked.

Staring at him and trying to contain the shiver of fear that quivered through me, I whispered, "What do you want?"

That was what it boiled down to.

He wanted something from me, but Jesus, I had nothing to give.

"I-I can clean your house—"

"Why would I want a thief in my home?"

I flushed, bitterly aware that I'd left myself open to that attack. "The circumstances—"

"What if another 'circumstance' cropped up? Would you help yourself to my widescreen TV because you couldn't feed your brother?"

"What do you want? Because evidently, you think I have something to give."

His top lip curled up as he folded his arms across his chest. "So unassuming." He tilted his head to the side. "You have no idea, do you?"

My brow puckered. "Look, I know you think I'm stupid, but I'm really not. I was desperate." I heard the plea in my voice and hated myself for it. There was no entreating this man to do anything.

"You keep on using that word," he retorted. "*Desperate*, but how desperate?"

"What do you want from me?" I cried again, unable to take his tormenting for much longer.

He patted the desk. "Sit here."

I reared back. "Huh?"

"Sit here."

All of a sudden, it hit me. I shook my head. "I'm not going to fuck you."

"Good thing I don't want to fuck you either," he countered immediately, unoffended by my words.

I'd been slow on the uptake here, granted, but what the hell was he talking about?

He didn't want to fuck me, so why did he want me to sit on his desk?

Throat tightening, I stared at him and recognized that he looked almost bored by our conversation.

"If I sit there, what do you want me to do?" I inquired, voice husky.

"You're going to spread your legs and touch your pussy until you come."

For a second, my eyes bugged out, and how the hell I didn't laugh, I wasn't sure.

He said it so calmly, without so much as a hint of heat.

I wasn't a virgin, but I didn't go around jilling off in front of people. Especially not professors.

And certainly not professors who loathed the ground I walked on.

"Are you for real?" I rasped, my fingers tightening to the point of pain in the busted seams of my bag.

"Oh, most definitely."

4

———

PHOEBE

THE WAY he crooned those words made me think this wasn't even a sexual thing. It was about dominance.

He wanted me to do this to humiliate me.

To belittle me.

I just didn't understand why.

What had I ever done to him to make him want to do this to me? To treat me like I was a dispensable pawn in his personal game of chess?

My heartbeat pounded in my ears with a dull throb that had pain slicing through my nerve endings.

Shuddering, I stared at him and asked, "Why?"

His smile was cool, calculating, but his voice was like silk, and dangerous for it as he threatened, "Because if you don't want to lose everything, you'll do as I say."

The words made me feel even more like a dog who was being trained.

When I didn't immediately leap up to do his bidding, he whispered, "Is there a reason your brother depends on you and not your mother? Is she dead?"

Eyes flaring wide at that, I bit out, "You leave him out of this."

"He's part of the problem, isn't he?" he retorted, as cool as ever. "His fate rests in my hands as much as yours does."

He wasn't wrong there.

Damn him.

I licked my lips. "P-Please, I'll clean anything, you can film me."

"Because I have time for that..." He cocked a brow at me. "I have time to let a filthy thief into my home and record her while she cleans the place, just to make sure she isn't stealing from me?"

"But why would you want me to," I motioned at the desk, "do *that*?"

He wasn't getting anything out of it.

Not with the repugnant twist to his lips that told me, more than his words had, that he didn't want to fuck me.

"Because I told you to. It isn't about 'want.' It's about obedience. It's about the fact that if you don't shut your fucking mouth and do as you're told, your shitty little world will come tumbling down around your ears.

"I've seen you steal from your workplace, and you've barely managed to get by in my class so a word in the dean's ear..." He smirked at me, a hateful twist of his mouth that I wanted to slap. "Then, there's your employer. After I explain what I saw, your boss will fire you, so what more do you think it will take for you to lose everything? And so close to finals too?"

As he dug the knife in and twisted, my nostrils flared with rage as I clambered to my feet. When I didn't spin around for the door, the most beautifully hateful smile curved his lips.

At any other moment, had a man graced me with a smile like that, I knew for a fact I'd be weak in the knees.

Instead, I was outraged and disgusted.

That smile was so beatific because he knew he'd won, knew that I was about to do as he asked.

My jaw clenched as I rounded the desk and hefted my not insubstantial weight onto it.

Almost as though he read my mind, he murmured, "Are you sure you're poor?"

For a second, I was speechless—were the stealing, the shitty book bag that had fallen to pieces, and the crap state of my clothes, not enough proof?

"W-What do you mean?"

"You're hardly starving, are you?"

I wanted to splutter, wanted to slap his face for the needlessly cruel words. It was as if he wanted me to hate him. Like he was saying it, digging in the knife, just to get a rise out of me.

The bastard.

"Cheap foods are nutritionally poor," was all I managed to grate out.

He hummed, and the tone of it was disbelieving. Like he didn't know that cheap, ready meals contained the worst kind of nutrition. As if I were bullshitting about that.

"You skipped a step," he carried on, settling back into his seat, rocking it as though he were in the middle of a lively debate.

"I-I did?"

"Can't get yourself off in your jeans, can you?"

My cheeks flushed with my misery as I jumped off the desk, because if I'd been happy about touching myself in front of him, I was less than ecstatic after his comments.

Was he about to remark on the size of my ass?

On the state of my panties?

Apparently, it was open fucking season on Phoebe Whitehouse today.

I was in the stocks and he was quite at ease throwing rotten fruit and vegetables my way.

Mouth tightening, I unfastened the fly of my jeans then began to drag them down my hips.

As I started, however, he murmured, "Turn around."

I closed my eyes, aware that his intention truly was to humiliate me, because he'd evidently read my mind.

This time, no amount of *tightening* stopped the quiver as my mouth trembled with my embarrassment. Toeing out of my sneakers, I struggled out of the jeans, trying not to bend down and kick my way out of them instead, but they weren't having it. They gathered around my ankles and stuck fast.

Mortified beyond belief, I bent over and quickly loosened them before twisting around, with my face bright pink.

The nasty sneer on his face said it all.

I was a disappointment. To a man who I hadn't intended on pleasing in the first place.

Cheeks burning with the scorch to my pride, I scuttled over to the desk and lifted myself back onto it once more. A fine tremor coursed along my body, making me preternaturally aware of every single fucking inch of it.

The ass that was too big.

The hips that were too round.

The belly that jiggled.

The tits that refused to stay contained by anything other than one of the ugly bras that 'big' girls had to wear.

The only saving grace?

He hadn't asked me to take off my panties.

Thanking God for that smallest of mercies, I reached down and began touching myself through that shield. Of course, I should have anticipated his next move.

When he shifted in his seat, I half-expected him to pull his cock out of his pants, even though I was under no illusion about how gross I was to him, and how this was simply a power play. But when I looked up, he'd moved only to open his desk drawer.

When he pulled out a pair of scissors, my eyes darted to his, and I felt fear at his move as I looked at him, then he passed them over to me.

"Cut them off."

"Cut them?" I choked out, and he narrowed his eyes at me once more.

"Your repeating everything I say is doing nothing more than irritating me, Phoebe. Do as I asked, please."

My hand was trembling as I reached for the scissors and, pulling them taut at the waistband, I cut through one side with a single snip.

When the fabric fell down, I bit my lip and moved to the other side, not stopping until they were nothing more than two flaps that were barely hiding my virtue from him.

His chair squeaked as he shifted back, and when I looked at him, it was easy to envisage him watching a movie. His arms lay relaxed at his side as he lounged at a comfortable angle, but his hands were on his belly, bridged as he rocked back and forth to the show going on before him.

He really was going to make me do this.

Not one single aspect of his features displayed guilt. Nor did he look grossed out anymore.

He looked satisfied.

Like a cat who'd dragged in a particularly irritating bird that he was going to enjoy torturing until its death.

I was that bird.

And I was way too young to die.

Closing my eyes, I sucked in a shaky breath and reached down to touch my clit. The angle wasn't right, and I felt awkward. Not only that, I was bone dry.

This was the exact opposite of a turn on.

"You won't leave here until you climax."

I didn't open my eyes, because if I did, I'd just want to shout at him, and damn him, he held the cards here.

So what if it was weird what he wanted from me? He wasn't going to tell my boss about my stealing, and things would return to normal—him glowering at me from his desk, making me feel insignificant with his grades and the notes he made on my papers.

God, how I longed for our relationship to revert to my simply dreading his lessons three times a week.

Sucking in a breath, I settled back on one hand, spread my legs wider, even letting one fall to the side of his desk so I could part them more.

Was I embarrassed?

Yes.

Did I think I could come?

No.

But I had no choice. I had another class soon. Crazy though it was, I had to get going.

Licking my lips for the gazillionth time, I tried to calm my breathing, tried to imagine I was in my bed at night, playing with my clit, and gently fingering myself until I climaxed.

My orgasms were never all that fulfilling, never all-encompassing, but on the rare occasions I felt the urge, they were a nice way to calm down after a busy day, a great way for me to tumble into sleep.

Breathing deeply, I focused on anything else but him and touched myself exactly how I did on those nights. I thought about a sexy man fucking me hard and fast, maneuvering me about the bed as though I were as lithe and slender as a little doll. I imagined his rough hands on my body, his firm tenet on my sexuality.

I thought about being pinned down and bitten, marked with his fingers and teeth, and I thought of *his* hand on my clit. I imagined he'd know exactly what to do with my pussy, would know how to make these tiny little poofs of an orgasm manifest tenfold.

Since my usual fantasies worked me over, I felt myself grow into the correct rhythm. With my eyes closed, I could forget I wasn't alone, could forget that a man who loathed me, who'd blackmailed me just to have power over me, was sitting there observing. Judging every move I made, probably critiquing me so he could fucking grade me.

Ridiculous though it was, my eyes popped open at the thought, and I wasn't surprised to see he hadn't moved.

Not by an inch.

His eyes had narrowed to the point that he was either asleep or he was watching me through the slits he'd made with them.

As that would be the most ultimate of humiliations, I chose to believe he watched me, because him falling asleep was somehow worse.

My mouth trembled again but I rolled my lips inward to stop them from quivering, and carried on working myself up, but I'd lost momentum. Lost it and was desperate to get it back.

Panicked, I studied him, replaced the blank face of the man who fucked me in my dreams with his mean one, imagined that snarl of his being put to better use as he gritted his teeth while he screwed me silly to hold off his orgasm. I pictured those hands, so strong and sure, stroking over my curves, making me come alive with each brush of his fingers.

I regained some control by using him to fulfill his demands, but it backfired spectacularly as the more I imagined him, the more power rattled through my bones like my body was a beat-up truck racing down a driveway riddled with potholes.

I shivered and shook, quivered and quaked, and all because I thought about those beautiful lips, lips that were capable of curving into the most gracious of smiles, curling about my clit, sucking me, slurping on the nub, and like that, I was done.

The orgasm came out of nowhere.

It hit me square between the eyes as I used my tormentor to get off.

I rode my hand, used the finger I'd slipped inside my gate to mimic his thick fullness to rock higher and faster. The heel of my wrist bumped against my clit, and my head tipped back as I allowed the climax total autonomy over my body.

It was, sickeningly, the best orgasm I'd ever had.

I could feel the heat sliding through my veins as the languor of release diffused into my system, making me relax when I should be tense in this man's presence.

When the rigidity in my body eased, and my breathing began to settle, he reached into the drawer once more and pulled out a pen and a pad of paper.

My cheeks, already red, burned hotter as he pushed the pad between my spread legs, not stopping until it was scant inches from my pussy.

"Write down your number."

His command had me frowning, and the lack of inflection in his voice extinguished any heat inside me.

He sounded like he was asking his waitress for his steak to be medium rare instead of well done.

Was that how little I'd affected him?

The question had me wincing.

What was wrong with me?

Why did I want him to be affected, period?

The man had just forced me to…

I gulped.

What?

Climax?

I shuddered because, in the end, I'd come hard and fast. I was pathetic. So pathetic. This wasn't about my pleasure, nor was it about enjoyment. It was his power-play over me, and I'd just fallen into his trap like a mouse who'd scented that creamy piece of cheese and who thought with its belly rather than its mind.

Not only hadn't I affected him when I didn't particularly want to, but my pride was also pricked and, to be quite frank, I was disturbed on a base level.

Alone in my bed, the most powerful orgasm I could achieve was sparkler-level. What I'd just felt with this bastard's eyes on me was more like July Fourth had gone down in my body.

Trying to steady my hand, I reached between my legs and grabbed the pen. As I scrawled my number on the pad, I knew one thing and one thing only—this wouldn't be the last time he forced me to do his bidding…

5
___

PHOEBE

THE NEXT DAY

I paused at my mother's slurred words, turned back to her and asked, "What do you care?"

She blinked at me, and I felt my mouth curl up in disgust at the state of her.

Her shirt was covered in only God knew how many stains, and her pants were just as bad but they were filthy too. Her hair made a rat's nest look clean, and I was pretty sure she'd stink of both alcohol and urine.

"I'm your mother. Of course, I care," she rasped out the lie, her eyes flaring wide as she tried to focus on me.

"I have errands to run," I told her, knowing that would get her to back off.

God forbid she ever pull any weight around this place.

"Get some beer for me," she ordered before slouching back toward her pit.

My jaw clenched as she settled in her armchair and let off a fart that had me scurrying out the door just to get away from her vileness.

How she got any man to fuck her for a fee was beyond me.

Saying that, I'd never seen the guys she'd picked up before, and had no desire to either—maybe they were as repulsive as she was.

Leaving Scottie with Cheryl for the rest of the afternoon and evening cost money I didn't have, but I knew I'd get some tips tonight and they'd have to go to Mrs. Linden's neighbor because I just couldn't leave him with Mom.

It wasn't ideal, but nothing about this situation was.

I had to suck it up, get on with things, and move on.

My first step was the laundromat. After I set everything up to wash, I waited until I could shove them in the dryer before running to the store down the street. I grabbed everything we'd need for the next few days. Some days, I eyed the fresh produce like I was eying up a Chippendale. I ate a lot of crap food, and longed for a time when a salad was more affordable than a crappy sandwich from a fast-food joint.

Scottie would eat better than I had as a kid, hell, even as I did as an adult. I'd see to it if it killed me.

But as I stared at the healthy stuff, it reminded me of the professor.

Of his words.

I felt fatter than ever, disgusting within my own skin because he'd made me feel that way. Ashamed of something that was literally out of my control. It was either cheap foods or nothing... Maybe he'd prefer me to starve?

Although, I guessed that begged the question of why he'd forced me to do what he had when I was so gross to him.

Just thinking of those cold eyes, that stern jaw had a shiver rushing down my spine.

Why was he so beautiful? How could someone so handsome, so picture-perfect pretty, be so mean? So hard and unforgiving?

I wasn't a bad person. I tried. I really did. And yet, to him, I felt like scum. Scum that he could do this to, that he could manipulate and use because I was desperate and he could take advantage of that.

My emotions were churning. Hatred for him warred with the intrinsic womanly pride every female had. I didn't want him to want me, hell, I should discourage it, but my ego was torn to shreds by his words. So, I put back some of the food I'd collected in my basket and grabbed the bare minimum I needed.

After grabbing Scottie's essentials, I headed back to the laundromat and saw that my stuff was ready to go. Folding it and placing it in my bag, I returned to my building with enough clothes and food for the remainder of the week.

Hefting it all up the stairs wasn't anything I wasn't used to, but I stopped on the third floor because that was where Janowicz lived.

As I approached his door, I braced myself.

Not only was our super a grade-A creep, he was mean too.

Still, he knew which hospital Mrs. Linden had gone to. Cheryl, the neighbor who'd been looking after Scottie, said she'd heard him outside when the ambulance had come.

I'd wanted to scream at her when she said she didn't know which hospital Mrs. Linden was being treated at—who heard EMTs and didn't think to ask after their neighbor?—but it was that kind of building in that kind of city. Every man, woman, and child were out for themselves.

Knocking on the door, I waited until the greasy lump appeared. His yellowed teeth bared themselves into a grin as he leered at me.

"You did my shopping for me. So kind of you," he mocked while scratching at his sweat-slicked chest.

I ground my teeth. "I want to visit Mrs. Linden in the hospital."

"I want a Thai bride." His eyes narrowed at me as if he sensed my disgust. "I'd settle for a Russian. Think you could hook me up?"

"Please," I added, hardening my tone. "Cheryl said you know where she is."

He shrugged. "Maybe I do. Maybe I don't."

"I just want to see if she's okay."

"Old bitch. It's time she died."

Janowicz disliked the residents who had rent-controlled apartments like Mrs. Linden who'd lived here for a long time.

Though his words hurt me, I merely whispered, "Please."

His response was another shrug as he scratched his dirty wifebeater-covered belly—did he have fleas or something? "It was either Brookdale, Brooklyn Hospital, or New York Community Hospital." His yellowed teeth made another appearance. "Damned if I can remember which."

When he slammed the door in my face, I was relieved. Three hospitals were a start. I just had to hope she was in one of them.

Believing that I'd find Mrs. Linden sooner rather than later, I carried on up the stairs. When I made it into my apartment, I tried to shrug off my sadness. Normally, I'd have food for Mrs. Linden too, and I loathed walking past her floor to get to mine.

She was my haven because I hated my apartment with a passion, and preferred to be with her and Scottie than up there.

I'd have slept there if I could, but I'd never crossed that line.

I didn't think my mother would give a damn if I ran off with Scottie. Maybe one day I'd try that and see if she cared about us at all. I had a feeling she wouldn't, but I wasn't ready to test that yet.

When I stacked the food in the grimy cupboards I cleaned every month—the nicotine stains remained no matter what I did—my mother lumbered into the kitchen.

"You didn't get any beer," she growled, staring in bewildered anger at my meager purchases.

"Didn't have the money for it," I told her simply.

It wasn't a total lie. I'd saved some money by buying less food, but I wasn't about to waste that on a six-pack. Not when Cheryl needed paying later.

"Bullshit," she spat.

I sucked down a breath, trying to keep my patience as I emptied the brown paper bag.

Facing the cupboards rather than her, I murmured, "Mrs. Linden is sick. I had to pay for a sitter."

"You mean you wasted money on a sitter when I was here?" Her hand grabbed my shoulder and she forced me to turn around. Her fingers were bony, digging into me like they were daggers as she got in my face. "How many times have I told you—"

When her spittle hit my cheek, I scrubbed at my skin where her filth touched me and snarled, "How many times have *I* told *you*? I'm not your personal shopper. You want beer? Go and buy it your goddamn self."

She narrowed her eyes at me, those eyes that were so like Scottie's and mine. Some days, it was the only physical reminder I had that she was our mother.

With her skeletal frame, skin that looked jaundiced, and her drawn features that had once been beautiful but were now just jaded and desperate, she didn't even look like our distant cousin.

"Don't be wasting no money on a sitter. I'm here, aren't I?"

"And some use you are. You'll leave him."

"I won't. I'm his goddamn mother. I know what I'm doing."

"The last time I had to leave him with you, you went out." My jaw clenched at the memory. "Mrs. Linden is in the hospital until God knows when, and I have to work. If you can't man up, if I can't trust him with you, then any money that goes to the sitter has to come out of our grocery funds."

I admit that I caved in sometimes and bought her stash regardless of my current hard stance with her. Why? Because I knew she whored herself out for her fix otherwise.

Truth be told, and as disgusting of a person as it made me, I didn't really care that she did that. But I *did* care that she brought the guys back here, in the same place my baby brother slept.

She licked her pasty lips. "I can look after him. It ain't too hard."

"Apparently it is, because you've managed to let me down every single time."

"If you grab me a six-pack the next time you're out, I'll do it."

Jesus.

You'd think I was Scottie's mother here. But luckily for me, his biological mom was willing to cut a deal with me—sheesh.

I narrowed my eyes at her. "A six-pack?" I sniffed, but then I thought about it, and realized it wasn't a bad deal if she could be responsible for once. "Fine. If you stay in and make sure he's okay, I'll get you two." Because two of the kind she bought were worth a damn sight less than Cheryl, and I couldn't afford Cheryl anyway. Hell, I couldn't afford the beer!

Her eyes lit up, revealing their once jewel-like beauty. "Great. I won't let you down."

I really hoped she wasn't lying because damn, I needed some help.

When she scuttled away like the cockroach she was, my shoulders sagged.

I was tired. Tired because I barely slept, tired because I worked so much, but mostly, I was tired of being the adult here.

Since Scottie's birth, things had grown worse with my mother, but it had been bearable because of Mrs. Linden.

Without my rock, I wasn't sure how I'd make it through the week, never mind much longer. Throw in this situation with the professor and the sword of Damocles hanging over my head, three words came to mind—God help me.

And I wasn't even religious.

6

PHOEBE

"MRS. LINDEN!" I cried, eyes stinging with tears as I rushed into the hospital ward.

It had taken me all afternoon to find out where she was being treated, and for each of those hours, guilt had filled me because I knew she was alone in the world, knew she had no family except for me or Scottie.

Her rheumy eyes were bleary as she blinked them open, and her face, tense with deeper lines than before, seemed to lighten as she stared at me and registered who Scottie and I were.

"It's good to see you, girlie," she rasped, her voice low and deep as she unfurled arthritic fingers and held them out for me to take hold of.

Before I could, Scottie giggled, grabbed her hand, and tugged the digits with his own. Her smile warmed my heart, and here, the only *real* mother Scottie and I'd ever known, chuckled as the baby squawked at her.

He was happy to see her, more than he ever was to see Mom. I couldn't blame him for that, because she was practically a stranger to him, but with our deal in mind, he'd be seeing more of the bitch who'd given birth to us.

Mom had actually behaved for the rest of the day when I'd

retrieved him from Cheryl's. I wasn't sure how long that would last, and knew her control wasn't good enough to rely on in the long run.

Even as fear for Scottie filled me, even as the cocktail of emotions my predicament with the professor stirred in me, I forced myself to focus on Mrs. Linden.

"I couldn't find you," I said, my voice breaking on a sob.

Her wizened brow furrowed as she beckoned me to let Scottie down. While the baby toddled over to her, wriggling until he was at her side, my heart cried out as he settled and, within seconds, fell asleep.

"He missed you," I whispered, guilt spiraling inside me until I thought I'd choke on it.

"And I missed him." She blew out a tired breath, then stared at me with dark, sad eyes. "Baby girl, I ain't got long left for this world."

"Don't say that," I chided, reaching for her hand and squeezing. "You'll get better. You always do."

"Ain't an 'always' no more, honey." She let her head rock against the papery pillow, and was it my imagination, or was her silvery white hair thinner and more brittle than before?

My stomach revolted as I took in the sight of the woman I'd known for years, who'd helped me with Scottie, sure, but who'd also been the only constant since Mom and I had moved into our building twelve years ago.

Without Mrs. Linden, I wouldn't have had the guts to try for college, and without her, I'd never have been able to care for Scottie too.

I loved her and she believed she was going to leave me.

The only person, aside from Scottie, who I loved, thought she was going to die soon.

I dipped my head and tried to evade those all-knowing eyes.

"It's my time, baby girl," she rasped, but I shook my head, unable to hear those words.

"You're talking like this because you've been by yourself," I countered, smoothing down her blankets to work off some of my nerves. "I could kill Mr. Janowicz. He could have told me sooner, but he's a mean, old…" I tightened my jaw because Mrs. Linden didn't like cussing. "Jerk."

I'd had to call the three hospitals he'd rattled off because of him, and had managed to find her by lying and saying I was her granddaughter. Our super didn't deserve the label 'jerk.'

At my words, she sighed and shook her head. "It's my time, honey."

Her tone was more insistent now, and all the more terrifying for it because she didn't even complain about Janowicz, was more bothered about me coming to terms with the fact she was dying.

I jerked at the sound of a loud snore, and Mrs. Linden rolled her eyes when Scottie, disturbed by the noise, began wriggling as he became more aware of his surroundings.

We were in a shared ward. At her side, there was the snoring woman, and the other cubicle had the curtain drawn around the bed. Straight opposite her, there was a woman doing a puzzle, and the final two were reading on e-readers. The scent of disinfectant was in the air, and the all-pervasive perfume of death was prevalent.

No wonder Mrs. Linden was feeling so uncertain—this place was hardly cheerful.

"You'll be home soon," I told her, but she shook her head again and patted my hand.

"No, baby. No." She reached up and cupped my chin, forcing me to look at her. "This ticker won't last much longer. The docs told me." She exhaled roughly. "I've made peace with it, but I'm frightened for you and this boy."

My eyes watered. "I love you, Mrs. Linden."

Her lips curved. "I know you do, and I love you. Both of you. But don't you think you could call me Enid?"

Throat tight, I whispered, "I love you, Enid."

She sighed. "That's better." Her hand curved around Scottie's chubby leg. "I missed this young'un, but I was even sorrier to have put you in a pickle. What did you do with him yesterday morning when I was brought in?"

"I figured something out," I replied, trying to sound nonchalant and probably failing considering she winced.

"You left him at home?"

I shook my head. "I didn't yesterday, but I'm having to now."

Curling her finger at me, she beckoned me closer. I leaned over her and couldn't scent her usual flowery perfume, but a clinical kind of soap instead—why hadn't I thought to bring her things with me?

God, I was so selfish sometimes. But when I'd finally found the right hospital, I'd grabbed Scottie then hauled us both over here on four buses.

Thoughts of perfume hadn't been on my mind—keeping Scottie comfortable, trying not to fall asleep before our next stop, and catching the right bus had taken all my mental capacity.

"In my cupboard, there's my purse. I want you to take it with you."

My eyes widened. "I can't do that!"

"Of course, you can, child. It isn't going to do me much good. Not where I'm going." Her smile was resigned, and I hated the tinge of relief I found there—had she been in so much pain that death was welcome? The thought crushed me. "There's a bit of money in there, not a lot, but you can take my keys. You take whatever you can and sell it. You won't get much, but maybe there's something that will pay for childcare. Even if it's for a few weeks, it's better than nothing." She shook her head. "Thinking of Scottie with your mother makes this old ticker race."

I reached for her hand and my mouth trembled as I whispered words I wanted to withhold but simply couldn't. "Please, don't leave me."

Both our eyes blurred as she whispered, "Baby, don't you think I'd stay if I could?"

My throat ached with the power of my sadness, and for a second, my body temperature plummeted as I tried to contain my sorrow.

Because I couldn't face her, not without bawling, I turned away from her and headed to the cupboard she'd pointed to. It was scratched and had been new back in the seventies, but I reached inside and grabbed her personal items.

"Could you pass me some water, honey?" she asked gently, her focus on Scottie who was fiddling with the hospital bracelet she wore on her wrist.

Nodding, I set her purse on the table then poured water into the sippy cup waiting there, and handed it to her. The tremor in her fingers was worse than before, and I watched the blue veins as she raised the cup to her mouth. They seemed to be duller somehow, and her skin was more papery than just a few days earlier.

With Scottie curled up next to her, his body so round and pink with good health, there was a stark contrast between the two of them, and grief choked me once again.

Because I couldn't sit still, I tidied her blankets again, which she'd rustled, and tucked her in, all while she cooed over Scottie who was half-dozing and making bubbles with his spit now.

It was gross, but it was amazing how a baby made things acceptable.

I'd been puked on, peed on, crapped on, and all of it now had the power to make me laugh a little—not that I had at the time, of course.

When I'd finished fussing, I returned to her side, and informed her, "I can't come tomorrow. I have three shifts, but I'll be back the day after."

She smiled at me and said, "Give the nurses your number."

"Why?"

But as the question escaped me, I realized that I already knew the answer—she wanted them to call me when she died. Wanted the call to spare me a trip to the hospital.

Oh, God.

I bowed my head, this time unable to stop the tears. She spoke so easily of death, spoke of it like she was heading out shopping for the afternoon, not leaving us forever.

I grabbed the blankets I'd just straightened, gripped them tightly in my hands, and tried to calm myself. Scottie was very sensitive, and I knew he'd sense my agitation, knew it would rile him up too, and the last thing anyone in this ward needed was a sobbing baby.

Her papery hand reached for mine, and she whispered, "Don't worry for me."

"I don't want you to be alone."

Her lips curved. "These past twelve years, I haven't been. Without you and this little monster, I might have, but you brought light to my life, baby. You've been my joy in these final years, and I can't thank you enough for that."

"I don't deserve your thanks," I rasped. "I've been a nuisance. Depending on you when you're sick—"

"You gave me purpose," she argued, instantly dismissing my words. "You gave me a reason to get up in the morning." She wagged her finger at me. "Don't take away from the joy you brought me."

I licked my lips, and unable to stop myself, did something I hadn't done in twelve years.

Even though I'd wanted to.

Even though I'd longed to some nights.

Mrs. Linden had never been affectionate, but I ignored that and reached over to press a kiss to her cheek. When my soft lips caressed her fragile skin, she released a deep sigh.

"I love you, child," she said again. "You've been like a—" Then she shook her head. "No, you *have* been a daughter to me. No 'like' about it."

Throat too full to speak, I whispered, "Love you too."

She reached up and patted my cheek. "You go now. I don't want you out much later. I know how long you have to travel to get here from our building but, please, don't forget to give the nurses your phone number."

"I won't," I murmured miserably.

"Now, put my things in your backpack," Enid directed, then she laughed at my bag. "The old one caved in?"

I nodded. "This is one I kept from high school." It felt like a lifetime ago, but it was scrawled with pen and littered with drawings I'd thought were good back in the day.

As I stored her few things in there, I watched as she hugged Scottie for what might be the final time, and he began fussing the second I hauled him into my arms.

My body ached with grief as I took a step away from her. Each one physically pained me. Our eyes caught and held, and her possessions were a heavy weight on my back as I put distance between us.

I couldn't tell her goodbye, but I didn't know what else to say. So instead, I reached up, and with my free hand, blew her a kiss.

Her smile as she caught it would live with me forever.

7

PHOEBE

WHEN MY PHONE buzzed the next morning, my one morning off a week before a nightmarish three shifts began later on in the day, terror whirled inside me.

When I saw the Caller ID was unknown and not the nurses' station I'd keyed in yesterday, I frowned and ignored it because I was in Mrs. Linden's apartment, going through her things, and didn't feel like being hit up for insurance or whatever else a telemarketer wanted to sell.

I felt like a gravedigger, like the filthy thief Professor Maclean had accused me of being, but I knew, as had Enid, that the second she passed, this place would be locked away from me forever and she wasn't wrong—I needed the money, and she wanted me to have it.

Enid wouldn't have lived in this building if she was a wealthy woman, but when I'd first gone into the apartment, I'd found a letter propped up on her dresser addressed to me.

Baby girl,

I'm hoping you get this letter, and that somehow, you remember that you have a key to my door—I'll never know why you always insisted on knocking, but I hope you remember before it's too late, because I'm not sure if I'll make it long enough for me to give you my keys.

There isn't much in this place that's been my home for too many years to count, but what there is is yours.

Check under the mattress. There's around three hundred dollars there for starters. I have a few pieces of jewelry that you might get a couple hundred for.

Please, take whatever you need. You know as well as I do that Janowicz will steal whatever he can.

I'm writing this as I wait on the ambulance. I could have called for you, but I know you'll be tired, and I knew, even more so now, that you'd need the rest.

Know this: you brought joy to my world when I was sinking in gloom. Before you, I was alone. With you, I had a family again. Thank you for that.

I love you and Scottie more than you know. Be strong for us both, go out there and achieve your goals, be who you were born to be.

When you can, take Scottie away from your mother. She won't argue. Leave her to her personal hell and make a life for yourselves with my blessing.

I wish I could see you grow to become the woman you were destined to be.

With all my love,

Enid

Hours later, my eyes were still wet from reading that letter, and though I'd had her blessing *twice* over, what I was doing still felt so wrong. I was rubbed raw by what the professor had accused me of, rightfully so, and this just made me feel even worse.

I gathered the money from under the mattress, hating that she might have scrimped and saved for this very moment—she'd intended on protecting me right from the very beginning.

As I moved around her small apartment, with its tired furnishings and the scent of her floral perfume still lingering in the air, it was hard to believe she hadn't passed yet.

Everything in here was ready to move on. Ready for this place to be empty, for someone new to live within its walls.

It killed me to think that soon, this apartment wouldn't be a haven away from my mother. Not just for me, but for Scottie too.

He'd never remember the woman who'd saved him far too many times to count, and I vowed to raise him with the many edicts Enid had passed my way, the recipe for pot roast she swore by, and the stories she'd told me as a girl—stories that had made me aspire to be an English teacher.

Gnawing on my bottom lip, I frowned as I peered inside a drawer in her dresser, feeling like a sneak for going through her things, for seeing stuff I'd never have dreamed of looking at if she were here.

Finding a scarf that smelled like her, I pulled it out and wrapped it around my throat. It was light and something she'd have worn to church when she'd been able to go—the priest came to visit her here now—and it would forever remind me of her.

With a sigh, and still feeling like a leech, I methodically moved through her things, finding some books I put in a box I'd brought from the grocery store, keeping a few figurines that I thought I might be able to sell on eBay—and God, didn't that load me with guilt—until I hit a chest of drawers that was loaded with clothes. They were definitely vintage, but I knew I could wear them.

There were gypsy-style tops and kaftans that would flow nicely in the summer, a couple of dresses that would fit as well. Considering any money would be going toward Scottie's daycare, I needed every cent I could and didn't have any to waste on buying weather appropriate clothes.

As I burrowed around for some more, I found a box. It was green leather and was slightly padded. When I saw the emblem on the front, my brows rose.

Rolex.

Popping open the box, it revealed a piece of paper that, upon further inspection, declared the matching 'his and her' watches to be authentic pieces.

My eyes widened and hope filled me. These had to be worth *something*, didn't they? Were they the jewelry Enid had mentioned in her letter? Otherwise, why hadn't she told me about them? They were buried under a lot of clothes, but surely she hadn't forgotten about them?

I wanted to visit her so we could talk about this, but I'd have to be at school in the next two hours. It was a forty-minute bus ride, so I wouldn't be late, but still, the urge to ask *who'd* worn the man's watch filled me.

In all the years I'd known her, she'd never mentioned a man.

Not a husband or a boyfriend.

Heck, she could have been a lesbian and I wouldn't have known. And there were no pictures tucked in frames that weren't of me or Scottie, so they were no clue.

Feeling selfish for not having asked, for her not being able to share that with me when I was the only person she saw on a day-to-day basis, I shoved it aside because those thoughts would get me nowhere.

Even as I tucked the authentication certificate back into the box, stroked my finger over the glossy faces of the expensive, vintage watches, I picked it up with great care and tucked it into my bag.

I wasn't sure what I was going to do with them, but leaving them in my bedroom for my mother to find when she was on the hunt for cash to get some booze was not on my agenda.

I'd have time, hopefully, after class to head to a pawn shop and pad out my bank account with something that would help me take care of Scottie on the regular.

It was weird feeling relieved and excited when this good fortune came at the expense of my one source of comfort. The incongruous emotions had me reaching for my phone when it buzzed again and answering without looking at the ID.

"Hello?" I asked, surprised to hear I sounded as dazed as I felt. The second I answered, I realized it could be the nurses' station and terror filled me.

"Why haven't you been answering my calls?"

The bark had me jolting in place. Even though I felt joy that it wasn't news on Mrs. Linden, I literally sat up straighter as tension bombarded me on all levels. "Professor?"

"Yes," he hissed. "If you think you can—"

"I didn't realize it was you," I blurted out, annoyed by his anger when I hadn't done a damn thing wrong.

This time.

"The second you put down the phone, input my goddamn name," he ground out. "Be in my office after class."

My heart sank to my stomach. "W-Why?"

"I think you know why."

And with that, he hung up.

It irked me to instantly obey, but he'd sounded so angry, and even though the Rolexes should ease my situation, I couldn't afford to lose my jobs or for him to disgrace me by telling my bosses.

Beyond anything, Lorenzo and Maria had been good to me. I didn't want them to think I was repaying them by treating them so badly. I'd been in a bind, and that bind wasn't of my own making.

Living so close to the poverty line made getting through each day the equivalent of walking across a battlefield. I'd gone to war and I'd been injured—Professor Maclean was intent on rubbing salt into my damn wounds.

I rushed out the door, locking the place up and leaving the things I'd collected in there except for the watches and the cash, both of which burned a hole in my bag.

Scottie was with my mom, so, as had always been my intention, I left directly for class and caught my bus just in time.

Was it stupid crossing Brooklyn with the Rolexes on my person? Yes. But how the hell would I get them to the pawn shop if I didn't take them in?

Thankfully, I made it to campus without much issue, and as I slunk into Professor Maclean's classroom for my one and only lecture of the day, I sat in my usual seat—right at the top and at the back. It never worked though. He always looked at me, and today's class was no different.

In fact, he stared at me more, and with each glance, a startling concoction of terror and nerves danced around my insides like a kalei-doscope of butterflies were fluttering around my stomach.

Would he make me do what I'd done two days ago?

Or would he ask me to touch him?

Was it wrong that I almost wished he would? Because if he did, I'd have something to accuse him of.

As it was, getting people to believe a sexual assault accusation was nearly impossible. But when adding that a hot professor had asked me to get off on his desk, I knew I'd be laughed at if I even tried to implicate him.

Mortification ate up any of my lingering nerves before it was quickly replaced with trepidation. I gnawed on my bottom lip throughout most of the class, and was relieved when we hit the final fifteen minutes without him looking my way more than twice.

Of course, I was stupid for relaxing, and should have known he'd never have been so generous.

"Ms. Whitehouse, what, in your opinion, are the value of journals and diaries to the writing process?"

When his eyes were on me, that lip of his curled up in a sneer, everything inside me just shut down in misery.

I couldn't think.

Couldn't even form words.

When he cocked a brow, and there were noiseless titters around me at my ongoing silence, I trembled in my seat.

Was I such a pushover that this man could make the ground beneath me quake just by raising an eyebrow?

I hated him at that moment.

He could have turned the question over to someone else, could have let me off, but he didn't. He held my stare like it was some kind of standoff in a Spaghetti Western, and just when it shifted into *beyond awkward* territory, I managed to whisper, "Journals can be an autobio-graphical tool, a self-efficacy or a goal-keeping tool, but also, a means of writing development. It's a way of expressing oneself through one's own voice, with, I suppose, the hope that, down the line, it will help convey a character's personality better."

He narrowed his eyes at me, and I imagined he was looking at the people close to me, wondering if they'd prompted me on what to say.

But I was alone. No one sat before, behind, or to my right, and at my left was the damn wall.

When he dipped his chin and murmured, "Ms. Whitehouse is correct. Sylvia Plath's journals are famous as they catalog the battles she had with her mental health, which were also chronicled in her literary works. John Cheever used his journals to…"

As he moved on with the class, taking the focus away from me, I still felt as though I were under his spotlight, still burned as hotly as though his attention, and the rest of the class' were on me.

With a sigh when he wrapped up the lecture, I waited, as I had Wednesday, for the hall to empty. When it did, I got to my feet and began the descent to the desk where he was closing up his attaché case.

Today, he wore a pair of jeans that cupped every inch of his lower half like a glove. They were a dark navy and his shirt, in a similar color, was spotted with random bright white dots. The dark navy contrasted well with the dark brown sports coat he wore, and the fabric was strange—coarse, somehow. Inviting touch so as to experience the texture against one's fingertips.

When he caught me staring at him, he cocked a brow at me. "It's rude to stare."

"I'm sorry," I replied, not meaning it.

He sensed it and grunted, then slipped his attaché case under his arm, and muttered, "Come with me."

Once again, I followed him out of the brightly lit hall and into the corridor. His back now in shadow, the light hit from the outside wall which was lined with windows, gracing me with a delicious glimpse of his ass.

Not that I should be thinking of his ass.

The man was repugnant.

Mean.

A bully who had set his sights on me.

But I wasn't blind. No matter the character, the specimen of maleness was beyond beautiful. He had the kind of looks that belonged in a classic portrait, and I could well imagine one of the greats, Da Vinci or Michelangelo, studying his masculine perfection and capturing it for the idolatry of future generations.

My thoughts were fanciful, but I was a fanciful person.

With my feet buried firmly six feet under, I was rational to my core, so beyond grounded it was a joke. But in my secret self, where I could aim high, dream of being anything I wanted, I wished to be a writer. Wished to be anything other than practical and sensible. It was why—how hideous was this irony? —I'd signed up for Creative Writing.

When we made it into his office, I stood just inside the closed door, hoping he only wanted to verbally mock me.

Before I could ponder my fate, he took a seat in his chair, and as he rocked back, he stated, "You should wear dresses more often." Before I could jolt in surprise at the compliment, he patted the desk. "Make yourself come."

Disbelief filtered through me.

I stared at him for so long his nostrils flared with agitation. It reminded me of a bull who'd been pissed off by that floating piece of red fabric a suicidal matador would wave in front of the massive beasts.

Taking that to be indicative of his temper, I whispered, "Why?"

"This again?" he ground out. "You may have time for negotiations, but I don't. If you want me to stay silent, hop on the desk and make yourself come like a good little slut."

My eyes flared wide. "I'm not a slut."

He sneered, "You're not good and neither are you little."

Hurt had me quivering where I stood. "Why do you want me to do this when you hate me so much?"

"As I told you Wednesday, I don't hate you." Those brown eyes of his would have given me frostbite if I'd been standing closer to him. "And I'm doing this because I can make you do anything I want. Now, get on the fucking desk and make yourself come," he growled, and he punctuated the statement by slamming his hands against the wooden surface.

The sound had me jerking in place and I scurried forward, not wanting to agitate him further.

My meekness irked me, but the sensation of being trapped was too overwhelming for my own good.

Before I hit his desk, I put on the brakes. Though I knew he was on the brink of growling out another command, he settled back in his chair as I pulled up the skirt of my dress and shimmied out of my panties.

The white fabric lay like a puddle of innocence on the floor, a state of being I was discarding by attending to his whims. But I shoved the strange thought aside as I clambered in front of him, because if I carried on thinking things like that, I'd never get off. And I was on a deadline. I'd start work soon. Cleaning at *Crow*, followed by two shifts behind the bar, and I wanted to go to the pawn shop first. I had things to do, and prolonging this agony wasn't on that list.

The second I was in front of him, I strengthened my resolve, parted my legs and dipped my fingers between my thighs.

I could do this.

One orgasm for his silence.

No big deal.

Ha.

When I touched myself, I focused on the 'V' of his throat that had been revealed thanks to the way the top button on his shirt was unfastened.

As I dipped my fingers into my pussy for lube, I realized I was wet. Not drenched, but slick enough to help me out.

What about this horrendous situation had made me wet?

I didn't have a mental argument over just how wrong my body's natural response was, instead, I focused on getting this over with.

I had to be grateful he didn't want me to suck him off or fuck him. This was mortifying and discomforting, a real lesson in humiliation, but that would be devastating because I didn't know if I could say no.

I was at an Ivy League college. The administration would fry me to a crisp if he went to them with what he'd seen. Especially since my grades had been dropping too. I was no valedictorian in the making, just an average student in a place of brilliance, whose one miracle had been the chance at getting a scholarship here. Asking for two miracles in my lifetime was just greedy.

Which all meant, God help me, that I needed to please him.

And for some reason, pleasing him meant pleasing myself.

Rubbing my clit with one hand, I used the other to pump two fingers inside my pussy. As a result, it didn't take as long for me to climax.

When release powered through me, my head fell back and my breath whooshed from my lips as I let myself come down from the high I hadn't wanted in the first place.

My body tensed as I pulled my fingers out of my sex, and when I did, he spoke for the first time since he'd commanded me to move on top of his desk.

"Lick your fingers clean."

Considering I'd never tasted myself before, I wasn't over the moon about complying but, sucking it up—not literally—I cleaned my fingers.

When I shot him a narrow-eyed look, I saw that he at least appeared a tad more *awake* than he had before. The other day, I'd been sure he was asleep, for Christ's sake.

We stared at one another. I wasn't sure if it was another standoff or if we were just transfixed, but for that moment, there was no hate in his eyes, and that was the only thing I could read.

I had no idea why, but I'd consider that a win.

8

PHOEBE

"SIX THOUSAND DOLLARS?"

For a second, I was sure I was going to pass out, but the pawn shop, who was already looking at me like Professor Maclean did—like I was a thief—would have been truly unimpressed if I'd fainted on his floor.

Still, my knees felt like cooked spaghetti, and I was pretty fucking certain that my entire body had gone way past *al dente*.

I blinked at the man who held *hope* in his hands, and whispered, "How do we do this?"

"You sure these are yours?" he replied, studying the proof of ownership once more with a weathered eye.

It would have been easier to lie, but instead, I pulled out the letter Mrs. Linden had given me. When he read it, he looked a little less distrustful.

"You live over on Eighth and Hargreaves?"

I blinked at the man who looked like a cross between an Elvis impersonator, and a brother in *Sons of Anarchy*—yes, that was how bizarre he looked. "I do," I confirmed.

"I know a Janowicz. If it's the same schmuck, he *is* a grave robber.

I can't blame this Enid for telling you to get in there first." He dipped his chin. "She passed over?"

My bottom lip quivered. "Not yet."

"I'm sorry," he murmured, seeming to sense how genuine my grief was.

"Thank you," I whispered. "Can you help me? I need the money for childcare."

He nodded and, with that, six thousand dollars less his fees were dropped into my bank account—away from my mother's thieving fingers, there to use on Scottie's safety.

As I left the seedy storefront that had smelled of musty paper and had been filled with items that once represented people's hopes and dreams—just like Enid's with those watches—for a second, I allowed myself to savor the freedom I now had.

Childcare was expensive, I knew that. I also knew that six thousand bucks wouldn't last long unless I was careful, but the way I'd been raised, careful was all I knew.

But at least now, I had a safety net. Some semblance of protection against the harsh realities of this cruel world. Mrs. Linden had done that for me. She'd done as she always had—tried to keep me safe.

There'd be no more need to cut things so close to the bone with money.

At least, not for a little while.

And, thank God, I could return the money I'd taken from the tips and the cash register at the coffee shop. That would definitely be a load off my mind.

My morning had been busy. First with sorting out Enid's things, and then with my class and *after*. My main goal today had been to deal with the pawn shop, but now that was done, I had about an hour until I had to get to the club where I worked.

Quickly calling my mother, relief flowed through me when she picked up with the delightful response of, "Yeah?"

"It's me. Everything okay back there?"

My mom huffed out a sigh. "You do know I managed to raise you, don't you? You turned out all right."

I refrained from talking about the times my school had called in CPS, and I'd been left to fend for myself, but it was hard going. Sometimes, I felt sure I could grab my mother by the hair and smash her face into the wall over and over again.

The violent thought usually stopped me from acting out on that urge. Mostly because I was sure it would do the opposite of what I wanted—give her brain damage and not shake some sense into her.

"Need me to come home before my shift?"

"I fed him and changed him. He's sleeping now," my mom grumbled, and I looked at the time on my phone a second, pulling it away from my ear and cringing because she was messing with his schedule.

Knowing it was too late to argue now, I mumbled, "I'll see you soon. Don't set the place on fire."

She hissed out, "I did that once."

"*Twice*," I asserted, but before things could devolve, I cut the call.

Sucking down air, I turned away from the street and stared at the box the pawn shop had already placed in the window.

I could have taken a loan from him, one where I could repay him at any point and get the watches back, but who was I kidding? As much as I loathed selling something Enid had kept all those years, I needed the money.

So it hurt to see the box in the window, and though I'd intended on calling her anyway, it dampened my heart some when I patched through to the nurses' station on Enid's ward. I had a thousand questions for her, but the nurse told me Enid was asleep, and had been complaining of some pain, so she advised it was best to leave her to rest.

I wanted to argue, say that Enid had a long time to rest but didn't have a long time to speak with me, but couldn't. Wouldn't.

Instead, I sighed, mumbled a farewell, and hung up.

Though I dawdled as I walked to my second job, I was still early, and while I felt like a spendthrift, I decided I was hungry and could afford to buy a burger from the joint next door.

It tasted divine. The beef was rich and juicy, and not like the stuff I bought to save money from the store. It exploded on my tongue, melting in my mouth while enabling me to savor the naughty goodness of all the accompaniments—oh yeah, it was go big or go home, so I had it topped off with bacon and cheese too.

Afterward, of course, I felt sinful, but fuck it.

The money wouldn't last forever, I knew that, but one burger wasn't going to break the bank.

Of course, the instant that thought crossed my mind was the minute I worried if it was. If it would break the bank with the trigger pull of me being slingshotted down a slippery slope that involved me making shitty choices when I couldn't afford one wrong move.

Hell, I'd already made one wrong move and it had led to this situation with the professor. That alone was enough to make me have palpitations, because *wrong* didn't even begin to describe what was going on with him.

As I sat in the restaurant, staring down at the meal I hadn't intended on eating, on money I hadn't intended on spending, dread curdled with fear.

The rash decision would have meant nothing to some people, but I just didn't have the means to splurge on things. Not even a burger.

For so long, my life had been one long round of drudgery, followed by more hard work, and I'd taken it on because I'd known, after college, it would be worth it.

This burger, though a small blip on the radar, represented the start of an attitude change I couldn't afford.

As a result, it made that curdling sensation in my stomach intensify, and made me doubly regret the meal I'd gorged on.

When I headed to the club, I threw myself into work, hoping to burn off the excess calories as well as disperse the guilt with the nastiness of cleaning the place before a double shift behind the bar.

Crow was a kind of club-cum-chill out space. The music was always too loud, the clientele too damn swank for their own good, and we'd been raided by the cops four times in the past year.

For all that I'd end up with a perforated eardrum and a brown nose from the, you guessed it, *brown-nosing*, I quite enjoyed it.

More than the café. There, the hours dragged by because though business was brisk, it wasn't like the bar.

Here, the second I'd grabbed someone's money, another client was shoving theirs in my hand to get the next drink. I had three people hollering orders at me while I served someone. Time flew. Not to mention, the tips helped me massively.

The café was more sedate, more relaxed, and I guessed it just didn't fit me as well as it probably should have.

I liked working late nights too. I preferred to be in the dark with music I enjoyed, rather than having to get up at the asscrack of dawn to pour snooty city types their cup of morning Joe before they trawled into Manhattan to start their day.

Crow was a long, thin rectangle, that was a pain to clean, but once it was done, that was it until next Friday—the only time I pulled this chore.

With housekeeping over, I had a quick wash in the restroom, then changed into the uniform in time for my next shift, which started with restocking the shelves before opening.

The bar stretched along the back wall, and working with me, there was a team of six serving the heaving crowds that surged inside the second the doors opened.

Beyond us, there was the dance floor that was overstuffed with humanity, and overhead, there was a kind of mezzanine with a VIP area—I never served up there. To be honest, I wasn't even sure who did.

In our white shirts, denim skirts, and high tops, the all-female team rushed here and there as we served on command. What the lofty bartenders in VIP wore was as unknown to me as the purpose behind Area 51.

Three hours into my shift, my manager tugged my arm. "Phoebe? Time to head upstairs. One of the girls has called in sick."

Sweat was beading on my brow as I reached up and swiped at it with my forearm. "Me?" I asked with a frown.

Michaela nodded. "Yeah. And before you argue, you're the girl with the most experience down here." Her slick, red lips curved with amusement like she'd known I'd argue and I hadn't let her down.

Blinking down at her, because I was quite tall, I grimaced. "Should I get changed into a different uniform?" I motioned down at my outfit, but it was mostly in an attempt to divert her attention.

Knowing how most bars like this worked, because I'd been around the block as I tried to get a job that fit with my lifestyle, seeing didn't mean believing—I knew full well that the uniform in the VIP section would be swanky *and* skanky.

Maclean was right—I was fat and the uniform probably wouldn't fit.

The burger churned inside me once more like a silent, pulsating warning, one that dared me not to heed my inner Scrooge again. Ignoring that side of me came with an accompaniment of guilt, and that was something else I couldn't afford.

"No, no need. You just stay behind the bar and let the others serve."

So, she was just as aware that I was fat.

Great.

There was no point in getting angry. This was NYC, after all. If you weren't young, beautiful, and most importantly, *thin*, you didn't exist. I was quite happy with being a shadow in the dark, and would have given my left tit for Maclean not to have shone a light on my path, one that illuminated me in his world, and one that guided me in a direction I hadn't chosen and never would have.

With a grunt, I dipped my chin at Michaela and headed toward the end of the bar where I could exit the enclosed space.

As I moved, however, she grabbed my arm and frowned at me. "Are you okay?"

Surprised by the genuine concern in her voice, I asked, "Yeah?"

"Are you answering my question with a question?" she mocked, amusement lacing her words now.

My lips twitched. "Maybe?"

She snickered. "Seriously, you okay? I expected more arguing."

"What's the point?"

That had her sighing before she squeezed the arm she'd grabbed.

"Tips are better up there," she assured me, and that had me perking right up.

I could offset the stupid burger if I got more tips than usual.

Her words had me pasting on a bright smile that wasn't totally phony. She snorted at the sight then slugged me in the shoulder. "Go get 'em, tiger," she teased, and I shot her a grin before darting off to start earning those bigger tips.

As I headed out from behind the bar, the sheer welter of humanity in the space, as always, overwhelmed me.

What people saw in these damn places bewildered me, but maybe that was because I saw this dump in the natural light.

With strobes and lasers, the mirrors in here looked pretty cool. There were huge figurines formed out of an opaque white plastic that glowed in the dark, seeming to throb in time to the music. The shapes were forged into icicles, which considering the heat from all the people dancing, was beyond ironic.

As I slipped into the crowd, a guy grabbed me, making me jerk in surprise. When I was hauled into someone's arms and twerked against, I scowled up into the stranger's face and shoved at his chest when he twisted me around.

With his cock pressing into my belly, disgust whirled inside me— who did that? Shoved their erection into a stranger's stomach and, for even more of an ick factor, ground it into the soft mound like I'd pleaded with him to do so?

Eyes narrowing, I shoved at his shoulders and when he didn't relinquish his hold on me, his smirk deepening in defiance, I spat, "I work here. You either let me go or I call security."

"Not sure they'll hear you," the douche retorted, his hands dropping down to cup my ass. When he squeezed my butt cheeks, I raised my leg and kneed him square in the balls.

When he howled, people around us snickered, but as I rushed off, I let him get caught up by the tide.

It wasn't the first time I'd been propositioned here, and it wasn't the first time I'd had to defend myself against unwanted groping, but damn, it was the first time I'd found satisfaction in kneeing someone in the balls.

Was that a good development, or a bad one?

And, when it boiled down to it, why hadn't Professor Maclean's repeated intimidation inspired a similar reaction in me?

Was it because he was beautiful when the guy on the dance floor was passably attractive?

With my thoughts making me uneasy, I headed up the steps toward the VIP section. Here, the lights were lower, and there was a private dance floor actual celebrities were known to frequent—not that I'd seen any, and not that I gave a damn.

Aiming for the bar, I froze when I saw Professor Maclean tucked in a corner booth.

My eyes widened at the sight of him.

What the hell was he doing here?

Was he keeping an eye on me or something?

It took everything I had not to walk over to him, to demand his purpose for being here, but then I realized how fucking stupid that was.

This was a club.

A popular one.

And while he was a college professor, he was the exact opposite of an old fuddy-duddy.

Why wouldn't he be at a club that was modern, trendy, and over-loaded with women who shook their nonexistent asses on the dance floor?

Though the reasoning made sense, it didn't cure me of my apprehension.

That I'd seen him in both my places of work this week was odd, right?

I bit my bottom lip then decided to push thoughts of him aside.

If he was messing with me or if it really was a coincidence, either way, I had a job to do.

When I reached the bar, I was hustled behind it, given less than two minutes to acquaint myself with the space, and was relieved to note the bottles were stored in the exact same layout as downstairs, just on a smaller scale and with a heavy focus on the higher-priced labels.

Up here, those weird glowing shapes were more of a feature—they were sofas, uncomfortable ones, and tables too. Those were the only sources of light, making it darker than usual, oddly enough, when I was already used to working in a nightclub where the major source of illumination was a laser.

I got to work, managed to shove aside thoughts of Maclean for the moment, and was staggered by a huge tip I got from someone who came up to the bar rather than waiting on being served.

When the same guy came back three times, with a massive tip on each occasion, my cheeks burned when I realized he was doing it for a reason—not because he was attracted to me, but to make his girlfriend jealous.

"It's working," I told him flatly, *after* I'd taken his tip. My eyes flickered over to the woman I'd seen him sit beside earlier. She was shooting daggers at me like I'd danced off with him into the sunset or something, and hadn't just served him his drinks.

"Good," was his gleeful retort, before he grabbed his order and returned to his date.

She shot me a triumphant look—like I gave a damn—and the second he was seated, almost knocked his drinks out of his hands in an effort to straddle his lap and kiss half his face off.

The tableau actually disturbed me on a base level. Made me wonder if she'd not been willing to put out or something, and his flirting with me—even though it had gone unnoticed in the face of my joy over his tip—had been used to manipulate her.

Men were douches, weren't they?

Grunting under my breath, I focused on the busy shift, and realized that though the tips were way better up here, I preferred the mania of downstairs.

Maclean waited in his booth the whole time I was there. He didn't dance. Didn't even make eye contact with me. Just stayed there. Silent. Present without being watchful.

It was weird, and I knew I was making it so but hell, he had me on edge.

He was using my stupid mistake against me, and with no expiration date except for graduation, my options were limited.

When, an hour before my shift was over, the hairs at the back of my neck stood on end, I knew who it was.

It was him.

I didn't even have to turn around to see him to know he was there.

My heart started pumping, and I could feel adrenaline surging through my veins. It was as though my body was viscerally aware of the threat he posed, and though he was danger walking, that wasn't my sole response.

Sure, I felt like I was in the middle of a race, with my lungs churning and my heart pounding, but my belly was tingling like someone was touching me. My core throbbed with a heat I couldn't deny.

At that moment, my body wasn't aware that he was the enemy. That he'd blackmailed me. All I remembered was how he looked that morning after I came, those beautiful brown eyes narrowed into slits as he studied me, watching me like I was his own personal movie, as he demanded I suck my fingers clean.

Wednesday, I'd been terrified. Today, I'd been angry.

But now, so shortly after he'd extorted his way into my life, I seemed to forget all that.

How could my body betray me like this? How could I be viscerally aware of this monster?

I turned around and saw him standing there, and when I saw the utter lack of *anything* on his face, just that calm studious expression that made me feel even more like an experiment, I realized how odd his behavior had been tonight.

He hadn't left the booth once.

Hadn't danced with anyone even though women had come to him and tried to entice him out—because yes, I'd noticed.

As he'd watched me earlier in his office, I watched him tonight.

And what I'd seen was just as perplexing as anything the man did.

He'd come to a nightclub to sit and read something on his phone? To ignore the hot babes who wanted to dance with him? Not even to hear the beat, evading it so successfully that he didn't even tap his foot?

No.

He'd come for me.

When I took in his handsomeness, a beautiful masculine face that belied the cruelty he was capable of, my breath was taken away from me all over again as I took in the look in his eyes.

Dear God, the intensity there set my nerves alight.

He saw me, I realized.

He saw *me*, and that was the most terrifying thing I'd ever noticed.

When he looked at me, his attention was nowhere else but on me, and it made no sense just as so much of what he did was actually illogical.

He hadn't touched me, seemed to loathe me, talked to me like trash, treated me like shit, and yet, I lit up like a fucking bonfire now that he was here.

The man down on the dance floor had inspired revulsion in me, yet this bastard had me tingling.

Surely, it was too soon for Stockholm Syndrome. I mean, he hadn't kidnapped me or anything, but he'd definitely hijacked my body.

Twice now, he'd made me come in front of him, and that was more masturbating than I'd done in a month.

Swear to crap, I didn't have enough energy to do more than scrub 'down there' clean in the shower most days. Touching myself was usually a great way to cure a migraine I didn't have time for, and they came along once every blue moon. But twice he'd forced me to focus on me, had made it all about me and not about him, and apparently, even though it was only *twice*, that was two times too many for my body.

It remembered him.

As for me? As if I could forget. As if I could forgive.

This man was doing me no favors by what he was forcing me to do, but like any prey in the crosshairs of a predator's focus, I was preternaturally aware of the threat.

With the music pounding behind him, and in the strange glow up here from all the weird furniture, his features seemed more pronounced than ever.

He had a wide forehead with strong brows that shadowed those dark chocolate eyes of his. His nose was smooth, bump-free, and his Cupid's bow was high, pulled taut almost, so that when he smiled, it flattened out, made him look like he was pouting—there was a reason half the females in his class sighed whenever he dared grin.

The thought had me gritting my teeth as I bit off, "Can I take your order, sir?"

"Yes, you *may*," he corrected, his eyes blackened pools that I could easily fall into.

Jesus Christ, you could take the professor out of the classroom, but you couldn't take the red pen and the grade book out of the professor.

Jerk.

"What would you like to drink?" I asked flatly, hearing my irritation and aware that he would too.

Why was my pussy melting for this bastard?

What the fuck was wrong with me?

"Can you take a bathroom break?"

My face paled. "E-Excuse me?"

"Not this again," he snapped. "You're a relatively intelligent human being, Phoebe." Huh, so I'd been upgraded from *moron* to relatively intelligent. Such sweet words a woman dreamed of hearing from a hunk like this. "I asked you if you could take a bathroom break. You haven't left the bar once."

So, he had *been watching me.*

"I-I can."

That smile appeared, and though it was sigh-worthy, it didn't inspire that in me. If anything, it made me trepidatious.

"Good." His eyes twinkled, and I knew the bastard was enjoying my discomfort. "Be a good pet, and go inside and bring me your panties, along with two fingers of Jack Daniels."

Before I could agree or disagree, he turned away from me, leaving me gaping at him, and wondering if I had the gumption to deny him his request.

For endless moments, I stared at his back, hating him and hating my response to him at the same time.

I didn't want him to touch me. *I didn't.* I didn't want him to coerce my panties from me. Didn't want him to be able to hold his threats over my head so he could force me to do things I didn't want to do. And yet…

When he left thirty minutes later, fifteen before I was done with my shift, my panties were in his pocket and I'd never been more aware of just how damn naked I was beneath my skirt.

9

———

PHOEBE

THAT NIGHT, when I made it home, I collapsed on my bed after checking on Scottie and kissing him on his chubby cheek.

As I lay there, still in my uniform, I stared up at the ceiling, wondering what was going on with me.

My body was behaving oddly.

So oddly.

I was wet.

Had been since I'd given him my stupid underwear, had been on the ride home on the bus, had been as I headed up the eighty-one steps it took to reach my apartment.

How was he controlling me from afar was wrong, wasn't it?

My face scrunched up as desire hit me. Having never had that much energy for sex, for even thinking about it, tonight, it was all that was on my mind.

Biting my bottom lip, I spread my legs on top of the covers and reached between them.

I'd done this twice now on his desk, and each time, I'd felt mortified. Alone in my bedroom, the mortification wasn't there, but neither was the drive to make myself come.

I touched myself, learning my body, the peaks and troughs of my sex, and then slipped a finger inside my gate. I was slicker than ever, and so aware of how thin my finger was and how empty I felt.

Just as I released my lip to give an exasperated and thoroughly frustrated sigh, my phone beeped a text alert.

No one except for work, my mother, the professor, and now the nurses' department at Mrs. Linden's hospital knew this phone number, and since it wasn't a call, I knew Enid was still okay.

When I reached for it, I saw the text was from the professor.

Mouth suddenly dry, I swiped into the message and felt my stomach sink.

Maclean: *Send me a picture of your pussy.*

A fine quiver rushed through me.

Did he want more leverage over me?

Or, God, would he jack off to the picture?

Even as anger struck me at his audacity, I felt myself gush, a slick droplet slipping down the lips of my sex in response to his command.

With my legs already parted, it was easy to take a shot. I sent it and waited with bated breath for a reply.

He didn't disappoint.

Maclean: *Have you touched yourself? Send a picture with your pussy lips spread.*

My nostrils flared, and rather than answer, I slipped my fingers between my folds, took a deep breath, and tapped my screen. Was it awkward? Hell, yes. But the shot was surprisingly clear.

I looked wet.

Drenched.

Bright pink and flushed.

Ready to be fucked.

My pussy clenched at just the thought.

After I sent that, I typed:

Me: *I didn't come.*

Maclean: *Don't you dare.*

I didn't reply, but instantly began to rub my clit.

Hard.

Where before, there'd only been the desire to explore, now I wanted to come.

God, I'd never wanted to come so damn hard in my life.

Don't you dare?

I'd show him.

My heart began to pound in my chest, my pussy pulsed with its incessant throb, and my whole body flushed as I neared a peak.

Then the phone rang, and when I stared at it, I realized he'd added me to a video call.

I could accept or reject the call.

Knowing I needed to see a shrink, I didn't hesitate over accepting the call. The second I saw his scowling face, his furious eyes, that snarled top lip, my head flung back as wave after wave of delicious ecstasy cascaded through me.

I was loud because my mother was flat out drunk on the armchair as usual, and I let myself cry out, moan, fully ride the delicious sensations that were whipping through me like a twister in Tornado Alley.

By the time I came down from the high, I was too languid to really care that there was a vein pulsing in his temple, and that his cheeks were hollowed from containing his rage.

I stared at him with sleepy eyes, unsure why the sight of him had triggered my orgasm and to be honest, uncaring too. And he stared back.

For endless moments, we didn't say a word, just looked at one another.

It was, bizarrely enough, one of the most intimate moments of my life.

My throat felt tight with the need to ask a thousand questions. Like why, even though he'd made this about sex and I wasn't about to complain about his stance, hadn't he once suggested that I do anything to *him*? Why was it all about me?

The thought had me biting my lip.

"I'll be at the café in the morning," he said, *eventually*.

I cast a look at the call length and saw that we'd been sitting, staring at one another for twelve minutes.

Twelve minutes of silence.

"Okay," I rasped.

"Don't wear any panties. I want you bare from now on."

I gulped—*from now on?*

My voice was strangled as I got out, "I won't. G-Good night."

He hesitated a second, then his mouth pursed before, curtly, he said, "Night."

The second he disconnected the call, I placed my cell on the nightstand again and slumped back onto the too-thin pillow that had needed an upgrade years ago.

Hygiene wasn't always easy when you lived hand to mouth. Did I want new bedding? Yes. Did I have the money to spend on it? Nope.

Of course, that had changed now, and once again, that urge to splurge hit me, as did the knowledge that once I bought anything that wasn't important, vital for my lifestyle, the guilt that attacked me would sour any joy I found in having new things.

Plus, it would let my mother know I had money, and with Linda Whitehouse, what was mine was hers and what was hers was hers.

It was beyond unfair and had been one of the major reasons I'd wanted to move out. Then she'd gotten pregnant, pretty much to spite me, I felt sure, and I'd been left caring for Scottie.

I'd even named him.

The second she'd popped him out, she hadn't even given that much of a damn to call him anything other than *son.*

God, the hate inside me for her was so overpowering some days. Others, I just felt shame, and then there was rage and annoyance.

I could attribute no positive emotion to my mother, and yes, that was sad, but I'd moved past that point.

I'd consider it a boon if Scottie and I never saw her again.

That thought had me closing my legs and curling onto my side.

A girl could dream, couldn't she?

I huffed, because dreams weren't for people like me. I'd already attained more than I'd ever imagined by getting into an Ivy League school, but even there, I was drowning in the weight of my studies, struggling to keep up. That dreams weren't for everyone was cemented home when at three AM, the hospital rang.

Mrs. Linden had passed away and the only family I had who loved me back, aside from Scottie, was gone forever.

10

────────

PHOEBE

THE NEXT MORNING, my eyes were red from crying and I knew I looked like one big, tear-swollen mess.

I didn't have much makeup, but I tried to blot it over my cheeks and ended up making things worse. After rubbing it off, I decided to just go to work looking splotchy.

So what if Professor Maclean was there?

Did I really give a shit if he thought I was uglier than usual?

Maybe he'd ask, maybe he'd learn why I wasn't the monster he seemed to think I was, but I doubted it.

He wanted to see me in his own particular way, and it didn't matter if I fell outside the bounds of that opinion.

When I headed into work, the place was empty except for Jose, the guy whose shift I was relieving, and someone in the corner.

Was that him?

I'd never really noticed before because the café was usually busy, and even though my job could have been easy, this was the quietest shift, so Lorenzo had me dashing in and out of the kitchen, getting things prepped for the morning rush that would hit later on. People could come and go without my notice, but I recognized the back of his head now that I knew it was him.

He'd been here before.

A lot.

A lot, a lot.

I couldn't say if it was every day, but now that I thought about it, I just remembered seeing someone always sitting in that corner when I came into work.

Did the man never sleep?

I know I sure as hell didn't sleep enough, and last night had left me more exhausted than usual.

When I called out Jose's name, the professor turned to look at me over his shoulder. Because I was waiting on the move, I stared straight at him, and when he saw me, he frowned then turned back around.

"Hey Phoebe," Jose greeted, then, after a scant second, he jolted. "What's wrong? Have you been crying?"

"Mrs. Linden died last night," I rasped, aware that most people who worked around my shift knew of my circumstances. Sometimes, they'd had to cover for me when Scottie was sick and Mrs. Linden couldn't manage him, or there'd been that time, a few months back, when she'd fallen and I'd had to help out.

"Oh, honey, I'm so sorry." Jose patted my shoulder. "Where's Scottie? Who's looking after him?"

"Mrs. Linden's neighbor."

Cheryl had agreed to look after Scottie for thirty dollars for eight hours. Not a bad rate, but considering I was paying her under the table, and she was at home anyway with her two kids, I figured it was better than nothing, and though I was going to let my mom care for Scottie at night, trusting her throughout the day too was just asking for trouble.

But, all told, it might be cheaper for me to stop working at the café period.

Two hundred bucks a week on childcare wasn't sustainable, and I needed every cent of what I earned here for living expenses. I had to figure something out before the money Enid had given me hemorrhaged. Working from home would be for the best, but hell, who didn't want that kind of job?

Still, that was for another day. For the moment, I *could* pay Cheryl, so I just needed to get to work.

And hopefully, Professor Maclean would distract me from my misery.

Of course, I should have realized there was no 'hopefully' about it.

The professor was here for blood, and like a shark, he circled around me the instant Jose had left with a tired yawn and the promise of an empty bed to climb into.

I envied him.

God, I just wanted to go to sleep too.

He left his booth and headed to the counter where I was wiping down the small mess Jose had left behind. I didn't mind cleaning up after him. Jose was a disorganized worker, but he didn't have a problem with me running a few minutes late. We had a good relation-ship on that score—I cleaned up his mess, he didn't mind if I wasn't always punctual.

Symbiosis in the workplace. What more could any employer hope for?

When Maclean approached me, I stopped mopping up crumbs and discarded coffee grinds and turned to face him.

"Good morning, sir, how *may* I serve you?"

His eyes were narrowed slits as he stared at me—seriously, did the guy know how to do anything but glower when it came to me?

"I'll have a café latte."

"No please or thank you?" I retorted, staring stonily at him.

His top lip twitched as he passed me a twenty-dollar bill. "Keep the change. That's 'thank you' enough." When I took the note, his other hand shot out. "Use the bathroom and insert this."

My body tensed at the strange object he passed me, but though I practically lived like a nun, that didn't mean I was stupid.

"Would you like me to stick a dildo inside me before or after I serve you coffee?" I snarled at him, aware that my cheeks made a beet look insipid in color.

"Before." He smirked at me. "Don't be long."

I glowered at him and took a look at the *thing*. It was bright pink, had a 'C' shape that was thick at one end, and had a kind of tab on the other, which, I assumed, sat on my clit.

It looked like a spermatozoon had gotten high on LSD and had ingested a crap ton of cherry Kool-Aid.

Mouth tightening, I shot him a look, saw that wicked glint in his eye that I was coming to learn spoke of his amusement, and with a huff, turned on my heel and retreated to the bathroom.

On my way there, I kept my back to him and questioned, "Watch the storefront?" I was supposed to lock the door when I was 'alone' and needed to use the restroom.

"Of course."

I nodded and headed on to the bathroom.

Was I irritated that he hadn't asked me why I'd been crying? Yeah, I figured I was. But also, whatever he was doing with me wasn't about him caring about how I felt, and I got that.

Still, the situation presented me with an issue.

I was drier than toast and no way was that thing going inside me in my current frame of mind.

Plunking the toilet seat down after spraying it with the disinfectant bottle there, I wondered how the hell I was going to do as he asked. The last thing I wanted was that thing inside me, but staring at it like it knew the answer to world peace wasn't going to get me anywhere.

Realizing I needed to clean it, I got up, headed back out of the stall and to the sinks. Washing the toy with the liquid soap, I dried it off with a paper towel, stared at it, then looked at myself and whispered, "How the fuck did this even happen?"

Shaking my head, I retreated to the stall once more, dropped my pants to knee-height, and tried to think about sex. The good stuff. Ya know, the stuff I hadn't had.

Seriously, I'd had more orgasms with Professor Maclean glowering at me than I *ever* had. I'd never had a penetrative orgasm, and the two experiences I'd had, had been with a boyfriend who'd ended up in jail for eight years on a grand larceny charge—apparently, I had shitty taste like my mother.

"Okay, thinking about Shawn isn't going to get you wet," I muttered, so I did what had worked for me last night.

I thought of Maclean's stern features, of the tic in his jaw, the vein that pulsed in his temple. I thought of that bitterly snarled mouth and those eyes that could make me burn with both fire and ice.

Like that, I felt it.

Heat.

In my belly.

I released a shuddery breath and slipped my hand between my legs. I was wet, not like the Niagara Falls or anything, but enough to work this thing inside me.

As I leaned against the bathroom door, my head cushioned by my forearm, I touched myself, tried to get wetter, and only thinking about the schmuck tormenting me worked.

Christ, I needed more than a therapist, I needed to be tossed in the local asylum.

With the hot pink vibrator inside me, I got myself fixed up and went to wash my hands. As I stared at myself in the mirror, I wondered what he saw when he looked back at me.

My hair was wavy, thick and lustrous—probably my best feature. It was a dark brown and it complimented my skin tone, which was a warm olive. My eyes were green and, at the moment, they sparkled. Same went with my cheeks—they were bright pink from what I'd just been doing.

As I stared at myself in the dowdy uniform, with the black cap that shielded my forehead, and the apron that made me look frumpy, I wondered what on Earth he was getting out of this.

He looked like *that*, and I looked like *this*.

We were worlds apart.

I mean, last night, I'd seen those chicks on the dance floor eying him up like they were piranhas and he was a fresh meal. But not once had he looked their way. Not once had he gotten up to dance.

Gnawing on the inside of my lip, I shrugged off thoughts of how drab I was, how he had to be doing this for some kind of joke, and as I sucked down a sharp breath to spur me on, I headed for the door.

The second it was open, the vibrator turned on.

Even though I'd suspected as much, it still came as a surprise. A startled and breathy, "Oh," escaped my lips and I stared blankly at nothing as I felt the low-lying vibrations pulsing through my sex.

Unable to bear it, I clenched my eyes at the same time as I bore down on the toy, and when that happened, my face rearranged itself as the painful pleasure hit me.

It wasn't an orgasm, but Jesus, it was close.

The thought spurred me on and I realized I needed to make his coffee. I was a little brain-dead as I worked, making him his drink all while staring blindly into space when he messed with the different vibrations. He'd surge them up, then lower it to almost nothing.

The bitch of it was, the *nothing* hurt more than the whole-heap-of-something.

When I grabbed his drink, I hurried over to his seat, thankful he'd turned down the vibrations as I carried the hot coffee over to him, and whispered, "Here you go."

He grunted when his gaze flickered from his laptop to the beverage I'd set down before him. "I didn't ask for a cappuccino." He tsked. "Get me my latte."

His commanding tone got my back up, and I racked my brain, trying to think about his order but it was no good. I didn't remember.

I picked up the coffee cup, but he grabbed my wrist. "Leave it." With his other hand, he shoved a five-dollar bill at me. "Go and get the latte."

Dazed when, with my first step away, the vibrations surged higher, I felt the tremor all the way to my bones. Shuddering, I carried on walking, aware that he was watching me the whole time. Not just as I stepped away from him, but as I made his drink.

When I returned with the latte, he was polite. "Thank you." I nodded, intent on returning to my duties, but he murmured, "Take a seat."

In time to that demand, he sent the vibrations soaring high. Higher than before. So high, my knees buckled and I settled into the booth with relief.

His chuckle set me on edge, but his words calmed me some—he hadn't been mocking me. "So sensitive." His voice was a croon that worked on me just as hard as the vibrations did.

I blinked at him, aware I was a little dead-eyed. Licking my lips, I whispered, "I've never—"

"Never used one of these?" Though I didn't see how he was controlling the device, he fiddled with the vibrations as they surged high before sweeping low, and once again, my face crumpled as I felt his ministrations deep inside my body.

"No," I confirmed on a shaky sigh. These things cost the fortune I didn't have.

"This one is quite interesting. It's synced to a song."

Well, that made sense now I thought of it. He hadn't looked away from me the second I'd taken a seat, and the vibrations were all over the place, haphazard rather than remote-controlled, something that would fit with a deep, heavy bass. "Which song?"

His lips curved. "That would be telling."

Gulping, I whispered, "Can you turn it down a bit?"

"No." He tilted his head to the side. "Why do you look like you've been crying?"

Stunned that he'd asked, I whispered, "The woman who helped raise me and my brother died last night."

His eyes flared wide and he reached for his phone. "When?"

"About two hours ago." I grunted as the vibrations died down to nothing—was it weird that I considered that to be a respectful move on his part? "S-She was the reason I—" I sucked down some air. "I've never stolen anything in my life. But when she was taken to the hospital the other day, I had to arrange for childcare. I didn't have the money." My eyes burned with shame. Swallowing thickly, I murmured, "She died all alone and I couldn't go see her again because I was working."

I bowed my head, hating my words, hating how they'd made me feel.

I'd been sleeping while Enid had taken her last breaths on this plane. I'd been sleeping with a lighter load thanks to the gift she'd given me...

God, I hated myself.

When his hand gripped mine, it had me jerking back in surprise. Of course, I couldn't have just done it neatly. Nope. Couldn't have winded myself as I slammed myself against the cushioned wall behind me. Oh, nope. Too easy.

I knocked over the scalding hot coffee, managing to drench my arm in the stuff.

The instant the heat hit me, I yowled, and he stared down at me like I was a time bomb that he felt sure was about to explode.

As pain assailed me, I released a whimper and that seemed to work. He shuffled out of the booth and quickly hustled me onto my feet. Together, we rounded the counter toward the kitchen, and he instantly turned the faucet on the second we approached the sink.

When he stuck my arm underneath the cascade, he ordered, "Keep it there. Where's the first aid kit?"

Though I blinked at him, I pointed to the wall—it was right in front of him.

He shook his head. "Need glasses," he grumbled, more to himself than to me, I figured. But damn, I'd pay to see him in glasses.

As he pulled out bits and pieces from the kit, I let the cold water soothe the scald and chided myself for being an idiot.

The kitchen scented of freshly baked muffins and coffee from the front, but also, his aftershave... and as someone who adored Lorenzo's recipe for blueberry muffins, I could attest to the fact that Professor Maclean smelled better.

The place was typical for a mom-and-pop joint. Kind of grody, in need of a new layer of paint, but painfully clean to the point of being Maria's obsession.

When I cut him a glance, saw his brow was furrowed as he delved into the kit, I realized how out of place he looked and how much I fit in.

He was made for faculty events, boring cocktail parties in smart suits where other professors gathered together and talked about boring shit. He belonged in casual designer gear like the polo he was wearing —legit labels, too, not fake—and those shoes of his probably cost more than my past five pairs combined.

What the fuck was he doing messing around with me?

I was a student; he was my professor.

Wasn't this a breach of the rules?

As much as he was blackmailing me into keeping quiet about what he'd seen, didn't I hold leverage over him? I had proof of his calls, could attest to the fact he'd been in my place of work… Hell, if I got to the dean first, I could make it look like he was stalking me. Sure, they would probably laugh me out of the office, believe him over me, but there was still a threat.

So, why?

Why was he doing this?

When he headed out and began searching the counter for something, I watched him go. His thick dark hair was mussed up like he'd been running his hands through it over something hard he'd been working on. His brow was creased as he hunted down whatever he was searching for, and in his casual outfit, he looked all the more handsome. Enough that I stared at him and wondered what he'd look like without the clothes, without all the gloss—I bet he'd look even finer.

When he returned with saran wrap, I didn't argue. The wrap was basic 101 in scald treatment, but I was surprised he knew that. Most people didn't know first aid unless they *had* to know it for a job, and it made me wonder if, back in the day, he'd worked in a place like this, had strived to reach his lofty position.

Somehow, that made me feel better.

Made me feel less like a lost cause.

When he turned off the water, I winced because the heat instantly hit me. He gently dabbed the area with clean swabs from the kit, and moving fast, loaded my arm with a burn cream before rolling some Clingfilm on it and covering it up.

When he shoved a couple of Ibuprofen at me, I shook my head. "It isn't that bad a burn."

"Doesn't mean it won't sting."

He stared me down until I accepted them and put them in my mouth. Under his watchful eye, I reached into the fridge under the counter and took a deep sip of the water I pulled out.

He released a relieved sigh. "Good. It will feel better soon."

"What's happening here?" I whispered, his concern hitting me on the raw.

His lips twisted into a half-smile that looked the antithesis of amused. "That's for me to know."

"And for me never to find out?" I shook my head. "It doesn't work like that."

When he reached up and traced a finger along the curve of my jaw, I realized it was the first time he'd ever touched me intimately. Not just the comfort of hand-to-hand contact, but an intimate, personal caress.

My body froze into one huge piece of ice before it flowed molten hot as I shuddered at the simple, meaningless touch.

My response to him was beyond anything I could have anticipated.

But then, I'd never expected this. Any of it. Never thought I could feel so much for someone who was intent on making me miserable.

I was sick.

I had to be.

Who got off on being touched by the person who bullied them? Who made them do things no one should ever ask of another human being?

Me, that's who.

My eyes closed as his finger trailed down my jaw and across my throat. Every single nerve ending leaped up in response, and I shivered, completely in his control as he whispered, "That's exactly how this works."

And with that, he moved away, leaving me cold, alone, and wanting him.

11

PHOEBE

MRS. LINDEN, Enid, had arranged her own funeral.

I wasn't sure if that came as a relief or not. It meant that the State didn't rely on her nonexistent next-of-kin to settle the debt of her burial, and it meant that I wasn't obliged to help out—like she'd undoubtedly known I would.

God, I missed her.

I missed the cup of tea she had waiting for me each morning after I left Scottie at her place so I could drink it on the way to work.

I missed her telling me about *Jeopardy* and bitching about Mr. Gardner on the eighth floor who I was certain she had a crush on.

I missed her perfume that filled my nostrils when I hugged her.

I just plain missed her.

If there was one advantage of being overworked, underpaid, caring for a baby, preparing for finals, and being blackmailed by my professor, it was that my mind was all over the place.

I was grieving, and it was at the forefront of my mind, until something else got in the way. It was a low-level pain, like a toothache. Possible to ignore until you did something stupid like eat.

When the hospital told me her body had been moved to the funeral home, I contacted them and discovered her burial was two days away.

Though I was surprised at the swiftness, I was also relieved. Thinking of her in a fridge somewhere just made me uneasy. I'd watched way too many John Oliver vids on YouTube to not want her buried quickly.

Enid deserved to rest in peace. She'd lived a long life, and I wanted her settled. Silly? Maybe, but she was my mother, and that was that.

The only black I owned was my uniform from the coffee shop, and it felt weird wearing that, but I didn't have a choice. I paired the black pants with a white tee-shirt, and used one of the wraps I'd found in her apartment to cover up. I also wore the scarf I'd taken, and before I hauled Scottie into my arms, I took a deep sniff of it, aware that today I was going to get closure before I was even ready for it.

Of course, Scottie instantly played with the scarf and his gurgles had me smiling as I carried him downstairs and began the short walk to the funeral home.

It was only twenty minutes away, and I was too used to carrying Scottie and hauling beer kegs that I didn't even feel the strain as we walked. He made it easy on me by being fascinated by city life as he so rarely went out, and it kept him quiet.

It seemed apt that the sun was shining today, and I tilted my head back, using a pair of shades that I'd taken from Enid's place to enjoy the light breeze and faint warmth on my face.

I'd taken the morning off from the coffee shop and, since it was Tuesday, I didn't have any classes until three, so I was as free as I ever got.

Brownsville was one of the only places in Brooklyn that hadn't been totally gentrified, but it still cost a lot to live here. I was used to its shabby ways, and believed this was home, even if my apartment had seen better days.

As I approached the funeral home I hadn't even known was there, I actually realized where I was.

A few years earlier, there'd been a huge drive in the area to save Our Lady of Loreto—a Roman Catholic Church that was over a century old. I'd found it pretty sad at the time, but Enid had been distraught over the loss of the parish.

Now, affordable housing was being constructed in the area—not that I could afford it. When the city council tried to make stuff affordable, who was it affordable for?

As I asked myself the question, Scottie tugged so hard on the scarf around my throat that I almost choked. Wheezing as I laughed, we both engaged in a tug of war over the fabric that I won.

I bopped him on the nose with my lips as I headed into the funeral home. I was, all told, surprised when I learned Mrs. Linden had opted for cremation. She'd been a traditionalist in many ways, but I'd expected there'd be more of a service than there was. Especially since she was Catholic.

When I headed into the room where Mrs. Linden, who'd yet to be cremated, was resting in a closed casket, my heart wouldn't let me walk over to where she lay.

She wasn't in there.

She wasn't.

I refused to believe it.

She'd live on through Scottie and me, and I'd make sure of that.

There were a few people milling around the room, drinking the cold tea that was supposed to be warm, and small glasses of sherry. It felt wrong. Weird. There was a dead body in the room, and it was like…

I sighed.

Overthinking this would get me nowhere.

I settled Scottie on my hip and sunk into the background. A priest came and went around the room, talking to people, and I sank deeper into the shadows, not wanting to see him. I'd never liked Father O'Neill, and avoiding him was a top priority.

Perching on the windowsill, I let the hours drift by. I stayed until the end, until the people who owned the funeral home asked me to leave.

Begrudgingly, I did, and was both relieved and disconcerted to know that Mrs. Linden had given them my contact details to collect her ashes when they were ready.

Wondering what I'd do with them, where I'd spread them that would mean something to her, I headed out, my thoughts elsewhere.

When, on the path outside, I found Professor Maclean waiting on me, my eyes widened in surprise.

"What are you doing here?"

His mouth pulled taut. "You told Jose at the coffee shop a Mrs. Linden had died. It didn't take much to find out where her funeral was."

He'd gone to that much effort for me?

For a second, I just gaped at him, then Scottie blew a raspberry on my cheek and slapped the other, which told me I'd been gaping for a lot longer than I'd meant to.

Clearing my throat, I muttered, "This is my brother, Scott."

Maclean blinked at my brother, then stared at me. "You have the same hair."

My lips curved. "Yeah."

I stared down at the curly mop on Scottie's head, one that matched my own. My hair was a pretty nice color, but it was the mass of curls and waves that set it apart.

Maclean cleared his throat. "I wondered if you'd like to go for something to eat."

I frowned at him. "Why?"

"Because you've just been in there." He grimaced as he motioned at the funeral home. "Hardly the nicest way to spend your morning."

"Enid deserved my time. I just wish I'd…" I didn't finish the sentence.

"I'm sure she understood," he said softly, and I knew he was right, but that didn't make me feel any better about the situation.

"She's the first person who's close to me that has—"

"Died?" he supplied, shoving his hands into his pants.

I nodded as I stared at him, miserably wondering if God was playing a joke on me.

In his jeans and sweater, he was wearing normal clothes, and yet managed to look like a dark angel as he stared at me. His perpetual scowl wasn't in the picture for once, and that was why I wondered if God had a hand in this, because that had to be a miracle, right?

Maclean and his scowl went together better than candy and Halloween.

When I stared at him, eying that luscious dark hair that my fingers itched to touch, he murmured, "Lunch?"

"Please." My voice was hoarse with emotion and really, the last thing I should be doing was inviting company, especially *his*. But I had to eat, and I'd prefer eating with him than alone.

If I was alone, I'd think about Enid, and one thing Maclean had shown me was that he was good at distracting me.

"Do you want anything in particular?" he asked, and I heard a hint of awkwardness in his voice, one that made me wonder if I'd misheard it because this walking specimen of perfection couldn't be awkward around little old me, surely? "For the child?"

I shrugged but found myself amused and touched that he thought about Scottie's needs. "I'll try anything once. Something light? I'm not really that hungry."

He hummed and motioned for me to step by his side so we could walk together. When his hand came to my elbow, like something from an old-fashioned movie, I felt my cheeks burn with heat and was grateful that Scottie was a distraction.

"How's your arm?"

Surprised he remembered, shyly, I told him, "It's fine. It didn't even blister."

"I'm glad."

Falling silent then, he used his hold on me to guide me down the sidewalk and over the crosswalks, and though it could have been a demeaning move, I knew he was trying to be nice to me so didn't take it as him thinking I couldn't walk without help.

It was to my shame that my brother was so goggle-eyed about the city. I never got much of a chance to take him out, and Enid hadn't been able to manage the stairs all that often, so he was inside most of the time.

The traffic, the people, the restaurants and shop fronts, kept him occupied as we walked in a strained silence.

At least, the silence felt strained to me.

I wasn't sure why he was here, or what he wanted from me. Just that he wanted something... The devil didn't come bearing gifts without a price in mind.

Still, the feel of his hand on my elbow sent heat billowing through me, warming me up from the inside out.

When we reached a vegetarian restaurant, I was surprised when he walked me inside and we took a seat. It was a small place, all whites and creams with scrubbed wooden tables. On the back wall, there was a mural of a jungle scene that fascinated Scottie.

As we were seated, a server came out from the back and, spotting the baby, dragged a highchair over. I settled Scottie in it after shooting the waitress a smile of thanks, and noticed the professor's gaze settle repeatedly on it—not Scottie. But the high seat.

Weird.

But then, what wasn't weird about Professor Maclean?

"I have a little girl about that age," she said with a smile, and I didn't correct her assumption that Scottie was my son.

"He's almost a year old," I replied, aware of how proud I sounded. Like I'd had a hand in the passage of time. But, and it was a huge but, without me, I had no idea what would have happened to him. Not with my mother as a parent.

I'd already endured her proficiency at motherhood, so I was grateful he wouldn't have to as well.

The waitress and I made small talk about babies for a few minutes until she handed us the menu, took our drink orders, then retreated to serve us. As she went, I looked at Maclean, aware he'd been studying me throughout the conversation.

"What is it?"

He shrugged.

Well, this was going to be a great meal if that was the level of chat he was capable of.

And I wasn't wrong.

Once our drinks arrived and the waitress took our orders, we were pretty much silent until she served the meal.

He just stared at me and did this thing with his hands—tapping them against the table in a way that could have indicated boredom but seemed more like a ritual of some kind.

Because I was embarrassed as hell, I played with Scottie and kept him occupied with the small rounds of bread the server had given him to gnaw on.

"What are you doing about his care now that your friend has passed away?"

The question startled me because he'd been so silent, it had been easy to think he was just bored and regretting his decision to be a decent human being for once.

Well, twice.

Since Enid's passing, he hadn't been horrible to me in class.

"Her neighbor is looking after him for the moment."

"I thought she charged?"

His cocked brow had me wincing. "She does, but Enid left me a few things."

"Like what?"

I narrowed my eyes at him. "I didn't steal—"

He raised a hand. "Did I say anything about stealing?"

"No, but I wanted to preempt you before you did." My jaw clenched. "She was looking out for me, and because of her, I at least don't have to worry about Scottie for a little while."

"Is it sustainable? A few of my friends are parents and they always complain about the cost of childcare."

Were we really having this conversation?

"I don't think I have much choice," I said stiffly.

"Why doesn't your mother take responsibility?"

"She's an alcoholic."

I tried to force some enthusiasm for the salad I'd ordered—he'd already accused me of being well-fed once, so I didn't want to give him ammunition a second time.

He grunted. "I see."

"I doubt it," I retorted shortly.

"What did Enid leave you?"

I wondered if my pain was visible on my features. "A pair of 'his and hers' Rolexes. I had to pawn them. But they were enough to help me get through college, so that's something. After I graduate, I can hopefully get a better job." I blew out a breath, feeling stupid for having such limited plans. "I guess you're used to people knowing what they want to do with their lives."

"Not everyone can afford ambition," was all he said, and even though his tone was cool, I actually appreciated the words.

"No," I agreed. "You're right. We can't all go where the wind takes us on a whim."

"That's probably one of the most fanciful things I've heard from you." He rubbed his chin. "And I've graded a lot of your papers."

Given me shitty grades on them too.

Not that I said *that* aloud.

"Even this realist is capable of whimsy," I mocked, spearing the lettuce leaf on my plate like I had a personal vendetta against it. And I didn't. I loved fresh vegetables because I rarely got a chance to indulge in them.

"Where would you let the wind take you?"

I snorted. "Why would I tell you? You'd just mock me."

He shrugged. "I'll tell you where I'd let it take me."

My eyes widened, and even though it was stupid, I fell for the bait.

Hook.

Line.

And sinker.

"Where?"

"France. I used to dream of owning a vineyard there."

"Why?" I questioned quietly, bewildered by the softening of his features as he stared down at the table.

"It was just a dream, now it isn't, but I'd still like to live there."

"Why France in particular?"

"I visited when I was a boy. My parents took me. We went to Paris, headed down to the South of France and attended a couple of the showings at Cannes… It's a memory that always stuck with me."

If I'd needed a dose of reality, I had it then.

That kind of vacation spoke of money. Not that I hadn't realized that. Everything Maclean wore showed wealth, and his office at the university was the same. Filled with furniture that had a sheen to it, a gloss of money.

If I'd needed a reminder that I was nothing more than a toy to this man, I'd had it.

"Well? What about you?"

Could I tell him? Should I?

He'd probably just scoff.

I stared down at my plate, uncertain and nervous, terrified even of his mockery.

He'd done nothing but hurt me and humiliate me, so why I wanted his approval in this when I knew I wouldn't get it, was beyond me.

"I'd like to write romance."

His facial expression didn't alter. "That isn't a place."

So literal.

I sighed. "No. But you can write from wherever, can't you?"

"I suppose," he replied stiffly, like he was fighting hard not to respond to me.

God, did he want to laugh but was trying to be kind because of Enid?

Mortification welled inside me, and I was relieved when Scottie squawked loud enough to make me jump.

I hauled him out of the highchair and bounced him on my knee for a second, and then I said, "I should go."

His smile was tight. "Is it customary for you to leave before you or the person who invited you for lunch has finished eating?"

He wasn't wrong, and yet, I didn't know if I could stay here much longer.

"Why did you bring me here?" I whispered, staring down at Scottie's hands that were tearing into a piece of bread.

"Because you needed to eat." He gritted his teeth, then slipped a hand into his pocket. When he retrieved a piece of paper, I stared at it and frowned at the words.

"What is it?"

"A friend of mine is looking for someone to transcribe her notes." He cleared his throat. "She works through this site so you need to apply on there. Maybe you could build up a clientele so you could work from home?"

Whatever I'd expected him to say, it wasn't that.

I stared at the paper, then back up at him. "Thank you," I whispered.

His mouth twisted in that way I recognized, and although I expected some cutting remark, he merely answered, "You're welcome."

Because of that, I didn't try to leave again.

12

PHOEBE

TEN DAY LATER

I GULPED when Professor Maclean had me stand up in class.

I hated when he did this.

Since when was Creative Writing the equivalent of Amateur Dramatics?

When I clambered down the stairs to the base of the auditorium where he loomed over his desk, looking like Pluto reborn with the command he had of the platform, four of us hovered there, awkward as fuck. It was a stunning contrast to his confidence, and increased my awareness of the man's power.

I was ninety-nine percent sure that he did this to make us miserable, and because I was getting to know him, even if it was obliquely, I figured I wasn't wrong.

Though his face was always stern and expressionless, his eyes held a wicked intent that reminded me of those moments after I came when his eyes would catch mine and I'd be left gasping like a fish speared on a hook. Great imagery there, but yeah. He looked like sin incarnate, and I looked like a dying fish.

Yup, sounded about right.

What made this worse, of course, was the text I'd received this morning.

Maclean: *Remember, no panties. Wear the vibe.*

No 'good morning,' just an orgasm as a threat. *Go me.*

"I want you to think about the importance of italics and why overusing them can be irritating," he stated, his voice toneless as he intruded upon my thoughts, but hell, I was sure he was messing with us.

Mostly because I *knew* I used a lot of italics in my work.

Was this his way of getting back at me?

When I looked at the piece we were reading, I frowned at it. It was by 'unknown,' which didn't put me at ease as I scanned through the text that was littered with italics.

"Ms. Whitehouse, I think you should start, followed by Mr. Hudson as Jericho, Ms. Lewis as Holly, and Mr. Markham as Johnson."

Was it just me? Was I the only one who heard the croon in his voice when he said my name? That dangerous purr that put me on edge? He didn't caress the others' names, only mine, and fuck, it made me feel alight with the way he put extra emphasis on mine.

Some days, he did this. Made me feel like I was the only person in his world. Then, on others, I felt like the nobody I was to him. The non-entity that a person like me was to someone of his stature— because I didn't give a damn what anyone said. He was more than just a professor. He had status and money. It was evident in every move he made, every syllable he uttered, and in the things he wore.

He reeked of it.

Nervously, I swallowed and when I tried to speak and failed, I cleared my throat, knowing full well that he'd never let me get out of this, and of course, the second I opened my mouth, he did it.

The bastard.

He turned on the vibrator.

I wanted to glower at him. Wanted to kill him with the death rays that were attached to my eyes, but I couldn't. Wouldn't. Didn't want to give him the satisfaction.

Which left me with a huge problem.

The setting was on one of the highest, and my body was already primed from how he'd been using it off and on during class.

He didn't do it often, but occasionally, I'd get the command in a text before class, and I knew to prepare myself for the misery.

I hated that he was sporadic with it. Some days, when he texted me, he wouldn't use it. Others, he'd overuse it. Leaving me totally hanging, unsure of his intentions. Of course, that was exactly what he got a kick out of.

My uncertainty.

My inability to plan what he was doing.

Bastard.

Sure, he'd been *nicer* since Mrs. Linden's funeral, but nice and Professor Maclean weren't words that went together often.

"The truth *is*, Jane *deserves* to die." The words were pretty strong for an opening line, and the use of two italics definitely made it weirder when they were uttered aloud.

"Nobody *deserves* to *die*," the guy next to me said.

"*Everybody* does *something* in their lives that is worthy of the *final* punishment."

I winced at how many damn italics there were and how, in the running of the dialogue, it sounded even funkier.

But of course, that wasn't the whole reason for my wincing and flinching. I wasn't sure what song he set the vibrator to, but the heavy bass killed me.

In fact, nope, that was too simple a word.

It didn't just kill me, it *annihilated* me.

Blasted my nerve endings like an atomic bomb, making it impossible to stand upright, to focus on the text in front of me.

When it was my turn again, my voice was reed thin as I stated, "*I* think *you* shouldn't be talking about such matters. It isn't a *servant's* place to do so."

The spotlight shifted off me, and for a second, I was relieved. Grateful. The vibrations died, lessened for a moment, then of course, just as I began to hope he didn't want me to orgasm in front of the entire class, the vibe turned onto the highest setting.

My shoulders dropped, my chin lifted, and I knew my eyes sparkled as I stared at him.

Right at him.

Our gazes clashed, held, and my jaw firmed as I tried not to moan, tried not to shudder with the power of the sensations coursing through me.

Only staring at him, letting him hold me visually, got me through, which was messed up considering he was the one tormenting me.

My body began to tremble, shaking from the inside out as the pleasure he'd forced on me made itself known.

"Ms. Whitehouse, is everything okay?" he asked, frowning at me, back in the role of professor and not my tormentor.

My throat was tight as I whispered, "Stage fright."

He hummed. "Just a few more lines to go."

I read my part, quickly scanned what I missed because he was enough of a bastard to ask us about the text, especially when I missed it thanks to him, and I realized he'd planned for me to come when there was a chunk of the dialogue where I wasn't required to speak.

Ugh.

Why did he do stuff like that?

Just when I could call him a bastard, he did something kind of nice.

Although, was that really *nice*? Wouldn't it have been nicer if he didn't text me before class and ask me to insert a fucking vibrator so he could torment me with it, while I was in a lesson where he was supposed to teach me something for the crazy fees I paid to study at this Ivy League joint?

He was blurring the lines again.

Confusing me.

Making me want something I shouldn't want.

During the mornings when I saw him in the coffee shop, he'd tip his chin at me when the place was quiet, and I'd come over with a café latte for him and a cappuccino for me.

I'd sit there, awkward at first, while he worked.

We didn't talk.

It wasn't something we did.

But I knew why he did it.

He didn't *want* to talk to me. He wanted me to take a rest. A quick one. With the tip he handed me when he paid for our coffees, I'd bought Scottie a teddy bear and had paid for groceries all last week thanks to that money.

It smacked of charity, but equally, it didn't.

I kind of deserved it for the crap he was pulling with my body. Making it work against me.

Damn him.

When the segment was over, I knew I was hobbling slightly as I headed back up the stairs to where I was seated. It hurt to walk up there, and I regretted sitting right at the top because, oh boy, I was sensitive.

I wanted nothing more than to take out the damn thing just in case he pulled another stunt on me, but mostly, I was just feeling hollow.

That was my biggest issue at the moment. Not the bills that were piling up, or the fact that I was going to have to hand over a couple of hundred bucks to Cheryl tomorrow. It was the fact that I was empty inside when I came, and I was tired of it. So tired of it.

What he was doing was wrong. He was blackmailing me, but what was weirder was that I wanted him to take it up a notch. This was turning consensual and that was terrifying. But what scared the hell out of me was how I was tired of him using my body as a marionette doll. I was tired of him being the puppet master. I needed more, and whether he was going to give that to me was another matter entirely.

It was so strange, I knew that, but I wanted him inside me. Pumping away over me while his body was a heavy weight over mine.

Just thinking about it had the power to make me shudder as I slumped in my seat.

I wasn't sure how much longer I could take any of this, and not for the reasons that most women would think…

Not a single part of me wanted this to be over. I just wanted more of what he wasn't offering, and if that didn't make me as much of a screw up as him, then I wasn't sure what would.

13

———————

PHOEBE

AS I STARED at the job offer from the professor's friend, I had to wonder if it was too good to be true. I had no idea if the rate was above average or not, just knew that it was more than I could make at the café in an hour.

The only trouble was I'd never transcribed notes before.

Not that I was going to tell the professor or his friend. Especially not with that kind of money on the table.

My jaw worked as I hovered over the reply. It all seemed straight forward. Payment through PayPal, Elizabeth would provide me with a link to a cloud where I could access the images of the diary she wanted transcribing and upload completed transcriptions. Payment would be made when ten new documents were uploaded and the accuracy checked.

I could work from home.

Stay with Scottie.

The two hundred I had to hand over to Cheryl in the next ten minutes burned in my pocket.

I couldn't afford to hand that over to her, but I had no choice. She was really good about me bringing him down so early for the start of my shift at the coffee shop, and she never complained if I was late back from school. But the money was just more than I could afford.

The Mrs. Linden-sized hole in my life was felt more than ever. Not just through the money I was hemorrhaging, even with the little fund she'd gifted me, but in every aspect of my life.

I was depressed, overworked, tired, and it was getting weird with the professor.

Not on his part—well, no weirder than usual.

But with me.

I wanted him, was starting to crave him because he was the only aspect of my life that wasn't predictable. That the threat of money and my debts didn't loom over.

Could someone have Stockholm Syndrome without having been kidnapped?

That was how I felt anyway.

Like he'd taken hostage of my body, had kidnapped it, and had made it his.

Just thinking of him made me hot and bothered, and what was irritating me the most was how he still hadn't touched me.

God, that was driving me insane.

It was like I had fire ants strolling down my damn nerve endings because he avoided touching me so much that I was even more sensitive than usual.

I blew out a breath and hit 'send' on the acceptance email of the job offer. Maclean had saved my ass, and I was sure he knew it, but it surprised me that he didn't lord it over me.

He was like that, after all. Quite capable of using my actions against me, but he hadn't mentioned it since the day of Mrs. Linden's funeral a few weeks back. And it wasn't like he'd forgotten.

At the coffee shop last week, he'd asked me if I needed a lift to the funeral home to collect her ashes, and me, being the sucker I was, said yes in the hopes that he'd touch me. Maybe hold my hand.

Christ, you knew you were desperate when such a simple touch was a craving. But the only person to hug me was Scottie, and the only person to care for me was, bizarrely enough, the professor.

And he did.

He bought me coffee, left me tips for food. He'd share his breakfast muffin with me on a morning, and had made that offer of a ride to the funeral home… No, he wasn't Mr. Darcy in the making, but hell, Lizzie Bennet had hated Mr. Darcy at first.

Before she married him.

Not that that was on the cards for the professor and me, but still. I understood her about-face, even if I'd always thought her a pansy-ass for it before now.

Walk a day in my shoes…

I hauled Scottie off the floor where he'd been crawling after I vacuumed it earlier and, tucking him onto my hip, headed into the kitchen. I bypassed my drunk-as-fuck mother and grabbed the gear my boy would need for the day.

Cheryl blinked blearily at me as she took Scottie from me. He settled on her hip with a pout that, I knew if I didn't leave soon, would morph into a tantrum. And that was the last thing any of us needed at this time in the morning.

Because of that, I shoved the money at her, and felt guilty at the relief in her eyes—she needed the money just as badly as I did, and yet I was about to take it from her now that I had this new job.

Her ratty robe was threadbare as Scottie plucked at it with displeasure.

"Thanks, Cheryl," I said, aware that guilt made my tone husky. "I might be late this afternoon. I have an appointment."

I didn't say why, but my post-class meetings with the professor were starting to take up more time, and I wasn't about to complain.

"No worries. He'll be here right as rain, won't you, bud?" she teased, and grinned at me when Scottie huffed like he wasn't her bud, and like he disagreed about the 'right as rain' part.

Her tired eyes held a lightness that was in direct correlation to my stress—she felt better for the money in her hand, while I felt all the worse for it.

I waved bye at them both and quickly got out of there. Knowing the professor would be there added a buoyancy to my step, one that made the walk to the café go quicker.

When I made it inside, I scanned the coffee shop and was astonished to see he wasn't in his regular spot.

My heart sank, but Jose was coming around the counter the second I was inside.

"Thank God," he grunted. "I have to go. If I don't get to bed, I'm going to die."

I snorted at his melodramatics. "See you tomorrow."

He yawned and scurried out, leaving me in an empty café.

Well, there were about five patrons, but it was empty of the one man who counted.

Worry for him hit me, and I knew that was stupid, but I couldn't stop it. He was here every day. His presence had been unwanted at first, but now, he made me feel safe.

I blew out a breath, aware once again how strange this was getting, but what perturbed me the most was that I didn't want it to stop.

The second I was behind the counter, I texted him.

Me: *Are you okay?*

No instant reply.

He was always on his phone. I'd noticed that.

After his trip to *Crow*, I'd often seen him up on that mezzanine, in the same spot. Now that I knew where he was, I knew he had a bird's eye view of the club's layout—including me.

He was watching me.

Another shaky breath escaped me as I accepted the truth.

He was stalking me.

Only, I didn't feel endangered. Didn't feel like I was unsafe. If anything, I felt safer. With his eyes on me, I felt untouchable. And yet, he wasn't here.

Why wasn't he here?

The panic inside me was like a bubble that was on the brink of bursting. I didn't know what to do or what to say. I tried to call, but he didn't answer, and as my shift dragged out, I knew I'd never been happier that I had a class with him today.

Even if he still tormented me within the hallowed walls of the lecture hall.

However, when I made it to school, there was a note on the door.

Class canceled.

My eyes widened and I rested my hand on the note.

Did that mean he was sick?

It would explain why he hadn't been at the café, and it would also explain why he hadn't answered his phone.

That he was sick, somewhere in the city, and I didn't know where he was or if he was okay, had pain spearing through my belly.

Legitimate pain.

Did he need me?

Christ, did he need anyone?

My jaw worked as I stared at the note. I was angry with him, I realized. Angry and stressed out because he hadn't contacted me.

I grabbed my cell and dialed his number again.

No answer.

My heart sank. I needed to hear his voice, and if I sounded needy, then fuck, it was how he'd made me.

I did need him.

And yeah, it was nuts, but maybe I *was* nuts.

Maybe that was just me and how I was, especially around him.

Throat tight, I bit my lip as I left the building and headed outside. I only had the one class today, and though the sun was shining and everything was bright and warm, with every other student scurrying around on their own schedule, it bypassed me.

The day was darker because he wasn't in it, and that was as terrifying as it was true.

14

PHOEBE

"WHERE WERE YOU?" I demanded, the second Jose had left the following morning.

His eyes were red-rimmed and his face was drawn. He *did* look sick, and that he hadn't contacted me told me just how little I meant to him.

And yet, I had to mean something, didn't I? Otherwise, why would he be interested in me?

He looked like he was in a mood. His eyes were brooding, and his mouth was drawn tight as he peered over his shoulder at the thankfully empty coffee shop.

"Sit down," he commanded, and that note in his voice made my blood sing.

Why?

Only God knew.

I released a breath as I sank onto the booth. "Were you sick?" I asked the second I was opposite him.

"Spread your legs," he demanded as coolly as he was ordering a fucking coffee.

I ground my teeth. "No," I spat. "I want to know where you were."

He cocked a brow at me. "It doesn't work like that. Spread your legs."

My blood quickened as it usually did, and it pissed me off even more that he was using my body against me.

When I glowered at him, my mutiny written into every line on my face, he murmured, "A day's absence and you forget how it works."

The purr was back, and fuck if it didn't instantly get me hot.

My stomach rippled as my hips rocked against the bench seat in response. I truly felt pity for Pavlov's dogs at that moment. I knew what it was to salivate at will.

Okay, different kind of *salivate*, but still. Those poor pooches. And God help me, I was just as bad as them.

"Are they spread?" he inquired, stirring his steaming cup of coffee that he'd evidently just ordered.

Except, when I stared into the brew, I realized it wasn't coffee.

It was yellow.

I frowned at him. "Since when do you drink chamomile?"

"Since I caught a stomach bug at a faculty meeting." His mouth tensed. "Are they spread?"

Because he'd answered me for once, and because I knew now that he'd been ill and was here, even though he still looked rough as shit, I did as he asked.

When he lifted his cup, he peered over the rim at me. "Are you wet?"

I hated that he knew my body so well.

How did he? How could he?

He'd never touched it. Had never even caressed me, and yet, he knew me better than Shawn, my ex.

It almost made me mad at him, and then I recognized how stupid that was. But this was a seriously confusing situation, and it had me on edge in ways that a woman in my position couldn't afford.

Or, at least, a woman who'd been in a position.

I was handing in my notice today when Lorenzo made it into the coffee shop before I left, and even though I was freaking out, I was also psyched. I wouldn't have to worry about Scottie being with someone he barely tolerated, and I could earn what I needed to get by while staying at home.

I mean, being at home wasn't as marvelous as it might be for some, but I'd take it if it meant I didn't have to hand out thirty a day for someone to care for my baby brother.

When he took a sip of tea, his patience irked me to the point that I stared back at him. Stared and stared until I almost drowned in his eyes. Until I almost wanted to.

My heart began to pound in my chest, my blood felt like it was boiling, and everything inside me felt as though it was turbocharged just from that one point of connection.

But it wasn't enough.

I needed more, but also, I didn't need this at all.

Closing my eyes, I broke the connection then reached under the table, slipped my hand up my skirt, and touched my panty-less pussy.

I was, as predicted, wet.

Blowing out a hard breath, I opened my eyes again, looked at him and whispered, "How do you do this to me?"

He didn't smirk at me, didn't even grin. If anything, his jaw worked and I wondered if this pained him as much as it did me.

What would it take to make him need more from me?

Even as that crossed my mind, though, I knew it was stupid. Maclean, despite being a bastard and mean with it sometimes, wouldn't hurt me.

I was safe.

Safe within the monster's clutch. Bewildering, yet true.

As I played with my pussy, I stared at him as though we were a regular couple having a regular drink together at a regular coffee shop.

But nothing about us was regular.

Nothing.

At all.

My pussy was wet, desperate for his touch, his cock. So eager for it, I—

The thought occurred to me, and I didn't know why it hadn't until now.

I could touch him.

He didn't have to touch me first.

He reared back like he knew what I was about to do, and I couldn't stop myself. Connected with him through our gaze, I licked my lips and began to sink under the table.

The second he understood what I was doing, his nostrils flared and he ground out, "Stay where you are, Phoebe."

I shook my head and disappeared under the tabletop. I felt his tension from afar, felt it and wondered at it.

Why wouldn't he want me to touch him, to give him pleasure? After weeks of watching me satisfy myself, surely he needed more? *Craved* it as much as I did?

My own mind was working against me. I needed to touch him, needed him to feel as much as he made me feel.

It was a compulsion, a desire so strong that it was more than I'd ever felt with my ex. This was almost as heady as an orgasm, for God's sake.

My hands rested on his thighs, and I felt the tension within him. What I also recognized, however, was that while he might claim he didn't want me to do this, he wasn't moving.

He hadn't shifted out of the booth, and he was still sitting where he'd been.

Was that the green light?

Did I need one?

My nails dug into his crisply ironed dress pants. The man wore clothes that some might wear on a night out, and this was just to visit a crappy coffee shop in my neighborhood.

Part of me wondered what he'd look like on a date night, and another part of me didn't give a fuck because all I really wanted was to see him naked. No clothes, no barriers, nothing between us.

Christ, I wanted that as much as I wanted his dick.

When my hands smoothed over his pants, his tension transmitted itself to me again, but I ignored it. I had to. I needed this more than he did.

As I reached his abdomen, I found his belt buckle and began to unwrap it. When I rubbed a hand over his shaft, feeling the thick bulge that was proof he wanted me, a sob of relief escaped me. I pressed my face to his leg, so fucking happy that I wasn't alone in feeling this exquisite need.

He felt it too, but he was fighting it, and that was what I didn't understand.

Maybe would never understand.

I shuddered as I started on the buckle once more, and just as I reached for the zipper, just as the lines began to part and the scent of him in these close confines overwhelmed me, the bell on the door sounded.

This time, my eyes did grow moist with tears, and I scurried out from under the table, terrified I'd be caught, but even more terrified at what I'd see in his eyes.

The craving for him was so powerful that my body ached with it, and I knew, without a shadow of a doubt, he was going to punish me today.

As I served the four customers who came in as a group, I wasn't surprised when my phone buzzed in my pocket.

Maclean: *Insert the vibrator.*

It was in my bag as it always was. Charged and ready to go.

When I could, I headed to the bathroom and released a moan as my fingers slid through my slickness. I filled myself up with the silicone dick and thought of the heavy weight of his. How it would feel in my hand, skin to skin, how it would taste against my tongue.

I imagined his body atop mine, thrusting, rutting against me like a beast from what I made him feel.

My fingers slid against my clit, and just as I was seconds away from orgasm, the vibe started.

A startled gasp escaped me.

How did he know me so well?

It was like he was attuned to me.

I cried as I orgasmed then. Cried because it was either that or scream as the pleasure raked down my nerve endings.

It wasn't enough. Wouldn't be until he was there, inside me, not this fucking piece of plastic, but it took the edge off, and I was surprised, truth be told, because he wasn't a kind man, and what bewildered me was the fact that I didn't want him to be.

I liked him just as he was—*weird*.

15

PHOEBE

A FEW DAYS into my new job, I had to admit a few things.

One, I felt guilty.

Not only had I left Lorenzo and Maria in the lurch, even though it was with their blessing when I explained my situation, but Cheryl had looked like she was going to cry when I told her about the change of plans.

That she needed the money as badly as I did was a given, but though my hands were tied, it didn't stop me from feeling bad about it.

Two, I missed seeing the professor at the coffee shop in the morning.

Without him to start my day, I felt like I was going into withdrawals. Like he was a drug I was addicted to, and didn't know how to buy.

Three, I was loving the change in Scottie, loving even more that I got to spend his birthday with him.

Working from home meant I could sit with him, and let him roam around my bedroom and his as he was refusing, more and more, to stay in his crib.

I often sat on the floor, my laptop on my knee as I watched him. He seemed to be flourishing with how much time I could give him now, and considering he was missing Mrs. Linden as badly as I was, it made me feel like I was doing something right at the moment.

As for his birthday, I got him some stuffies that he adored. What with my being around more and the teddies, his smile had never been wider.

He had to stay in the crib while I was at school, and on the nights when I was at the bar, Mom was home. She wasn't a responsible adult, and she spent half that time drunk off her ass, but he was asleep and she promised me she wouldn't leave him.

I should have known she couldn't even keep that simple promise.

A few nights after she'd repeated that promise to me over another payment of a six-pack of beer, I returned to find Scottie sobbing his heart out. He sounded like he was in agony, those tears were soul-deep, *wounded*, and they pained me. Physically.

After a quick scan that showed me my mother had left him because she was nowhere to be found and hell, the apartment was tiny so hiding was out, I went into the bedroom, smelled crap, and saw his arm was torn up and bandaged badly. And for the first time in my life, I was at a loss.

I stared at him as he stared back at me, his cheeks bright red from the fury he'd worked himself into, his tiny hands curved into fists that were white from the strain.

Then, he broke my heart.

Literally burned it to ash.

"Ma-ma."

His first word.

Was he calling me that or was he saying that Mom had done this to him?

Okay, that was allotting a lot of brainpower to an eleven-month-old, but he called *me* mama?

Oh, God.

And I'd left him.

I'd left him with that bitch who'd birthed us both.

My mouth quivered as I shot forward and hauled his stinky butt into my arms. Sure, he smelled of poop, but beneath that, he smelled like mine.

And, for all intents and purposes, he was.

I was the one who'd rocked him to sleep, who'd fed him and burped him, who'd changed his diapers and cleaned up his puke. I'd been the one to fret over his vaccinations, who'd worried about daycare…

Me.

I *was* his mother, and I needed to start acting like one.

Staying here was a no-no. I saw that now. I'd been running on hope and a prayer as I had for the past twenty-one years of my life where my mother was concerned, and I knew that the time had come for me to break ties with her.

This was it.

She'd really fucking done it now.

Maybe I should have reached this point before, maybe I should never have left it until this moment, but I'd been thinking like a sister. Reacting instead of acting. I'd had no money, no prospects without my degree, and I was young. Those were my excuses, but no more.

It was time to woman up.

I soothed him until he calmed down, and the second he didn't fret as much, I got him cleaned up as much as I could and tossed his dirty diaper into the trash.

Leaving him for a second to roam around his bedroom floor, I closed the door to run into the bathroom and set up the baby bath. When it was ready, I headed into the kitchen to grab a quick drink of water and saw the broken glass on the carpet again, along with some droplets of blood.

How many fucking times did I have to tell her?

How many times would it take for her to learn not to break shit? And why the hell had she let Scottie crawl in here in the first place?

I'd put him down for the night before I left for work, goddammit.

Not wanting to leave Scottie for too long, I left the kitchenette that stank of old beer, ignored the crappy living room that smelled of cheap liquor that had soaked into the carpet, and returned to Scottie's room.

Hauling him into my arms, he giggled as I blew a raspberry onto his cheek. When he settled on my hip, the rightness of *everything* just sank into my bones.

I could do this.

We could do this.

I needed to get away from my mother, needed to stop her toxicity from seeping into Scottie's life.

Resolved, I washed him up, looked at his arm and was relieved to see the cut was tiny but the blood had made it look worse than it was, especially since my drunk mother hadn't bandaged it properly.

It would scab over quickly, but the rift between my mother and her children never would.

Enough was enough.

I'd reached my limit.

Or so I thought.

After an hour of sitting with Scottie and comforting him until he could sleep, I was dead on my feet when I finally made it into bed.

Professor Maclean hadn't texted me as was his usual way, and I found that disconcerting enough to keep me staring up at the dark ceiling longer than I should.

Tomorrow, I didn't have to get up for anything except for Scottie. My shift at the bar started at nine, so I had the day to work on the transcriptions and try to figure out my next move.

I'd need to start relying on Cheryl again, but at night this time, and the next thing was figuring out somewhere to live that was close to the bar.

Because my brain was whirring with thoughts, I was awake longer than my tired body wanted. Still, if I'd been asleep, I probably wouldn't have heard the giggles coming from the living room, or the masculine grunts a few moments later.

Mom had given up her bedroom for Scottie when he'd been born, so the living room was literally where she ate, drank, and slept.

Now, she was apparently fucking in there too.

I didn't say anything.

It wasn't the first time I'd heard her having sex with some random.

Christ, I'd probably been 'there' for Scottie's conception too. But damn if it wasn't going to be the last time I had to endure this.

As I heard her crying out to God as she faked an orgasm—because *no one* came that fast, not even me with the professor watching and stoking my embers—my phone buzzed. I reached over and something inside me settled when I saw it was him.

I stared at his text for a long time.

Maclean: *What are you doing tomorrow?*

Why did he want to know?

Any other man, I'd have thought he maybe wanted to hang out with me. But this was the professor. He didn't want *that* from me.

I wasted about twenty minutes before I replied, and even then, my heartbeat sped up because I was keeping him waiting. The tiny ticks had turned blue so I knew *he* knew I'd read the messages.

Because I wasn't in the habit of lying, I texted: *I'm moving out. My brother and I can't live with my mom anymore. She's dangerous for his safety.*

Maclean: *What happened?*

His reply was astonishingly quick, and it made me wonder what he was doing. Made me question if he was lying in bed, in the dark, his body bared beneath the sheets as he spoke with me.

Even as riled up as I was, as angry and unsettled over my intentions for tomorrow, everything female inside me stirred at the thought.

I'd never seen him so much as discomposed, yet he'd seen me in so many various states of discombobulated it was ridiculous.

As I stared at his question, I wondered how much I should tell him.

He'd threatened me.

Had said, "I hold the worlds of you and your brother in the palm of my hand."

But this was the man who'd appeared at my side after Enid's funeral.

Who'd tended to my arm when I'd scalded it.

Who'd suggested the transcribing in the first place.

Would he really do anything to separate me from Scottie?

I gnawed on my cheek as I deliberated how I should reply. Though

I barely knew him, I knew enough to know he wouldn't be happy with a non-answer, and silence would only piss him off further.

Like he'd read my mind, my phone buzzed, and I snorted out a laugh when I read his next message.

Maclean: *Waiting.*

God, he was such an asshole.

His nose was bump-free, which led to the question of how the fuck had he reached this point in his life without someone breaking it for him?

Despite myself, I was amused by his arrogance, and it prompted me to answer with the truth.

Me: *I came home and he was all alone in the apartment.*

Maclean: *She'd left him?*

My jaw clenched.

Me: *Yeah. And he was bleeding from a small cut and was a mess.*

Just thinking about that mess made rage swirl inside me. As well as terror.

Tonight could have ended so differently. Could have derailed in so many different ways that my heart sped up as I contemplated the numerous and varied incidents in which Scottie could have hurt himself tonight.

Maclean: *What's your intention?*

Me: *I don't know. Not really. I don't have anywhere to go, but I know I can't stay here.*

There was a long pause, and I wondered if he'd fallen asleep. It was late, late enough that the fucking in the living room had turned to grunts and snores.

I settled my phone back on the nightstand, not expecting a reply tonight, hell, not expecting a reply at all.

What was there to say?

But I wasn't ready for sleep. Not when I was thinking about the next steps I was going to take.

I had to get Scottie out of here, that was for damn sure. He couldn't stay around the poison that was our mother.

When my phone lit up my bedroom, I jolted out of the daze my sleepy brain had fallen into, and when I read his message, I just gaped at it for a solid minute.

Maclean: *You can come stay with me until you get back on your feet.*

Was he for real?

I couldn't stop myself from typing: *I thought I was a filthy thief.*

Maclean: *You were. Now you're not.*

It was such a typical response from the asshole that I had to shake my head.

Me: *I couldn't impose.*

Maclean: *Wouldn't have made the suggestion if it was an imposition.*

As I stared at the screen, wondering if he'd lost his mind, I subsequently wondered if I'd lost *my* mind because instead of refusing, I replied: *If you're sure.*

Maclean: *I'm sure.*

And that was how, the following day, I climbed into a taxi with the minuscule amount of possessions I owned, my brother in his car seat, and headed for Williamsburg—one of the best neighborhoods in Brooklyn.

PART 2

THE MIDDLE

16

NICHOLAS

I'D NEVER CONSIDERED myself an idiot. If anything, I'd considered myself as being relatively smart.

As a Rhodes Scholar, I'd read Literature at Oxford, and now was one of the youngest to have tenure in my department. It wasn't my dream job, but I enjoyed it.

For the most part.

At least, I had.

Until Phoebe Whitehouse had walked through the doors of my lecture hall and had changed everything, then had compounded my misery by electing to sit in my class.

Did every love story begin with stalking?

I hoped for the heroine's sake that wasn't the case, but Phoebe wasn't a heroine and I sure as fuck wasn't a hero.

As I stared at the picture of her slick pussy, I imagined her fingers fucking herself, thought about her moans when she came in my office, and remembered the scent of her when she climaxed.

My cock instantly hardened but I ignored it, as I always did. Even when my heartbeat throbbed inside the shaft, even when I felt like I'd fucking explode, I ignored it.

I had to.

It was a sweet, delicious agony, but the trouble was, I'd just invited my sin in the flesh to come and stay with me.

That was what made me a fucking idiot.

But what the hell was I supposed to do, see her on the streets?

The reason I followed her around most of the goddamn time was to make sure she was safe, so her wandering around homeless went totally against that. Plus, I might be able to sleep more than two hours if she was here, under my roof, protected.

That thought alone created a welter of emotions inside me. Want and need curled around the persistent desire for her, as well as my body's craving for REM sleep. The four combined into a cluster that had me leaning back on the bed and staring up at the ceiling.

I'd intended on watching her come tonight. Had intended on making her video herself, but when I'd arrived home late from a faculty meeting and had found Gina bawling on my front step, things had gone awry.

Suddenly, the need to torment Phoebe as she tormented me hadn't been there, it had been replaced with the simple desire for her company.

She was, in her own way, a bizarre combination of complex and simple. I knew she didn't realize her own power, and that was the only thing that made this situation bearable.

I'd seen a lot of bitches walk through my classroom doors—fuck, I'd married one. So I knew the type who believed they walked on fucking water. They had more men panting after them than a pet store full of dogs, and they knew it and milked it for everything they could get.

Phoebe, in another life, might have been that girl, but this life had knocked her around, and while a part of me wanted to lift her up, force her to see what she was for herself, another part was selfish.

If I kept her as she was, she'd stay the same.

She wouldn't change.

And I hated change.

God, I fucking loathed it.

Someone hollering in the distance had my head twisting to the side as I looked out of the window. I couldn't see much, thanks to a large tree beyond—not that I was about to complain—I loved that tree. I'd buried Cara underneath it, and watching it grow from a sapling to a strong and hardy pin oak always filled me with satisfaction.

Death didn't have to mean the end.

I rubbed my belly where the start of my own particular 'ending' had been, the scars were thick ridges that had me gritting my teeth.

Forcing my thoughts away from those memories, instead, I focused on the idea of Phoebe and her brother living in this sterile place I called home which, before they arrived, I'd have to clean as well as set up somewhere safe to store my gun.

I thought about how long it would take me to baby proof the apartment and set an alarm. With that done, I leaned back in bed, then a couple minutes later, reached for my phone again and set it a half-hour earlier.

Sure, I had a housekeeper who came once a week, but she wasn't due for another four days, and this place wasn't safe enough for a baby so I'd have to work on that tomorrow.

No one had lived here with me since Rosa and Cara had died, and Gina had moved out, and because of that, I was getting a rep among my few friends for being a confirmed bachelor.

I wasn't.

I'd been burned, literally, and had no intention of it happening again.

That was why I hated Phoebe.

She was walking fire and she didn't even fucking know it.

My jaw clenched as I thought about her earlier that day.

Over the weeks, she'd started finding it easier to come. At first, she'd been tense and it had taken her a while. Now, it was disappointingly fast how quickly she reached orgasm, even though a part of me was pleased by that too.

She'd taken to plunging her fingers in and out of her cunt, whereas at the start, she'd inserted one and had kind of left it there. Now, though, she was greedy for her release and fucked herself with those slender digits that were callused from her work.

I wanted those fucking hands around my cock more than I wanted my next breath, wanted to ram myself inside her, give her the pleasure she craved with my body, but I wouldn't.

Couldn't.

It was both heaven and hell to have her watch me back. For her eyes to be open, trained on me, as she made herself come.

Some days, the urge to tongue fuck her had me almost tearing off the leather on the armrest of my deskchair. Everything inside me wanted more, but that was why I held back.

And those were the days I was spiteful.

Mean.

I hated myself for it, and watching her shoulders droop as I denigrated her, twisted me up as much as it did her, but words were weapons.

I'd learned that a long time ago.

Still, today hadn't been too bad. I'd been busy, aware of the faculty meeting, and hadn't had time for her to really get herself off in front of me. I always made time, of course, but I'd been glad for her speed, and had enjoyed the show even though it had frustrated the life out of me.

There was one advantage to her living here, I guessed.

I could watch her more often.

Hear her more often. Have her make more noise, and not risk my position by making her do the crazy things I needed from her in my office.

I could take advantage of her closeness, not have to rush things, or worry about where she was and with whom.

As the thought sank in, and my eyes began to close with the promise of sleep, I recognized that maybe I wasn't so stupid after all.

17

NICHOLAS

HAVING RECEIVED a short text from Phoebe, I knew she was on her way.

My home wasn't exactly ideal for a baby, but it was clean now. *Safe*. I couldn't have her or her brother who, even though I loathed children, was quite cute—it helped that he looked like a miniature Phoebe—on the streets.

When I'd learned she had a baby, I'd hated the infant immediately. My disposition had improved the second I'd learned he was her brother, and my jealousy had been further alleviated when I'd seen him outside the funeral home.

With all that hair?

With those sparkling green eyes?

Phoebe in the flesh.

How could I not find him adorable? Even if he did make a mess and a lot of noise in the restaurant I'd taken her to, he'd done it with a smile that reminded me of her.

I should have known then I was doomed.

Still, my loft wasn't child-friendly. As I stood at the doorway, trying to picture what she'd think, I had to wince.

The open floor plan was split into two sections. To the left was a doorway that led to the bedrooms, bathrooms, and the kitchen and utility room, but directly ahead was a raised platform that was separated from the living area by a wall.

Once upon a time, the walls had been blank, then I'd stumbled upon a Yayoi Kusama print in a store and had bought it, framed it, and placed it there.

Whenever I walked in, I saw the print first and it reminded me of both Phoebe and myself.

The print was almost like a cross-section of a cell. With its endless dots and looping shapes, scarlet eyes, and the spiky perimeter that reminded me of dripping blood. But what resonated were the faces. I guessed they were crude, but one watched the other and that was me watching Phoebe.

In that print, I saw infinity.

An endlessness to the obsession I had with her.

The need to watch her seemed epitomized in that print, and it was the only bolt of bright color in the entire place.

The table and chairs were dark wood, modern in style. The living room consisted of a navy sectional on a thick-pile cream rug.

Opposite was a fireplace that ran the length of the wall, and above it, a TV that I never used. Beside the sectional was a small stand that carried a lamp, and in the corner was my desk. Its twin was in my office at the campus, as was the desk chair, and it was neat. Most of the paperwork was housed within the drawers and never on the surface.

I often sat there, staring out at the tree opposite my building, unable to relax in a place that was my home and yet, felt detached to me.

When the buzzer to my door sounded, I jolted in surprise as I realized how long I'd been peering around my apartment.

Knowing she was there, I felt a curious buzz churn through me. It was a mixture of nerves because I wanted her to like the place even though I didn't, and also, relief.

She was here.

She hadn't run.

She'd be safe and I could rest.

My heart calmed when she buzzed again, and I pressed the release, coolly stating, "Yes?"

It was amazing how cold I sounded, not just *cool*, when I felt anything but around her.

It was like I was constantly running a fever in her presence, and hell, maybe I was.

She was my own personal sickness in the flesh, and I adored her for it.

"Professor?" she answered, her voice faintly high-pitched, her nerves bleeding through and as always, because I was a sick fuck, that calmed me down. "It's me."

"Who's me?" I asked, my lips curving even while my tone was stern.

She cleared her throat. "Umm, Phoebe? Phoebe Whitehouse?"

Like there was any other Phoebe, any other *woman* who was allowed here.

This was, did she but know it, her place.

"I'll be down in a moment," I informed her.

"Oh. You don't have to. If you don't want me to come up, it's ok—"

"I'll be down in a moment," I repeated, interrupting her without compunction.

I knew her confidence issues wouldn't resolve themselves with me barking at her all the damn time, but my barbs were a means of self-defense.

If she was going to live with me, though, and I fully intended on keeping her here, I'd need to stop that.

Her hesitations and stuttering irked me.

She was glorious.

A creature made to be worshipped.

Such glory did not stutter.

Such a being did not whisper her way through difficult statements.

Resolving myself to not being curt with her, even if that made for a few awkward conversations where I couldn't speak what first came to mind, I cut off the intercom, grabbed my keys, and headed out of the door.

I was only two floors up, so I always took the stairs, and when I saw Jackson, the doorman, both eying her up and staring at her things with snobbish dismay, the beast inside me reared to life.

Glowering at him until he dipped his chin and turned his head away, I stared at Phoebe, looked at the sleeping child in the car seat, and then at the four bags she had with her.

Blinking at the sight, I asked, "Is the rest in the taxi?"

Her cheeks bloomed with heat. "Um, no, this is everything."

Everything?

Their lives, their *worlds*, were in these four bags?

Jackson coughed. "Sir, I paid the taxi."

I cut him a look, retrieved my wallet, and gave him a fifty.

"It was thirty dollars," Phoebe squeaked.

"Keep the change," I told him, ignoring her.

When she flushed again, I sighed, then held out a hand. "Take it," I urged, when she stared at the key resting there.

As her fingers brushed against my skin, I realized that was the first voluntary, non-sexual touch I'd ever had from her.

My cock leaked pre-cum from that single, caressing touch of the tips of her fingers against the tender skin of my palm—so innocent, yet so powerful.

My jaw clenched, but I hid my agitation by ducking down, grabbing two bags under my arms, then clutching the other two by their handles. I didn't wait for her to follow, just left her to carry Scott as I headed back up the way I came.

When I heard her tentative footsteps against the stairs, I sighed in relief and remained silent as I led her to my apartment.

Backing up so she could reach the door first, I motioned at it with my chin when she made it up the stairs.

Keeping her eyes downcast the way she did always irritated me, even if I understood why—if you kept your eyes trained on the ground, you remained a stranger to the world itself. You could blend into the shadows, and slip through the cracks until everyone forgot about you.

Of course, she hadn't slipped through *my* cracks.

I'd seen her.

Seen her and made her the center of my universe.

As she opened the door, she released a sigh as she went inside, and I followed her in. I didn't wait for her to look at the place, to critique it, but headed down the hallway to where my personal torment had begun.

There were four bedrooms in the loft.

I could easily have put her in the room the farthest away.

Instead, I put her beside me.

I liked to torture myself.

"You can use another room for Scott if you want," I rasped, my voice loaded with the strain that having her here, so close and yet so fucking far, would present.

Her smile was faint. "Call him Scottie. I don't know if he'll answer to Scott." Then, she cleared her throat and mumbled, "I wouldn't want to put you out even more so he can just sleep with me."

She'd been putting me out for years and hadn't known it—why should this be any different?

My life had changed that day I'd seen her on campus, and when she'd ultimately signed up for my class, it had gone from bad to worse.

I ignored her and placed her things in the bedroom.

It was a woman's room, and I'd left it as Gina had decorated it because it seemed pleasant enough.

The back wall was lilac with a print of a blue leaf in a black frame in the center. It hung above a sleigh bed made from rich oak, and housed a matching dresser and nightstands. There was a comforter rolled up on top, as well as fresh sheets stacked there for her.

It was probably rude of me not to have made up the bed, but feeling cotton that was about to touch her would have been an effort in torture.

Yes, I knew I was a freak.

It wasn't like I needed the reminder.

Eyes shuttering at the thought, I turned to her once her bags were on the floor and murmured, "I'll let you get settled in."

She blinked as she looked at the room, then to my retreating back, managed to get out, "Thank you, Professor."

It was stupid, so stupid, but I couldn't stop myself. Couldn't have withheld the words if I tried as I turned to look at her over my shoulder. "Inside these walls, Phoebe, you may call me Nicholas."

When she gnawed on her bottom lip and whispered, "Thank you for helping me, Nicholas," I almost came in my pants.

This was going to be more of an issue than I'd originally anticipated.

"You're welcome. Treat it like your home."

If it looked like I fled the bedroom, that was because I did.

I got the hell out of there as quickly as I could and headed to the kitchen where I downed a shot of tequila. Did I give a fuck that it was ten in the morning? No. I'd stopped giving a shit about the bounds of normal society when my wife had divorced me on the grounds of cruelty when, if anyone had been treated badly, it was me.

And I had the fucking scars to prove it.

My jaw tensed as thoughts of Gina flushed to the surface. It was odd timing for her to show up last night. She had a habit of hovering around the place, flirting with whichever doorman was on duty and sneaking up here. I'd long since stopped getting pissy at the doormen though. They were only men and Gina was sex incarnate.

All she had to do was flash a hint of her cleavage at some walking dick and he'd get a hard-on.

I'd thought Phoebe was like my ex.

But she wasn't.

She was her antithesis.

She didn't know her beauty, didn't know how desirable she was, and I wanted to keep her. Wanted to keep her for myself and no one else.

Lust for her had me tightening my fists, but the sound of a baby squawking had me stiffening in surprise. Though I knew Scottie was here, the noise stunned me.

These walls were hallowed. A crypt, a sanctified place that was both memory and reminder wrapped into one unhealthy ball.

This place was where everything had started to go wrong.

After the divorce, I hadn't sold it, hadn't moved on and moved out.

I stayed living here, stayed within these walls because they never let me forget what a woman could do to a man.

This place was borne of misery, not of joy, so the sweet gurgling giggle took me aback.

Not in a bad way, but a good one.

It was *that*, more than anything, that surprised the shit out of me.

18

NICHOLAS

SHE STUCK to her room for most of the day, and when I slinked past —way too many times than was healthy—I heard Scottie giggling or silence interspersed with the clacking of a keyboard.

Scottie's existence had surprised me. I thought I'd known everything there was to know about her, but I'd never seen her with him. Not once. Of course, now I knew why.

Mrs. Linden.

A neighbor.

One who Phoebe grieved. Who had gifted her with the pair of Rolexes that currently sat in my desk drawer.

I didn't appreciate how much of her world was inaccessible to me. I hated not being in the know. But she led a relatively quiet, if, busy life. She worked more than I liked but I'd thought her reasoning was the same as every other college student in my class—student loans. I'd never imagined she had a baby brother she was caring for, and I'd never known her mother was an alcoholic.

In truth, my behavior wouldn't have changed *had* I had access to this information, but I intended on using this enforced proximity to learn everything I could about her.

With her having quit her job at the coffee shop, I was relieved that she only went out at night. I believed the café was far more dangerous than the bar because she was tucked safely behind the counter and surrounded by security, whereas at the coffee shop, she was left alone with a cash-filled register and only patrons to protect her.

Of course, it didn't always work out that way. Just recalling that night when I'd seen one of the clubbers grab her and haul her into him made rage seethe inside me. Before I'd been able to go to her, protect her, she'd protected herself.

I'd never been happier to watch a man nurse his balls because Phoebe had damn well handed them to him. Still, knowing she could protect herself, didn't ease the inherent need within me to keep her safe.

It was a compulsion.

One, I feared, was linked to my ex. I didn't want Gina back, but Phoebe was like a fresh start, a new leaf, one I wanted to make sure didn't rot and perish away to dust.

That obsessive need had led to me creating the transcribing job for her. I paid her above average rather than a high rate, because I didn't want her to suspect I was behind the new position.

I knew enough about her to accept that she would reject any charity, so I'd dug out my old diaries, the books I'd handwritten, and had scanned each one then sent them to her.

I had thousands of them.

Before Rosa, when my muse hadn't dried up and had been more than a withered sack, I'd been quite prolific. I'd never needed to be published, had just found joy in getting the story down on paper.

At the end of a long day, when Gina had been reading or primping or going out with her friends, I'd found a simple joy in sitting on the balcony attached to the apartment, watching the world go by, and writing down my thoughts and the stories that inspired me.

I was uneasy with her accessing those intimate moments, but I was even more discomforted with how hard she was having to work. Now that her mother had revealed herself to be unreliable, I was doubly glad.

Making a mental note to scan more of the documents later on for her to transcribe, I lay back on the sofa and drummed my fingers against the cushioned leather.

Phoebe Whitehouse was in my loft.

Inside, I was probably as excited as I'd been at my first frat party.

Outside?

I was still. Calm. Quiet.

That was my life now.

The old Nicholas had died that night, and this one was born from those ashes.

I didn't like the new me. In fact, in many ways, he disturbed me.

I never imagined I'd be a stalker, and my only consolation was that I didn't stalk randomly, just the one woman.

Of course, when I phrased it like that, I sounded just as psychologically deranged as any run-of-the-mill whack job who followed Lady Gaga from concert to concert.

But I wasn't.

Was I?

I didn't think I was, even if I was obsessed with her. But my obsession took the form of ensuring she was safe, untouched. I'd never hurt her.

Ever.

Verbally was another matter entirely, but physically, she was safer with me than without.

When she stepped out of her room, rupturing my philosophical musings, I tensed, wondering what she was doing. There was a connecting bath so she was either hungry or she was seeking me out. I looked at my phone and saw that it was too early for her to be heading out to work.

Would she leave Scottie with me?

While it was an imposition, I wouldn't have minded—a fact that surprised me.

I hadn't held a baby since Rosa had passed away. If anything, I'd gone out of my way to avoid children, yet here I was, inviting one straight into my inner sanctum.

Her footsteps were soft, light, and I thought back to when I'd called her fat, and wondered what world we lived in where she believed me.

She was perfection in female form. All rounded and soft. Smooth curves instead of hard lines.

"Professor?" she whispered, and her scent seemed to follow her.

"I told you to call me Nicholas," I rasped, and knew that she jerked in surprise at my hard tone and hated myself for getting a thrill out of it.

It was delicious to me when she responded out of fear. If anyone was scared, it was me. I was the one who was obsessed. I was the one who was terrified about being found out, and yet the object of my obsession was frightened of annoying *me*.

Irony was best served with a side of pussy, I found.

And if it was her pussy?

God, I'd lap that up every damn day of the week.

She cleared her throat. "Nicholas."

"Yes?" I tilted my head to the side and found she was studying me.

She wasn't scared though.

If anything, she was eying me like I did when I worked hard not to eye her.

She was attracted to me. I knew that. She saw the face and not the demons within.

Why was it monsters were always hidden behind a beautiful form?

As she licked her lips, I fought a groan.

"What is it, Phoebe?" I demanded, knowing that if I didn't prompt her, she'd just gawp at me.

Though I scared her, she was as fascinated by me as I was by her. Even before my blackmail, I'd sensed her regard in class where she looked at me like I was a juicy steak, and she'd been vegan for a decade.

"I was hungry. Would you mind if I made us something to eat?"

My heart quickened at her inclusion of me. "You don't have to ask. I told you, treat the place as your home."

Her eyes shifted from mine and quickly darted around the place. I didn't have to be a mind reader to know that this loft was entirely unlike her old home.

"Yes, well… would you mind?"

"Feel free. I'd appreciate that." And I would.

Gina had never cooked for me.

I'd never wanted her to though. Not like I wanted Phoebe to cook for me.

To care whether I was full or not.

The nurturing side of her character was something I couldn't have anticipated. I saw her timid friendliness with others, her quiet humility, and the low self-esteem that had her darting through life like a hungry mouse on an assault course. She had a habit of running a few minutes late—understandable now that I was aware of Scottie—and would always help her colleagues out in a pinch.

She was, I knew, a good person.

She didn't, I also knew, deserve to have someone like me in her life.

Someone who'd taken advantage of what I'd seen, of her pocketing something from the till, and had used it to force a link between us.

As I always did, I'd intended on sneaking out of the coffee shop while she was in the kitchen. But when I'd been watching her, waiting for her to leave the storefront, I'd seen her grab the twenty from the tip jar and the ten from the register.

Disappointed wasn't the word, but even as I'd been angry at her, I'd known I could use it to my gain.

And here we were.

Five weeks later.

Phoebe and her infant sibling were in my loft, and she was offering to make me lunch.

Life had a strange way of turning out.

19

———————

NICHOLAS

I HEARD the door to the loft open, and as she'd done for the last few nights, she stepped out onto the balcony almost as soon as she made it inside.

I'd been kind, not wanting to scare her off, and had contained myself, but tonight the beast was riding me.

Hard.

With the snick of the patio door opening, I slipped to my feet and headed out of my bedroom.

Before I followed her, I went to her room and quickly dipped my head inside.

Though Rosa had been dead for four years, I still remembered the routine, and when, that first night, she'd started to get him ready with the intention of taking him to a babysitter she'd arranged, I'd told her not to be foolish and that I could manage a one-year-old.

Of course, I couldn't.

Of course, I'd lied.

I needed her to need me.

Wanted her to depend on me.

And if she did, then incrementally, I could relax. Loosen the taut reins I had on myself.

My throat was tight as I quickly checked on Scottie, who was a far easier baby than Rosa had been. But then, my baby girl had been spoiled for attention and I could tell that though Scottie was used to Phoebe's focus, he was also used to being left on his own.

A notion that both saddened and angered me.

How many other babies were like him?

Abandoned by their mothers, left to relatives to raise?

Phoebe was just barely an adult. Sure, there were younger mothers, but she wasn't his mother. She was his sister. Still, you wouldn't be able to tell.

When she left him, his face would turn bright red but he wouldn't cry. It was like his fury was internalized. I had to admit, I'd never seen anything more terrifying than a baby with his sense of control.

Rosa would have bawled her eyes out. Had done so every time we'd left her with my parents or Gina's. But Scottie was one of those babies who slept the whole night through because he was accustomed to being ignored.

A month ago, I'd have blamed Phoebe for that. Wanted to attribute something, *anything*, negative to her. But instead, I was sympathetic now. I knew how hard she worked, how hard she strived, and she'd done the right thing by taking Scottie away from her mother.

A month ago, I wouldn't have said this was a safe place for her. Not with me in the vicinity. But with Scottie here, I wouldn't do anything to put him in jeopardy. Would do nothing to unsettle him, not after he'd had a short life of being passed around from pillar to post.

It was hard not following her everywhere, hard staying at home while she went out to work at *Crow*, but it was getting easier.

Knowing Scottie was safe made my not keeping an eye on her bearable.

As I rubbed a finger down his cheek, he didn't stir, so I left him to rest and headed out to the balcony.

She was safe from me, but that didn't mean I wanted her to know it.

Nor did it mean I wasn't ready to see her pretty pussy again.

My cock hardened as I stepped onto the balcony where she was leaning over the railing and staring out into the distance.

From here, you could see Brooklyn Bridge and all the way over to the Seaport and the Lower East Side areas. I knew why she was fascinated by the view, but I was more interested in her ass.

I'd studied that heart shape so often that I could imagine what it felt like to hold it in my hands. But I wouldn't touch.

I couldn't.

"Thank you for letting me stay here." That she knew I was watching came as a surprise, and when I didn't reply, she turned to look over her shoulder and smiled at me.

To any other man, that wasn't a siren's song, but to me, it was. My own personal fucking torture.

God, the urge to take that smile away was ripe, and I was such a twisted fuck that the only way I could control myself was to hurt her. Verbally. To diminish her self-worth, to make her feel like shit.

What kind of a fucker did that?

Who made their woman feel that way?

The words burned on my tongue, evil and vile, but I *wasn't* that man. I wasn't. Not anymore. If she was going to be my woman—not that she was aware of that yet—then I couldn't treat her badly.

I wanted her.

More than I wanted my next breath.

If I pushed her away, it would kill me.

And so, though it was one of the hardest things I'd ever done, I held my tongue and moved toward her, coming within a hairsbreadth of her body, calmly saying, "You're welcome. But I've already told you that."

She hummed under her breath and the sound made me wonder what that would feel like if she was sucking my cock.

She turned to look at the view once more. "I miss her," she whispered.

"Mrs. Linden?"

"Yes."

I wanted to touch her, but didn't dare. "That's natural."

Christ, did I have to sound like such a fucking robot?

I despaired for myself sometimes.

I truly did.

Rubbing my forehead instead of reaching out to touch her, I amended, "I mean the pain will go with time, but embrace it while it's here."

I could tell my advice surprised her because she twisted to look at me.

"What do you mean?"

"I mean that the pain is your love for her. It won't die, it will only blossom with time as she becomes a part of your memories. But the pain and the love make them more deeply entrenched in your soul."

Her eyes widened. "That's a beautiful way to think of it, Nicholas."

I shrugged. "Hardly." Because I didn't like how she was looking at me, like I'd reinvented the wheel or something, I changed the subject and blurted out, "How was work?"

"Tiring." She hung her head. "I'm tired of working nights but the money is beyond good. The tips were crazy tonight."

She fell silent then, her gaze turned out toward the city that brushed her with its lights. Painting her in colors that merely illuminated her beauty.

For a second, I was a sycophant.

Nothing more than a worshipper at a goddess' altar as I breathed in the same cherished air as her.

"I need to start looking for somewhere else to live."

The words were loaded with embarrassment, and though my immediate reaction was to snarl at her, I didn't because I heard something in her voice—she liked it here, and was only making the suggestion because it was what people in her position did.

Phoebe, however, was unaware of her position. Her true position.

Without batting an eyelid, I murmured, "Spread your legs."

She reared back as was her way when I surprised her, but when she caught my eye, she saw something in mine that had her cutting off her response.

When she licked her lips, I knew I had her.

Her weight pressed harder onto the railing as she parted her legs and shoved her butt in the air—a sight that turned my bones molten.

"Are you wearing panties?" I asked, turning my head so I could whisper the words into her ear. The second my breath touched her, she shuddered.

"No."

"Good girl," I praised, both surprised she'd taken my instructions and made them a rule but also enraged that she'd been at *Crow*, panty-less for the past few days, without my protection.

God, if any motherfucker dared touch her... I'd call Jay and ask him to have his bouncers tear the bastards a new one.

When a breath hiccupped from her lips, I could practically taste her excitement.

Whatever it was about me, about what I said or did to her, it made her hot. It fizzled in her core, enticing her as much as another man's kiss might.

"Are you wet?"

"Y-Yes," she moaned, her head dropping as though she couldn't bear to carry the weight.

"Good." I fell silent, content to let her suffer, content to let her stay there in that stasis of misery, a state I existed in perpetually because of her.

Hungry for her.

Ravenous for her taste, for her touch.

The sound of her overexcited breathing was like a caress to my cock, and my lips curved in a smirk as I stared over at Manhattan.

I could live there if I wanted, but I preferred Williamsburg. Preferred looking at the beehive than being a part of it, and I especially appreciated the seclusion of this balcony that allowed me to behold the magnificence of NYC while tormenting the woman who tormented me with every breath she took, knowing that no one else could see her.

"P-Please, Professor."

At any other time, her failure to use my given name would have pissed me off. But now, it fit.

I hadn't thought it would.

Hadn't imagined I'd like the reminder, but appreciate it I did.

"Please what?" I inquired coolly.

"L-Let me touch myself."

Her words sent relief crashing through me. I might never be able to touch her, might never trust myself with her, and I'd feared the change in circumstances would make her think our unusual arrangement had changed too.

"Why?" I questioned, like I was asking her to defend a statement she'd made in my class.

And fuck if I wouldn't be thinking about this the next time we were on campus.

"Because I need to come."

"Do you *deserve* to come?" I queried.

She was quiet for a second. "I worked hard today, so yes."

Finding myself amused by her retort, and well aware that my amusement laced my reply, I said, "Then, by all means, find your pleasure."

A whimper of relief came from her parted lips, and I wanted to taste it so badly that it took everything I had not to make my move.

Instead, in the city lights, I watched her lift her skirt with one hand, not stopping until she dragged it around her waist, and with her pussy bared to me and the terrace, she slipped her fingers between her thighs.

The second skin touched skin, she moaned, and I closed my eyes. The scent and power of her was so overbearing that I couldn't stand to look at her for a second.

Her fingers moved fast, faster than usual, and she didn't plunge them inside her pussy, didn't fuck herself, just focused on her clit.

She worked herself high, hard and fast, and just when she was about to come, I breathed in her ear, "Stop."

I felt her temptation to disobey me, felt it, longed for her lack of obeisance, but instead, she paused, and as her fingers stopped, she mewled in distress.

"Suck them clean," I ordered her, as I'd done many times before. "What do they taste like?"

"Salty. Sweet." They were her usual answers. But she surprised me. "Need. Want. Desire."

"Desire for what?"

She exhaled roughly. "You."

The single word ignited fireworks in my soul. But she couldn't have me. Not in that way.

"Make yourself come."

A disappointed moan escaped her, and I realized she'd been asking me to fuck her.

How I wanted to.

How I fucking needed to.

I clenched my jaw, and the second she cried out with pleasure as she found her release, I walked off, left her outside with her climax to keep her company, because if I didn't, there'd be no saving either of us.

20

———————

NICHOLAS

THE SCENT of bacon filled the air when I awoke the next morning, and as I'd discovered, my stomach stirred at the same rate as my cock when I thought of Phoebe cooking in my kitchen.

If the fridge was stocked, she cooked, and that was a decided advantage to having her living here.

While I could be accused of sounding chauvinistic, I was already red for dead with the whole stalker shit, plus, I'd been known to buy bags of Iceberg lettuce, eat it straight from the wrapper, and call that a salad.

I needed all the help I could get.

Phoebe wasn't exactly a gourmet chef, but I appreciated her time and effort, and loved that she wanted to feed me.

Gina hadn't been like that.

Which was another way they were different, another way in which I could find relief at the lack of similarities between my ex and Phoebe. What had triggered the compulsion, no longer drove it.

Phoebe was fire enough on her own to spur me on.

As I rolled onto my belly, I shoved my cock into the duvet, appreciating the ache it caused. The masochistic pleasure was all I was allowed when I was punishing myself for being a creep, so even as I enjoyed the pain, I enjoyed the timid knock on my bedroom door even more.

She'd taken to doing that—knocking on the door to wake me up.

Not even the lightest sleeper in the world would hear that tap though.

"I'll be out in a minute," I called out huskily, and hearing the swift click of her footsteps, knew she was scuttling back to the kitchen.

She was an odd one, that was for sure.

Half terrified of me, half aroused by me.

I knew she liked it when I tempted her, taunted her even. Knew she liked to challenge me and reveled in testing my control.

Maybe the two of us were just the perfect amount of weird to suit one another down to the ground.

The thought put a smile on my face, and since it was a Monday morning, smiles should have been illegal.

I didn't bother showering, just grabbed a robe and dragged it over the tee and briefs I slept in. Knotting the robe loosely at my hips, I yawned as I stepped into the hall and heard Phoebe singing.

Fucking singing.

I didn't care that it was a nursery rhyme, one that was her attempt at wheedling Scottie into eating something, it just set my nerves on red alert.

I found that the many memories of Rosa were battering me on all fronts, but what I was surprised by was how well I dealt with it.

My daughter had been gone far longer than I'd had her, but that didn't diminish my pain any. Didn't diminish Gina's either. It was why she'd gone crazy, after all. Losing Rosa had fucked with her already fucked-up head, and had turned her from a successful lawyer who was on the right trajectory for DA, into a whacked she-devil who'd given me more physical scars than mental.

I'd stopped telling people about losing Rosa, mostly because I got that old, 'no parent should ever have to lose a child,' shit. Most said that to try to make me feel better.

It didn't work.

Rosa's death would be a perpetual ache inside me.

Gina's betrayal would be a rip in my control that I'd forever try to repair.

But those imperfections in my character were what had made me *me*. I wasn't happy with who I was, didn't approve of how I treated Phoebe, hated myself for having stalked the poor woman even if it could be argued I was helping her now, but I'd survived.

And there'd been points where, honest to God, survival hadn't seemed likely.

The song I'd once sung Rosa rang around the kitchen walls, but I tried to let it soften me, not harden me. For all she'd been a transient presence in my life, Rosa had brought joy. In fact, though I mourned her to this day, she'd given me more joy than grief, and that was truly saying something.

So, when I made it into the kitchen, I sang along with Phoebe. She faltered for a few notes, but when I cocked a brow at her, she rallied around and continued with her song.

And, wouldn't you know?

The little booger started eying the mush Phoebe had put on the plastic plate in front of him with more interest—seemed he liked a show with his meal.

My nose wrinkled at the food. "What is that?"

"Banana and oats."

"You made it yourself?" I asked, eying the ramekin jar on the counter.

"Yep. It's easy. He usually likes this. I don't get why he's being fussy."

Sardonically, I informed her, "He's a man. I'm sure he just likes variety."

For some reason, that had her cheeks blanching and her gaze instantly darting away from mine, and when I put two and two together, I had to hide a smirk.

So, she was worried that *I* needed variety.

Interesting.

Rather than remark on it, I moved toward Scottie and hauled him into my arms. He cooed and beamed at me, his cheeks coated with more mush than his plate, and I held him higher up so that he could look down at the world.

"Now try and feed him."

Her attention was back on me, exactly where I wanted it. But the softness to her gaze had me thinking shit I shouldn't be contemplating, and not just because I was holding Scottie.

I had no right to her. Even if she was, in my head, mine already.

She fed him from the small dish and laughed when he munched on it, accepting the food now that his scenery was more interesting.

As I held him, he wriggled slightly and I tightened my grip, not wanting him to fall.

It felt good, him being in my arms, her feeding him. It felt like this was my family, and God, how I wished it was.

When Scottie had finished, I settled him back into the highchair I'd had shipped in, and started on some of the bacon she'd fried for me.

When she turned around and began poaching me a damn egg, I had to say, "You really don't need to make me breakfast, Phoebe." Her shoulders tensed. "I mean, don't get me wrong, I appreciate it, but you're not my servant."

She looked at me over her shoulder. "You don't have to help out with Scottie, but you do. You didn't have to let us stay here, but you did. Cooking you something for breakfast and dinner is nothing."

I sighed because I heard her resolve. "I'm grateful."

"No more than I am," she retorted firmly, and I enjoyed that hint of steel in her voice. Enough that I settled back in my seat and watched her bustle around my kitchen.

This hadn't been somewhere Gina and I had ever really been interested in. It was pretty minimal with steel backsplashes and plain, raw ash cupboards that opened with the press of your palm against the door.

Everything was hidden behind those doors, the fridge, the ovens, even the dishwasher. When you walked in, very little gave away that it was a kitchen. It might even have been a utility room for all it was decorated.

As I watched her, though, I realized it didn't fit. Maybe because Phoebe didn't fit in here.

It was too modern.

Too simple.

Phoebe wasn't a simple person. She was chaos in a slowly moving world.

I doubted she saw herself that way, but that was something I appreciated in her.

For every action, Newton said, there was an equal and opposite reaction. That was what happened around Phoebe.

Men stopped and checked her out, but she didn't notice the traffic jam that backed up because of her. Her kind smile could light up a room, but to her, because she was deep in thought and had her gaze trained on her feet, she might as well have been tucked in among the shadows.

She didn't expect the world to stop turning for her, but she should.

Last night, after she'd complied, after she'd obeyed me, and after I'd managed not to whip her with my words for the feelings she inspired in me, I realized I needed to build her up, not drag her down.

Even if it put me in emotional peril.

The world had already had its ill effects on her. She should be bubbling with confidence, the life and soul of any party, but she wasn't. She was too tired from all the running around she did.

But that needed to change.

I'd come to realize that.

By bringing her here, everything had changed, nothing was the same. Including me. And our relationship.

So, even if building up her esteem, forging the walls of her confidence meant I lost her in the end, I'd do it. Because to me, she was *the* woman and I didn't want to be the bastard who brought her down.

Some sacrifices were worth making, and because I wasn't good enough for her in the first place, this was less of a sacrifice than it might have been otherwise.

"You're looking at me funny," she chided, as she placed my breakfast on the table in front of me.

"Just thinking," I replied easily, switching my focus to the eggs, bacon, and grilled tomatoes and mushrooms on my plate.

This came after yesterday's oatmeal, and then some kind of chia pudding the day before, something that had told me she'd raided my cupboards to find them—my PT had insisted they were a great way to bulk up a shake, but I loathed them.

Somehow, she'd made them palatable.

Another miracle.

"About?" she tested, her gaze darting to mine before retreating to her plate. She had an egg white omelet, no bacon, and more veggies.

Boring.

Even as I wondered if she was trying to eat healthy because of me, or if it was simply because she had the run of the food in the cupboards, I said, "Just wondering what you're going to do while I'm at work today."

"Get some transcribing done. Your friend sent over a lot more sheets last night." Yeah, and it had taken me over a fucking hour to get that done. "I'm not sure where she gets all her notes from!"

Maybe I was a glutton for punishment because I asked, "Are they boring?"

"The notes?" When I nodded, she frowned as she chewed on her omelet. "No. The job is, I guess. It's tedious, but I like the way she thinks. Doesn't she show them to you?"

I snorted. "No."

The brisk answer had her shrugging. "Shame, because the stories and insights are good. I wonder what she's going to do with them once they're transcribed."

"Publish them, probably." I scratched my chin as the lie tripped easily from my lips. "I have another faculty meeting tonight. I won't be back in time for Scottie. Do you have a sitter?"

"I found an app. I couldn't afford it before, but you pay to subscribe and the sitters are registered locally so I can make it work."

I frowned. "That's not ideal, is it? They could be anyone."

She reached up and pinched the bridge of her nose. "I'm not sure what else to do."

Because I wasn't either, I fell silent as I pondered the situation, then, when the solution came to me, asked, "What about a nanny?"

She gaped at me a second before cascading into giggles. "N-N-Nanny?" she spluttered, going so far as to slap the table which, of course, had Scottie mimicking her until it was like being at a Blue Man concert without any blue men in the vicinity.

I stared at her with a frown. "What's so hilarious?"

"How can I afford a n-n-nanny?"

And that set her off again.

"I'll pay," I offered, huffing at her humor that came at my expense.

"You damn well won't." Like that, her amusement switched off and she glowered at me. "Scottie is my responsibility, not yours. I'll work something out."

"It seems impractical—"

"Maybe it is, but that's the reality for a lot of women in my position." She blew out a breath, then, eyes softening, said, "Look, I appreciate the offer, but I can't allow myself to depend on you. I can't. If I do, then when I leave here, it will be too hard to go back to the way things were before."

I wanted to tell her that she was never leaving here, but that would make me sound like a kidnapper.

I wasn't that bad.

Yet.

Pulling a face, I raised my hands and said, "Do what you must, but if you need help, I don't mind."

"No, but I do."

How had I failed to see how proud she was?

I wasn't sure if I appreciated that in her or not.

She was right, to an extent. In her circumstances, it would be foolish to grow dependent on something that had no roots.

Which meant, I swiftly realized, that I needed to make those roots, and fast.

21

———

NICHOLAS

Fuck.

I did.

I wasn't sure how I stopped myself, didn't know how it was possible, but as she hopped onto my desk like this was a regular thing to do in your professor's office, lifted her skirt and showed me her pussy, my mouth watered with the need to suck on her clit, to slurp up her juices.

Because yes, she was wet.

Very wet.

And I wanted that all over my goddamn mouth.

My nails dug into the leather armrests on my desk chair as I watched her touch herself. The bloom of pink had gone from her cheeks now. She was no longer embarrassed, instead, she was turned on by what I had her do.

Her eyes glinted; they weren't cast down with mortification. Her skin was rosy, to be sure, but with desire and heat, the flush of pleasure.

The thrill of the forbidden had yet to bore her, but I wanted more. Truly, I did.

Could I have it? Would she want it if I offered it to her?

She bit her bottom lip then trained her eyes on me, letting me know, without words, that she was really fucking *me*. That her fingers were my cock.

I was so out of practice, so out of the game that I didn't know what to fucking say or do.

But the promise *was* there, waiting for me.

Shuddering, I closed my eyes and gritted my teeth. I felt like a caged bear. One who was made to dance and perform, one who was forced to do unnatural things by my owner—*her*. And in this, not touching her was the most unnatural thing I could think of.

Then she signed my death warrant.

"Please," she whispered, the words low, breathy. Softer than a moan, more heartfelt than a murmur.

As she drew the one-syllable word into two, I bit off, "Get down, bend over, put your face to the desk, and stick your ass out."

The excitement that overtook her almost had me panting. Her tits swayed beneath her shirt as she hurried to comply, and when her ass was inches away from my face, when I could smell her delicious pussy, I gripped the armrests once more.

If, and it was a huge if, I was going to do something to her, it wouldn't be here, and it would take longer than the time I had to give her before my next appointment.

I was tempted to use the vibrator on her. Hours and hours of fucking research had gone into that toy. I'd had to make sure it was not only the best, but that it wouldn't hurt her. That it was safe enough to be inside her while I toyed with her endlessly. But even that kind of penetration was more than I could handle.

"Get yourself off," I commanded, and her whimper of distress was like being sucker-punched in the belly.

"B-But…" She mewled.

"Do it," I ground out, and breathed a sigh of relief when she edged her fingers under her belly and awkwardly rubbed herself.

Her legs were shaking by the time she climaxed. It took her a little longer than usual, granted, but I appreciated the different view, enjoyed the more subservient pose.

With her glistening flesh so close to me, it was a severe effort in restraint as I watched her thigh muscles tense and strain to stay upright, inadvertently pushing her pussy lips together.

I wanted so fucking badly to slide my cock between them. To spear myself inside her and thrust into her so deeply she didn't know where I began or she ended.

Because I couldn't do that, I whispered instead, "Stand up."

I gave her a few moments to comply, and when she stood, I saw from her dazed eyes that the orgasm had been deeper than usual. No wonder she was swaying on her feet.

I couldn't resist.

I had to taste some small part of her.

"Kneel between my legs," I urged her, my voice a silken promise.

Like day flowing into night, she slipped to her knees and sat there, looking up at me through bright green eyes that sparkled, even through her slumberous satiation.

I let myself get lost inside them, allowed myself to be lost inside *her*, and then, I broke my own protocol, leaned down, and allowed my lips to brush hers.

The way she moaned was something I'd never forget. It was seared into my brain, into my memory banks. I'd remember this until the day I died, and even then, it would be as much a part of me as my bones.

My hands were shaking as I lifted them, cupped her soft cheeks, and finally allowed myself to touch her. To connect with her.

Our mouths were trembling, her lips softly parting as I thrust my tongue between them. As we were united that way, the guttural groan that escaped her sank into my very being, and I swallowed it and her breath.

Her fingers settled upon my knees, and the close touch, after four long years of *no* touch, had me jolting into awareness. But before I could begin to fear she'd move her hands farther up, her nails dug into my adductors, high up on my inner thighs, biting through the thick denim of the jeans I wore as she took her pleasure out on me.

I thrust into her, tasting her, savoring her, knowing she tasted and savored in return.

That one kiss was better than a night of sex with Gina.

It was better than a thousand blowjobs, a million hand jobs.

It was everything, and yet it was nothing.

Just like our connection.

It was less than it should be, and on its way to being more than I'd ever anticipated.

As I devoured her mouth, she tore into me, and the only thing that stopped us was the knocking at the door that signaled my next appointment.

When I pulled back, startled, I reached up and wiped my mouth.

"Wait a minute, Jarrad," I called out hoarsely.

"Sure thing, Professor," was his cheerful reply. A reply that didn't suit my frame of mind. That didn't resonate at all with the ground-trembling, earth-shaking kiss that had just decimated everything, razing it to nothing, only for it to be built up once again.

She stared at me, drowning me with those big green eyes, looking at me as though she believed I had all the answers.

But I didn't.

This was us breaching that thousand-step journey, and did she but know it, she'd made her choice.

And God help us both.

22

NICHOLAS

THE NEXT TWO days were a study in torture.

She cooked, studied, went to her classes, worked. I put up with having a strange woman, the new sitter, in the place when we were both out, wanting her to lead her regular life so she could see how much better it was when she was with me.

And though I could sense her contentment, through it all, she watched me.

Phoebe was waiting.

In her own way, she was an innocent, and I knew she was letting me make the first move. But even though she seemed to think I had all the answers, I didn't.

I was as goddamn terrified as she was.

One night, as I sat at my desk, the windows wide open so the light breeze could slip into the room, I stared at Scottie who stared back at me.

Although she'd first insisted on keeping him in her room, I knew babies liked to explore. Hell, more than that. They needed to.

Scottie, as a result, was now in the know about every nook and cranny in the loft, and I was getting used to tripping over him. As he stared at me from the ground, gnawing on his fist, I wondered what he was thinking.

Wondered if he cared that I'd had to vacuum the floor three times before I let him go on it. Wondered if it mattered that I'd been on my hands and knees disinfecting anything I thought he might touch.

Rosa's death had been genetic, but I'd be damned if Scottie—

My jaw clenched at the thought, and the urge to get up and clean something else, to make sure it was sanitized enough for him rode me hard.

He had to be safe. As much as Phoebe was. I couldn't lose another one. Couldn't lose someone else.

This child had been in my life a ridiculously short amount of time, and yet, he and his sister had taken over my world.

For too long, my days had started and ended with thoughts of Phoebe. But now, Scottie was there too.

It made strange emotions unfurl inside me.

I'd locked myself away from most people after my divorce, not wanting to let anyone in, because when I did, I knew they'd let me down.

Most had believed Gina's bullshit over my side of the story, but a few had gone to bat for me. Jay was one such person. He'd gone from simply family to friend that day. But I'd lost a lot of kin in the aftermath, and it made me wonder if it was because of Gina's accusations or because of how I'd treated them.

My propensity to snarl at Phoebe was a habit.

A bad one.

I couldn't hide from that anymore.

Whenever she got too close, whenever she touched a raw nerve, I'd snap at her, say something mean to make her cry.

Hadn't I done that this morning?

Wasn't that why she'd run off to her bedroom?

She'd been in such a fluster that she'd left Scottie out here with me, and it was why I was certain her kid brother was glowering at me with all the disdain a one-year-old kid surrounded by unicorn soft toys was capable of.

I couldn't even think of the words that had spilled from my lips without cringing, and Scottie had been there to witness it. He didn't understand, granted, but he judged me for it nonetheless.

My introspection wasn't going to improve matters. I had humble pie to eat, a good two or three slices, and I would, easily, because I was a bastard.

A real shit who didn't deserve this woman or this child in his life.

Who deserved the solitude that had been caving in around him these past few years.

Who'd dug himself into a well of despair so deep that he didn't know how to get out of it, but knew the woman he'd hurt this morning was his salvation.

My jaw worked as I got to my feet. Scottie scowled at me as I bent down and hauled him into my arms. He squawked, displeased by the move, and probably not happy with being so close to me, but that was the shit thing about being a baby—you went where you were carried.

Still, he settled on my side like he was born to be there.

It was eerie how well he and I connected.

I got the feeling the kid didn't like change, that he was grieving Mrs. Linden, and then these past few weeks of endless alterations to his routine were definitely not something he approved of, but with me, he seemed settled, and that made me content.

It had been so long since I'd felt anything other than stoic that the warm feeling inside me had taken me all this time to recognize.

Nicholas wasn't happy.

Nicky had been, but Nicholas? No.

I knocked on the door, and waited for her to let me in. When it took a while, I pressed my forehead to the wooden plank and called out, "I can't apologize to the door."

"The door would listen. I won't," she rebuffed, but I heard her tears, knew she was still upset, and I couldn't blame her.

I'd mocked the paper she'd handed in the other day.

Why had I done that?

Why did I target her writing? Downgrade and downplay it when it was some of the most refreshing work I'd read in years?

I wasn't jealous.

I just—

Hell if I knew what I was. It confused even me.

I closed my eyes. "I'm sorry," I whispered.

She didn't reply, and the silence from her room was deafening. She didn't make even a peep of sound, so it made it feel as though I were talking to an empty room. Then, I heard the patter of her footsteps, and I released a heavy sigh of relief. Scottie's hand slapped my cheek, almost like he knew Phoebe wouldn't give me the beating I deserved, and I took the smack.

Fuck, I'd earned it.

Pulling back slightly so I didn't lean on the door, I waited with bated breath for her to open it. When she did, she stood staring at me with tear sore eyes.

I'd done that to her.

Me.

I sucked down a breath and whispered again, "I'm sorry."

That had her tensing. I realized she hadn't anticipated this conversation, and I wasn't sure if that made me an even bigger bastard or not.

"Why do you do that? Why do you say the things you do to me in one breath and then do something crazy like let me stay here and not pressure me to find somewhere else to live?

"How can you hurt me with your words, but hold Scottie like he's yours, and offer to get a damn nanny for us?" She gulped, and the tears clogging her throat hit me like another sucker punch—I'd experienced so many of late that it was a wonder I was still standing. "Why, Nicholas?"

In the face of her earnestness, it didn't even occur to me to lie.

"Because I'm scared."

"Of what?" she sputtered.

"You. Me. What you make me feel," I rasped, aware that she didn't have a clue how I felt about her.

"You're confused about hating me?" she questioned, her brow puckering.

I was confused about fucking loving her. But I couldn't say that. She'd run away from me if I did.

No, the truth was too unpalatable.

Some thought the words 'I love you' were as big a cure as a 'sorry' was, but they meant nothing. Not really. Not unless they were gifted and received with heartfelt intention.

I licked my lips. "I don't hate you. I've told you that before," I retorted. "I don't want to feel anything for you—"

"But you do?"

Before I could answer, Scottie—my new BFF—squawked and took her attention from me to him. She stared at me for a second, then sighed and reached for her brother.

When the kid was settled on her hip, I watched as she lugged him across the room and set him up in the crib I'd insisted on buying for him—something she'd only agreed to when I'd bought a travel one, and had told her that she'd regret it if he fell out of bed with her one night.

I could have left them to it. I'd made my apology, after all, but I didn't want to.

I was sick and tired of being on the outside looking in, of watching her from afar, needing more and not daring to grasp it.

Instead, and feeling as though I were bridging a thousand-feet-wide chasm, I stepped across the threshold and closed the door behind me.

Was it strange that I felt the need to herd her in, to contain her?

To me, she was like a kaleidoscope of butterflies—impossible to capture.

But how I wanted to.

I wanted to be the one to cage her because I knew that was the only way a fucked-up monster like me would ever be able to hold her.

As it clicked closed, her head whipped around so she could look at me over her shoulder.

I kept my back to the door and stayed silent until she carried on tending to Scottie.

"He's asleep," she muttered after a few moments.

Christ, that was quick.

"Come to the living room and talk with me?" I requested huskily, watching her back stiffen.

"About what?" she replied with a tired sigh. "There's nothing to discuss."

"Please?" I asked again, ignoring her refusal.

She huffed out another sigh but stepped away from the cot and moved toward me. I opened the door for her and stepped out behind her, and the second I closed it once more, I grabbed hold of her and pressed her into the wall.

Before she could do little else than squeak, I was on her, and thank fuck, she was on me just as fast.

Her hands were in my hair, pulling at the strands as though she wanted me closer but Christ, there was no getting any closer. Her lips were on mine, my tongue in her mouth, and I fucked her. I fucked her there like I couldn't fuck her pussy, and goddamn, but she loved it.

In my arms, she was a wild thing. Anything but the tame and calm woman who'd managed to raise a baby who wasn't her own, and hold down several jobs while going to college.

This woman was electricity, and I wasn't scared of touching her. If anything, it drove me higher and faster than any other kiss I'd experienced.

I pushed my cock into her belly and raised my hands to grab at her own. I knew she'd try to touch me soon, and that couldn't be tolerated.

Not now, maybe never, but I needed to bind her to me, tie her to me in ways that no other ever could.

With one hand clasping her wrists, I used the other to smooth my palm down her leg and hooked her behind the knee, urging her to grip my hips. When the other mimicked the first, I rocked my cock into her core, letting her softness brush against my hardness.

Fuck, even through several layers of clothing, it felt good.

Better than good.

Heaven.

I stopped fucking her mouth and pulled back to catch my breath. This was about as much sexual contact as I'd allowed myself in the past four years and I didn't want to come too soon. But shit, it was hard.

As I pushed my dick into her softness, I pressed my face into her throat. I couldn't stop myself from scenting her, from breathing in deeply and absorbing every bit of her smell. It filled me to overflowing, making me never want to be apart from her, making me want to take it into my body so that our scents were combined into a new one, one of our making.

She struggled against my hold, her arms twisting, hands writhing with her need to touch me back. But I didn't let her. Instead, I ground my dick into her cunt, reveling in the low moan that escaped her at the pressure.

"Get yourself off," I ground out against her throat, then, I nibbled on the tender skin there and bit down.

Hard.

Hard enough for my teeth to leave marks, for there to be a bruise in the morning. Hard enough for me to remember the claiming, for her to see it later on.

She whimpered in pain before she began to rock back against me. Her butt bouncing off the wall as she wiggled, this time not to escape me, but to facilitate her orgasm.

I felt and sensed the difference in the tenor of her breathing, in the way her tits bobbed against my chest.

That she used me filled me with delight. I loved it. Fuck, I loved her.

When she screamed in my ear, I let myself go.

For the first time in four years, I came.

My seed spilled into my pants, my shaft throbbing as it celebrated an orgasm, as it reveled in the close proximity of her pussy. I wanted more. I wanted in her. Just the thought was enough to make my cock twitch, but I contained it.

Barely.

My breathing was hard and rough as I came down from the high, and her own was sweet and soft, still a little ragged, but she was like molten gold in my arms. Sinking into every part of me, merging with me until I wasn't sure where she began and I ended.

The Japanese believed in *kintsugi*. That a piece of pottery didn't lose value once it was broken. If anything, it gained it. A broken pot, for example, was bound together with a special gold lacquer, high-lighting the flaws, celebrating the imperfections, reforging it so that it was useful once more.

She did that to me.

Sank into every crack in my nature, bound herself to every broken shard, making me a better man than I was before. Not new, not perfect, but if anything, perfectly imperfect for her.

The thought resonated with me in a way that made me feel like I could breathe easier for the first time in years, and I released her flesh from between my teeth, enjoying her whimper as I pulled back. The move had my cock burrowing into her soft flesh while I stared down at her.

"That's what I'm afraid of," I admitted.

Her eyes widened, the dazed emerald orbs grew clearer as she worked through my words.

"How could you be afraid of that?" she whispered back. "It was beautiful."

My jaw tensed. "You don't understand."

"No. I don't. Explain it to me."

Her irritated tone had my lips twitching, but I closed my eyes and shook my head.

"I'm not ready."

She gritted her teeth. "Well, I am." When I didn't reply, she wriggled in my grasp then grated out, "Nicholas. Talk to me. Please. Help me understand."

I thought about her words. Thought about whether it was possible for her to understand, and then I thought some more—about showing her my scars, revealing the mental ones as well as the physical, but I just couldn't do it. No gold would make those better or make them less hideous.

I'd hidden them for so long. From the world, from myself even.

When I showered, I refused to look at that part of my body, just scrubbed it with soap to make sure it was clean.

How could I share *that* with her, this beautifully perfect creature?

The answer was, I couldn't.

Wouldn't.

And so, I released my hold on her hands, and pulled back and away.

I used words to keep my distance from her, but this time, the words I needed to say, the truths I needed to reveal, were something I wasn't ready to disclose.

23

NICHOLAS

WHEN I TURNED the key in the lock a few days later, the sound of voices came as a surprise to me.

I knew for a fact that the sitter shouldn't be here until tomorrow night, and though it should have been impossible because I could count the number of friends I had on one hand, Phoebe had even fewer.

Hell, I was pretty sure her only friend had been cremated a few weeks ago.

As sad as that made me feel, it also made me wonder who the fuck she'd brought to my apartment.

Was she with a guy?

Had she brought some random home to—what? *Punish me?*

Whenever I didn't do what she wanted, she sulked.

It was an irritating habit I wanted to spank out of her, but if I spanked her, the desire to fuck her pinkened ass would be too overwhelming.

I couldn't deal with the temptation, even if she did wear on my last nerve with the silent treatment she'd gifted me with since I hadn't explained myself to her.

But if she thought she could bring someone here to get back at me, I'd spank her until next fucking Tuesday.

As I rushed inside, intent on beating the crap out of anyone who thought they could take a taste of what was mine, I heard the other voice.

And it was no stranger's.

"Fuck," I whispered under my breath, as I closed my eyes in anger.

Rage whirled around inside me like a twister, and I took a few moments to calm down because if I didn't, I'd do something I'd regret.

Not because I minded hurting Gina, but because I didn't want Phoebe to see that side of me.

It was a side only Gina could bring out of me. A side that was born from the mutual grief we had over our daughter, but also from the past experiences we'd shared—all of them bad.

Like it always did when she was around, the skin on my belly, hips, lower back, and butt began to itch. Tingle with reaction. It was unnerving and made me want to scratch the still delicate skin, but instead of doing what I wanted, I stormed down the hall.

Realizing Gina was in my fucking bedroom, I came to a halt in the doorway and saw she was in my bed—naked as the day she was born.

As for Phoebe, she was standing at the foot of that bed, gawking at my ex.

But as I saw the two of them together, for the first and most definitely for the last time, it hit me how unalike they were.

In my mind, they'd been like twins. Both with rich dark hair, bright green eyes, and a body made for sin.

But they were so dissimilar it was a joke.

Gina's brown hair was from a bottle, and her skin was overly tanned to the point of being sallow.

Phoebe had warm, olive skin, and her hair was a lustrous brown that glinted red in certain lights and chestnut in others. Her eyes were like gems, not dull like Gina's. The difference was like that of a beryl stone and chalcedony.

From the very start, I'd seen the two of them as so startlingly similar that I'd almost believed they were one and the same person.

Except Phoebe was younger, fresher, born to remind me of everything I'd lost, a secret torment I had to exorcise from my life—not that it had worked.

She'd become my obsession when, at best, I'd been mildly curious about Gina.

Because both women were arguing, snapping at each other like feral cats, I had a chance to catch my bearings, to overcome my surprise in the pair's appearances.

As such, my tone was cool when I interjected, "Is it that time of the month again, Gina?" I tilted my head to the side when both women startled at the sound of my voice. "You know, the one where you come and make a fool of yourself in front of me?"

Phoebe jerked in surprise at that, but Gina's brow furrowed. Against my navy-blue comforter, her nakedness was all the starker. But I'd long since lost any interest in her tits and ass. Nothing about her intrigued me anymore. Nothing.

At the foot of my bed, looking hurt and confused and angry, was the possessor of every ounce of intrigue I'd need for a lifetime.

Unlike Gina, who was brash and trashy even though the clothes the bitch had discarded on the floor cost twice as much as everything Phoebe owned in the world, my woman looked simply put together in a pair of well-worn jeans and a thin cotton tee that let me see her bra through the grain.

Phoebe looked the innocent, while Gina appeared a slut.

Night and day, the pair of them.

And for the first time in Gina's presence, when I sucked down a breath, it was loaded with relief because I was free of her. Entwined utterly by someone else now. We'd always have the tie of Rosa, but Rosa was gone, and I had to live. I'd survived long enough, and life was beckoning me with its siren song.

"Nicky," Gina crooned, her voice loaded with faux seduction. "Don't be like that." She cut Phoebe a look. "Is this your new plaything? I'm not possessive." At my snort, she scowled before tacking on, "Anymore. I'll play with her too."

Phoebe stiffened at her words, staggering back a few steps as though trying to evade their meaning.

Though I wanted to go to her, wanted to comfort her, I didn't. Couldn't.

Gina turning up at my place had happened once too often, and it was time I cut the cord for real. She'd crossed boundaries, and I'd let her. Was I afraid of her? The question gave me pause, made me wonder if I had been. If, deep down, I was scared of the ticking time bomb she represented to me.

But I was no longer the Nicholas of before. I had more to lose if I was caught up in a blast, but I couldn't live my life with this witch poisoning everything I did.

And so, I bit off, "Unfortunately for you, *I* am possessive. I'd share her with no one, and certainly not a slut like you. Get the fuck out of my bed, Gina."

Her green eyes glinted with stony rage. "She's seen them, has she? That why you're so worried about keeping her? Because she puts up with how gross you are beneath those pretty clothes?"

"The scars you inflicted, you mean?" I retorted, sounding cold and unaffected, when inside I was a tortured animal. Phoebe knew about the scars now and the second Gina fucked off, she'd ask about them.

Maybe would even want to see them.

Could I show them to her?

Show her what only I'd ever seen and been repulsed by?

Gina huffed and sent her hair flying over her shoulder. "Will you never forgive me for that little mishap?"

Still waters ran deep, or so they said. But at that moment, I could have throttled her. My body began to shake, the muscles trembling as a rage so acute flushed through me.

"Get out."

I whispered the words when I wanted to scream them. Whispered them when I wanted them to lash her with the pain and misery she'd reaped on me.

"Nicky," she chided softly, but her voice was small. A squeak in comparison to her usual strident tones.

"I'm Nicholas. I'm no longer your husband—by your own design. You have no right to be in this apartment anymore, no right to be anywhere near my life." I gritted my teeth a second before biting out, "The next time you pull a stunt like this, I'll get a restraining order. You're the lawyer. You know how this works. Now, get out."

Her nostrils flared but she scurried to her feet, too audacious to grab the sheets to cover up. I got an eyeful of a body I'd have killed to possess once upon a time, but as I looked at her now, I saw her for what she was.

She-devil.

A demon who sucked the souls from men, all for her own pleasure. Who hurt them without care, without compunction, who tried to take their will from them by using sex against them.

Was it any wonder she'd fucked me up in the head?

Was it any wonder my body responded helplessly to Phoebe and yet, mentally, I couldn't allow myself more than what we'd experienced in the hall?

Gina had tied sex with manipulation. Wrapped it up with so many knots that it had caught on, infected me, and I was doing the same to Phoebe.

Controlling her through her orgasms.

Making her want me as I tied her pleasure to me.

The thought had me shuddering, but I didn't allow my body to respond. Didn't allow my reaction to show, because if I did, Gina might take that as a sign. I didn't need her to think I wasn't deadly serious.

I'd tried to be kind, but she'd taken advantage. I had more than enough proof to take to the police, and getting a restraining order with my family's pull would be nothing difficult.

When she was dressed in a black pantsuit, she ducked down and grabbed a pair of five-inch stilettos. She gripped the straps with her fingers then strolled around the bed.

I didn't hear what she said, but she whispered something to Phoebe that had her brow furrowing as she flashed a glance at me. I didn't look at her. Instead, I stared at my bitch ex and watched as she sashayed toward me now that she knew she had my full attention.

I backed off to give her space to leave and followed her down the hall to the front door.

"You come again and I'll call the cops," I repeated, my voice cold with the bitterness that came from years of hatred.

"Oh, I'll *come* again," she replied, her eyes narrowed, her tone a sickening croon that made me want to snarl at her. "You're mine, Nicholas."

"You tossed *me* away, Gina," I countered, pushing myself into her space so that I could tower over her. "And do you know what?" I breathed against her mouth, sensing that she thought I was about to kiss her.

"W-What?" she whispered, pupils blown with a messed-up mixture of lust and smug satisfaction.

"It was the kindest thing you've ever done. Now, fuck off."

Her mouth gaped wide in bemusement, but before she could say a word, before she had a second to compose herself, I dragged open the door then grabbed her arm and hauled her out.

She let loose a screech as I moved, but I ignored it and slammed the door in her face. For a few seconds, she bashed her hands against it, screamed my name a couple times, but then I heard her cursing under her breath before she took off.

I released a relieved sigh and pressed my forehead to the cool door.

Overheated and uneasy, I wasn't sure if I was about to be sick or not. My stomach was certainly churning like I'd drunk a gallon of OJ and milk mixed together.

"She wants you back."

I rolled on my forehead to look at her. Her arms were folded around her belly, and she looked so fucking young that I felt ancient.

"She wants what she can't have. Always has, always will."

Though I *was* surprised that she wanted me, even with the scars. Not that she knew how bad they were. She hadn't seen them since those first hours at the hospital.

"What did she whisper to you?"

She gulped. "It doesn't matter."

I laughed and the sound was cruel and hard. "Doesn't it?" I curled my hands into fists. "Let me guess. Did she tell you that I'm a monster?"

Her brow puckered. "She's crazy. You should have heard the stuff she was telling me."

"You didn't believe her?"

She snorted, and the sound was so down to earth that I stared at her intently for a handful of seconds. Long enough that she turned pink.

"No, Nicholas," she told me softly. "I didn't. She's sick, isn't she?"

"She's high-functioning, but yes. She's sick." Fuck, who was I to judge? Wasn't I sick in the head too?

"Because of Rosa?" she queried, and the fact she knew my daughter's name meant that Gina had tried to tell Phoebe I'd killed our baby girl.

It wasn't the first time she'd pulled that lie. Only the coroner's report had my mother looking at me with ease. Yeah, Gina had convinced my mother that I'd—

Fuck.

My tongue felt thick in my mouth as I grated out, "She was insane before, but after Rosa died…it got worse." I licked my lips. "SIDS. One day she was there, the next she wasn't."

"I'm so sorry, Nicholas."

The bitch of it was, I heard the sincerity in her voice.

Oh, everyone *thought* they meant it when they said they were sorry for the passing of a loved one. But Phoebe truly did. Each word was imbued with her genuine sorrow on my behalf.

I released a breath but fell silent, unsure of what to say.

"She said I killed her, didn't she?"

"Yes." Simple. No bullshit.

"She likes to blame me for it."

"SIDS is impossible to protect against. For the first six months, I was terrified for Scottie—"

My throat felt tight as I twisted away from her. "I went in there that morning. Saw her. It's something I live with every day."

"I can't imagine," she replied gently, and I heard the soft padding of her bare feet on the raw oak floorboards. I tensed against what was about to happen, but when her hand pressed to my side, it felt good.

Right.

Like my heart could stop racing now that she touched me.

As she moved to face me, she asked, "What scars, Nicholas?"

This time, I turned my head away from her, but when she pulled at my shirt, dragging it from my waistband, I didn't stop her.

Her hands touched them first, rubbing over the puckered flesh that was uber-sensitive to the touch. That was difficult enough. But for her to see them made me feel sick.

They were repulsive.

Repugnant.

Just like me.

A true manifestation of my character.

"What happened?" she breathed.

My throat was tight, but I managed to grate out, "I was faithful to Gina, Phoebe."

She quieted. Didn't rush to tell me she believed me, didn't huff and say she didn't.

This woman, to whom I'd shown my worst side, didn't condemn or judge me.

She waited for the full story.

I appreciated that, even if my ego didn't.

"One night, she accused me of cheating on her. It came out of the blue, and I talked her down. Like I said, she'd been more unstable than ever since we lost Rosa, more erratic, but I understood because most days, I felt insane too." God, that was an understatement. I'd been sure I was losing my mind every fucking hour of the day. "Then, a week later, she woke me up with—"

"With?" Phoebe prompted me when I fell quiet.

"She had a tea kettle in her hand. Freshly boiled." Behind me, Phoebe tensed. "She poured it on my stomach—I was lucky. She was aiming for my cock. That was one target she missed."

"What the fuck?" Phoebe rasped, and suddenly, I was being hauled around, forced to turn so that my back was against the door and she was there.

In front of me.

Her eyes ablaze, her body tense, throbbing furiously with her anger.

"Why?"

"To clean me." A hard laugh escaped me. "Sterilize me… in two meanings of the word."

"I wish I'd torn her hair out while I had the chance."

I blinked, and found my lips were quirking at the thought of Phoebe, who I'd believed was timid, going Amazonian on my ex-wife's ass. "Why didn't you?"

"Because I don't have the right to—"

"Be possessive of me?" My eyelids felt heavy. "What if I wanted you to?"

She swallowed. "Nicholas, I—"

"You, what?"

My skin tingled where her hand rested on my belly. The skin was still red, even after all these years. Some parts were puckered, others were smooth. Where water had trickled down over the contours of my flesh, there were strange scars from where it had puddled and then trailed down like tiny tributaries.

My abdomen, hip, and lower back area were a mess. My butt bore deeper scars where they'd done skin grafts to heal some of the deeper wounds.

But though the scars were revolting, she touched the damaged flesh as though it were healthy.

Like it had been before.

Didn't it revolt her?

Repulse her?

Even though Gina claimed to want me back, went to these bizarre lengths to entice me, I knew for a fact she'd find them repugnant.

Had I been nuts enough to want her back, I'd have had to accept that she'd never be able to come to terms with what she'd done to me.

And yes, I was aware of the irony in that statement.

Her fingers spread out over my belly, touching me in a place that hadn't known another's touch in far too long. But she didn't stop there. She smoothed her palm over the bumps of my muscles, then reached up to cup my jaw.

"Tell me what happened."

I swallowed. "Why?"

"Because this is why you've been the way you've been. It's why you've chosen this path for us. I want to understand before I say yes to anything." She sucked down a shuddery breath. "You have to understand, Nicholas, I know I'm a pushover." Her smile was lopsided.

"No. You're not," I ground out, hating that she thought that of herself.

"I am. I let my mom push me around, let you push me around—"

"It's to my shame that you can lump us both together in that sentence." I sighed and though it was weird for me, strange to initiate contact like that, especially with my scars on display, I tilted forward until my forehead rested against hers.

"Tell me," she urged, not replying to my comment, and I didn't blame her. There wasn't much to say. No apology I could give for the way I'd whipped her with my tongue, lashed her with my actions.

"There isn't that much to tell. Honestly," I rasped when she shook her head. "We got a divorce a few months after this happened. She cited cruelty as her reasoning, used a few examples of me going off the rails at her in the aftermath of this."

She scowled at me. "Didn't you throw that shit back in her face in court?"

"Why would I?" I shrugged, and at her gasp, shot her a wry look. "I wanted to get divorced. The second she did this, I wanted her out of my life. And I planned for it.

"The nurses wanted me to have her arrested on domestic abuse charges, but I knew that wouldn't wash. They even called the cops in, but I told them it was just an accident.

"You have to understand Gina to know what she's like, Phoebe," I told her when she gaped at me, stunned by my words. "She's possessive. She doesn't give up something that she believes belongs to her unless she's playing a game. She called for a divorce because she thought it would make me toe the line. She didn't think it would ever happen.

"And, when I didn't fight it, didn't refute her ridiculous claims, just let it go ahead, she couldn't deal with it. That's why she keeps coming back around because her plan didn't work."

I'd even let it taint my relationship with my parents, had let them believe what they wanted to to get that poison out of my life.

It was worth it.

And they weren't worthy of me.

"Not because you want her to come around?" Phoebe asked, her voice small.

And there it was.

The reason.

Whatever bullshit Gina had spewed in Phoebe's ear, it had found its mark.

"Phoebe," I chided. "You've felt them, but it's time you looked at them. Maybe you won't be able to stand the sight of them, of me, after you look. But Gina? Gina, who values the superficial over everything else?" I shook my head. "She doesn't want me for me. She wants me because I'm the one who got away."

She licked her lips, and then she broke my heart when her eyes welled with tears. "I'm so sorry you had to go through that."

I blew out a breath. "I'm not going to lie. It's messed me up, Phoebe. I'm not a nice man."

That had her gnawing on the inside of her cheek. "I know you're not, but I like you anyway."

"Does that make you or me crazy?"

She surprised me by smirking. "I think it makes us both a little crazy." She pulled back after sucking down some air, then murmured, "Okay, you think this is a breaking point. It isn't. Let me see, and we can move on from this."

There was so much to move on from. So much she didn't know about yet, and so much I couldn't tell her, but this was phase one. An unexpected phase, because I'd never anticipated any of this happening, but if it helped me reach my end goal, I wasn't about to complain.

Phoebe wasn't Gina.

Not in looks or temperament.

I'd done her a disservice by lumping them together in the same box, by believing they were both shallow bitches just because, with their beauty, they could make any man fall to their knees.

Phoebe was good people. She was loving and nurturing, a hard worker, dedicated and strong.

Gina was a backstabbing narcissist. She only cared about herself, her wants, her feelings. In her mind, *she'd* lost Rosa. Not me. Like I didn't count because I was only her father. Like my grief didn't matter.

But it did.

It had forged me into the shit heap of humanity that stood here before a woman who was far too good for me.

Christ, I felt small.

So fucking small, and so imperfect and revolting at that moment.

Her hands moved the hem of my shirt aside, and I had to close my eyes, had to hide from her expression as she took me in in all my ugliness.

When she didn't gasp or rush off to puke, I eventually had to look at her, had to see what she was thinking, but what I saw was her looking at me with such a well of sadness in her soul that I didn't know what to make of it.

"They're bad," she admitted, making my heart sink. Then she reached up and cupped my cheek again. "But they're not as bad as you think they are."

I remembered them from after the accident—bright red, oozing pus after they got infected. There were smooth bits and crater-like flesh that had taken the brunt of the boiling water. Some parts were my natural tan, others bright pink even after all this time.

I knew they *were* bad, but I wasn't about to complain that she didn't think so.

Instead, I reached up and cupped her wrist. It hurt me to say this, hurt me to take that step forward, but I had to. Phoebe was in the dark here. She'd been dragged into my world without her consent. I'd black-mailed her into being here, dammit.

This was on me.

Not her.

I swallowed down my terror and whispered, "I need you, Phoebe."

Her shoulders dropped at that and her eyes rounded. "You need me?" she retorted like she couldn't believe it.

Yet more confirmation that we really needed to work on her confidence.

That's your own goddamn fault, Nicholas, I chided myself.

"Like I need air," I admitted as if I were confessing to murder in a priest's confessional.

"W-Why? I'm nobody."

I shook my head. "You're not nobody. You're everything."

Her bottom lip quivered, then she whispered, "I-I don't want to not touch you anymore. When you walk away from me, when you leave me to just come and I can't touch you, you make me feel cheap, Nicholas. I can't handle that. *Won't* handle that."

"I wouldn't let you," I replied huskily, letting my thumb rub the back of her hand, and Christ, it killed me to put this out there, but I had to because she was right…

What kind of relationship would we have with me bullying her all the damn time? With me watching her get off, reveling in her pleasure, but never letting her touch me?

I wanted her.

So fucking badly I could barely see straight.

I'd stalked her to keep her safe, and this time, I had to keep her safe from me but I couldn't.

Wouldn't.

Because now, I wasn't the biggest danger to her. If anything, she was dangerous to *me*.

She could break me.

Rupture me into a thousand pieces, shred me to nothing, destroy me, and I would have no choice but to let her.

"If you're not repulsed—"

She grunted. "You're beautiful, Nicholas. Beautiful. Sure, this is a little mar on all that perfection, but you're human. And because you're human and not a fallen angel, that means I can touch you without fear of getting burned."

I believed her. Those words ripped away the shroud of fear that had been clouding me, that had stopped me from taking what was mine.

A growl escaped me, one that throbbed with the longing I felt for her. The need that encapsulated every ounce of sentiment she dragged from me, both willing and unwilling.

Before she could change her mind, I reached for her, hauling her against my chest and dragging her into me. The second her body connected with mine, she moaned, long and low in her throat, as though I'd touched her pussy, rubbed her clit. She reacted to that simple caress like a woman starved of her man's touch.

Well, not anymore.

I tipped my head forward, not stopping until our lips were bound, merged into one. My tongue thrust into her mouth, fucking her there like I'd soon fuck her. My cock pulsed, aching with an arousal so intense only this woman could satiate it.

But she surprised me.

She didn't passively lay in my arms. Wasn't as timid as I'd anticipated.

That first time, she'd been hesitant. Unsure. Uneasy with her body and definitely unconfident with her sexuality.

But the weeks of rubbing herself off in front of me, of baring her cunt to my eager gaze, of coming on my command, had worked their wiles on her.

And the only thing I had to say to that?

Halle-fucking-lujah.

I growled as her hands grabbed my waist, squeezing there before moving down to grab my butt. She pressed me into her, holding on tightly so that the minute amount of space I'd brought between us disappeared and was swallowed up. She arched her ass though, rocking her pelvis back so that she could tunnel her other hand between us.

When I felt her hand on my cock through my pants, I had no idea how I wouldn't burst.

Jesus Christ.

This woman was my personal dynamite.

I groaned into her mouth, loving the vibration that tingled along our tongues. She grunted in response, then I felt her nip my bottom lip. Hard. Not tearing into the soft flesh, but marking me as I'd marked her before.

And I fucking loved it.

God, I wanted her to claim me, because that would make me as much hers as she was mine.

I shoved forward, only so I could twist us around and press her back against the door. Taking advantage of the new position, I reached up and cupped her tit, and the second I did that, her hand tightened on my cock.

Fuck.

My eyes would have crossed if they weren't closed.

I began rocking my hips, began thrusting into her palm, and just when I felt sure I was about to claim my woman for the first time against the front door, her cell rang.

And my entire evening went to shit.

24

NICHOLAS

"WHAT HAPPENED?" Phoebe sneered, and I realized I'd never truly seen her this denigrating, this angry and outraged. I mean, I thought I had, but I hadn't. "Let me guess, you fell asleep, drunk as usual, and were smoking at the same time?"

The woman sitting, coughing and spluttering into a ventilator, looked like the human equivalent of jerky.

Not because she was burned. She wasn't. But smoked, yes. She was brown and leathery, sweat streaked her skin, making white tracks appear here and there along the creases of her eyes and down her cheeks.

Her body was wrapped up in a silver blanket, and the fact she was huddled up, her knees wrapped against her belly underneath said blanket, told me she hadn't been burned because she'd be creased up in agony if she had.

At her daughter's words, however, Linda Whitehouse's head drooped. "It was an accident," she rasped, tucking the nebulizer out of the way so she could make her claim.

"Always is with you," Phoebe said with a scoff. "You know the only reason I answered?"

Linda blinked at her warily. "W-Why?"

"Because you hadn't called me since I moved out. You didn't give a fuck about me. And I figured this was someone in a hospital somewhere calling your emergency contact." She snarled, "How right I was."

"I-I need your help, baby."

"I'm not your baby, and I'm already taking care of the only child that is. I have enough responsibility without dealing with a drunken, deadbeat mother." Her top lip curled. "You'll get no more help from me other than what I gladly give Scottie. I only came here to tell you two things.

"I don't and never will forgive you for being a useless mother. And the only way I will ever let you into mine or Scottie's lives again, is if you complete the Twelve-Step Program and come to us clean. Otherwise, that's it. You're dead to us."

Before I could do little other than eye the frazzled woman on the smeared-with-charcoal hospital bed, Phoebe had grabbed my hand and was hauling me down the corridor we'd just traversed.

The ER department was busy at this time of the evening but Phoebe moved through it like the pro she was at avoiding crowds, thanks to her job at the bar. With my hand tucked firmly in hers, I let her guide me until we were outside.

The second the warm night air hit us, she almost folded in two, and that was my Phoebe. The one in there had surprised me. Not disgusted me, just had taken me aback.

Phoebe wasn't perfect, I'd never believed she was an angel, but her disdain for her mother had come as a definite shock—even if it was deserved.

But this Phoebe, the one who sobbed as she propped herself upright, whose tears sounded like they were being dragged from her kicking and screaming, was *my* Phoebe.

And she stood there, like the island she'd been but no longer was, holding up the tide, containing it all within herself, when now, she wasn't just one but a part of a pair.

Her tears killed me, decimated me, and under the blinking light outside the ER's reception area, I rearranged her pretzel-like form and hauled her into my arms.

She sank against me like I was a life raft in the stormy sea, and I let her, let her sob into me, let her drench my shirt with her emotions and took it for the honor it was.

Around us, people stared, but this was a hospital, and they misconstrued her grief.

They stared at us through a haze of cigarette smoke, some of them attached to IVs, others in wheelchairs. Some were surgically attached to their cellphones and peered up at Phoebe's sobbing with a glower for her disturbing their concentration. Others ignored us, too intent on their own problems.

Before us, the ambulances came in to dock, spitting out EMTs who shouted as they moved, wheeling in gurneys with patients who were bleeding and gasping for air. Some were silent, no lights required, as dead bodies were brought in.

Around us, the world was chaos, and even though Phoebe still wept, her tears had slowed down, and I felt like I was in a calm space with her as we looked out onto the manicness of the scene around us.

She brought, I realized, peace to me.

Funny how I only just recognized that.

Even when I'd followed her and had been stressed, my intention hadn't just been to make sure she was safe, because I saw now that it was because of how it made me feel to be around her.

Like she was my air and I was suffocating without her.

I closed my eyes at the thought, and pressed my face into her hair. Like she knew I'd abandoned myself to her, thrown myself all in, she curled tighter into my arms, huddling into me as though together, we could make anything right.

And hell, maybe she wasn't wrong.

Maybe the two of us together was the only thing that made sense in this godforsaken city.

When Phoebe had walked into my world by strolling onto my campus, she'd been like a living representation of my past. When I saw her, the flick of her hair over her shoulder, her silken smile, the sinuous curves of her body as she wielded them like a knife in a duel, I'd seen

Gina. I'd seen the bitch who'd controlled me, and I'd stalked that past. Had followed it to make sure I knew where it was at all times, because it couldn't hurt me then. *She* couldn't hurt me then.

When she'd compounded my belief in her wickedness by stealing, I'd taken advantage of that, and inadvertently, had welcomed the present and the future into my life, because Phoebe was both. And she could never know the true origins of our relationship. If Phoebe ever did, that was it. My life was over.

"Are you ready to go home?" I asked after a few moments longer. Peering up at the sky, I saw the clouds that had been threateningly dark all morning had moved over us, and looked set to trigger our own personal storm. I hoped that wasn't a harbinger.

"Home?" she whispered.

"Yeah." I bussed her forehead and squeezed her tightly. "Our loft."

She gulped. "We haven't talked about—"

A sharp laugh escaped me, but it wasn't mean or cruel. If anything, it was amused.

"You're mine, Phoebe Whitehouse. Don't you realize that yet?"

She pulled away from me, not out of my arms, but away enough that she could peer up at me. She was tall for a woman, around five-ten, but that was still short in comparison to my six-four.

As she stared up into my eyes, she whispered, "You've just seen where I come from."

And she thought that was an issue?

I snorted. "Gina's father heads a law firm, and her mother is aiming for Senate next year." When her shoulders dropped, I moved my hand there and rubbed one. "Hey. I didn't mean it like that. I was just saying, she supposedly came from good stock, baby, and look at what she did to me."

Her throat visibly moved as she gulped. "I hate her."

Gina? Or her mother?

When I asked, she whispered, "Both of them."

"Well, we never have to see either of them again."

She gnawed on her bottom lip. "If she gets clean, I won't turn her away."

I shrugged. "Okay. But only if she gets clean?"

We had enough psychos under one roof with me in the building. We didn't need an alcoholic too.

"Yeah. Only if she really, *truly* gets clean." She licked her lips then peered at the doors to the charity hospital's ER department. "I wonder where she'll stay."

"The YWCA, probably."

She nodded. "So, she'll have somewhere to go."

If they'd take her.

I didn't say that though, figured it wasn't necessary.

The trouble with addicts, you had to let them bottom out sometimes. Let them sink to the depths of degradation for them to realize they wanted more out of their lives.

Did it suck?

Yeah, it fucking did.

But it was the only thing that worked.

I kissed her forehead again and murmured, "My aunt was into prescription meds in a big way. Unless you let them fend for themselves, they'll never get clean."

"I know. I just—I don't like what she brings out in me."

I could understand that.

"She isn't my mom."

My brow puckered at that. "What do you mean?"

Phoebe stared up at me, her eyes burning, her chin set in a defiant slant. "Mrs. Linden was my mom."

Understanding struck.

I reached up and tucked a curl behind her ear. "Of course."

"Just like that?"

I smiled. "Just like that. We claim who we want in this life." Just as I'd claimed her.

She sighed, the fight seeming to have been stolen from her with my easy acceptance of her assertion—like I'd have argued.

From what I knew of Mrs. Linden, my woman and Scottie would never have made it without her help. For that, Enid would have my undying thanks—she'd kept Phoebe safe until I could.

She rubbed her forehead against my shirt. "Are faculty and students allowed to date?"

Tensing, I queried, "Do you want the truth?"

"Of course." Then, she sighed. "Oh."

"Yes. Oh." I cleared my throat. "On the downlow until the end of the semester?"

She hummed. "Finals are soon anyway."

I kissed her temple once more. "That they are. And don't expect to get any help with the answers," I teased, where once I'd have been cutting. "Kisses will get you nowhere."

That had her laughing. "That's a shame, but I guess I'll just have to keep kissing you anyway."

"Damn straight," I growled, squeezing her tightly.

"You're right," she whispered. "Let's go home."

And fuck, if those weren't the best words I'd heard all year.

25

NICHOLAS

"NICHOLAS?"

I twisted around in my seat and stared at her in the hall. "What is it?"

She licked her lips. "Aren't you going to bed soon?"

"I have papers to grade." I wasn't even lying. For once. I grimaced. "Things got a little derailed this evening."

We'd made it back from the hospital with no issue, and the sitter had relinquished Scottie's care back to us with a smile and a 'no worries' for the short notice. Scottie, because he was a sensitive little monster, had apparently sensed something was wrong because he'd clung to Phoebe all night.

I could hardly blame the kid.

At least he had a reason to want to be glued to her side.

For me, I'd just look fucking weird.

Still, I hadn't complained when she'd ended up having to take him to bed early and go down with him until he rested. I'd just gotten on with my work because I always had plenty to do.

I'd even graded one of her papers, and though it was strange reading through it without the bitterness of before, and the desperate longing that had entwined every single move I made around her, I realized how unfair I'd been in the past.

Her voice was clear, pure. Shy, just as she was, yet strong too. It was a beautiful representation of the woman herself, and the more I read, the more I wanted to read her other work.

She was due to get her short story to me this year. It was an evil assignment that I always gave my students. A thirty to fifty-thousand-word novella on a topic that meant something to them. I got everything. From solarpunk dreams of utopia, to philosophical rewrites of Romeo and Juliet.

I'd been blind, thus far, to her talent. And while I might sound biased again, this time with the joy of her having accepted me, scars and all, I wasn't.

It was to my shame that I'd hidden from her abilities.

Christ, that I'd hidden from her period.

Well, I was done hiding.

She stood there, with the hall light illuminating her gentle curves in her over-washed tee. With her legs bared and her body ripe, I felt everything in me harden in the face of her softness.

My fingers dug into the leather armrests as the desire to make her mine overwhelmed me.

Voice low and gruff with my emotions, I grated out, "Come here."

Her eyes rounded, and her tits bounced with the sharp throb of excitement. She scurried over to me, walking on her tiptoes in a way that reminded me of a dancer, and within seconds, she was in front of me. Without even asking, she slid to her knees and stared up at me from between them.

After she licked her lips, she whispered, "Nicholas?"

I hummed as I stared into her eyes, and though she was in control of this situation, I knew she wasn't aware of that.

And I wasn't about to tell her.

Leaning back in my desk chair, I felt like a pasha looking over his servant girl for the night.

Except, I didn't want any other servant girl. None except her.

Drumming my fingers against the armrest, I replied, "No, Phoebe." Her brow puckered in surprise at my words. "Spread your legs."

Her eyes clenched close as she obeyed, but I knew she didn't want to. Knew she was thinking of what she'd said earlier, of how she needed more from me than *this*.

"How wet are you?" I asked, my jaw like granite as I looked at the slick folds of her sex.

"Very," she admitted, slipping her fingers across her pussy, the breathiness of her words getting to me like nothing else.

I leaned forward. "Let me taste your fingers."

At that, her eyes flared open, and I saw the hope deep in those beautiful crystalline eyes. Her hand shook as she lifted it to me and the delicate digits traced over my mouth, shaping my lips before I let my tongue peep out so I could savor her flavor.

Fuck, she was like honey and spice. Those deep, intense notes made me want to feast on her, to fucking ravage her with the depth of my need.

And I could now, couldn't I?

She wanted that side of me.

Even if she didn't really know what she was getting herself into, she wanted that.

All of me.

A shudder ripped through me as I pushed myself off the chair and down onto my knees. The second I was there, she made a move to kiss me, but I carefully cupped her shoulders and ground out, "No. On your back."

She whimpered but complied, and I couldn't stop myself from shaping her legs with my hands before spreading them wide. I dropped down into a low crouch, and like a starving beast, I ate her sopping cunt.

Her flavor exploded on my tongue, and I let it intoxicate me with all that she was. This beautiful, delicious woman who belonged to me.

Me.

Mine.

I growled, loving her sharp squeal as the sensation made her throb, then I sucked on her clit as I shoved two fingers deep inside her pussy like I'd been wanting to do since forever.

She softened around me like a silken glove, and I gritted my teeth as I curved my fingers upward, raking down against the tender inner walls. A grunt escaped her, and then her hands sank into my hair, her nails digging into my scalp as she let me know her pleasure.

When her legs came up to cup my head, I grinned into her slick flesh, loving how fucking juicy she was with arousal for me. I sucked down on her clit in silent thanks, then sucked harder when she rocked her hips, arching her pelvis to get closer to me. As though even a scant hairsbreadth was just too fucking much.

And I concurred.

Any space between us was too much in my opinion.

Fucking her with my fingers, I scissored them apart a few times. My cock wanted in her so goddamn badly, but I knew I was big and from the feel of her, she wasn't. Spreading her was a joy, though, and going down on her was the fulfillment of a lot of fantasies.

Every time I'd watched her get off on my desk, I'd wanted to suck her down, slurp her up.

With her, I wasn't a gentleman. I was a beast. I wanted to ravage her, claim her with every base, visceral part of me.

Fuck, she twisted me up, churned me until I was a shadow of the man I'd been before.

Gina wouldn't recognize me like this. None of my other lovers would either.

With Phoebe, I was raw and ready. Hers. One hundred percent.

When she curved up in a semi-crunch, this time her hands on my hair were there to discourage me. She began mewling, "No, no, no. Your cock, Nicholas, need you. Please. Need you inside me."

Mid-suck on her clit, I stared up at her, saw the desperation on her face, that eagerness for me that was just as strong as what I had for her.

I lapped at her clit with the tip of my tongue, teasing it until tears leaked from her eyes.

I'd wanted her to come first, and it stunned the shit out of me that she was withholding her pleasure, that she was refusing to orgasm without me inside her.

Because that level of self-control deserved a reward, I reared back, and began shucking out of my shirt. As I did, I watched her look at me. But I saw no revulsion as my scarred abdomen was revealed.

When I unfastened my zipper, her mouth trembled, and the second I pulled out my cock, her eyes rounded.

Not wanting to strip anymore because I had scars on my hips as well, I grabbed a firm hold of my cock and began to jack off in front of her.

In time to each thrust of my hips into my fist, she panted, and I watched her lick her lips as though she couldn't wait to taste me, to savor me as much as I'd savored her.

I thrust into my fist to torment myself. I'd denied myself even this measure of release since I'd been watching her because I hated what I was doing and knew it was wrong.

But from that wrongness, this had spawned.

It seemed insane, and maybe it was, but it was perfect for me.

"Nicholas, I need your cock deep inside me," she whispered, her face flushed, her tits jiggling beneath her shirt.

"Take off the shirt," I ground out, ignoring her other words, and watching with satisfaction as she ripped it off overhead, leaving her bare before me. A vision of silken, olive skin that I wanted to come all over. I wanted my seed marking her from the inside out.

"Beg me," I whispered. "Beg me for my cock."

Her lips trembled, but though I could have mistaken it for sadness or fear, it wasn't.

It was lust.

One-hundred-percent lust.

She groaned, "Nicholas, I need you. I need you so badly. You're so fucking big and I'm so empty. I'm going crazy without you inside me. All these weeks, all this time, I've gotten off, but it's felt half-complete. Like I was missing something, and I was. You. I need you, Nicholas. I need you."

I dipped down, satisfied with her words, and as I pressed my cock to her slickness, letting it settle along the length of her cunt, I pressed my weight into her and whispered against her lips. "What am I to you, Ms. Whitehouse?"

Her eyes flared. "You're my professor, sir."

I grunted at that, loving that she wanted to play with me too. "You've been a very naughty student, Ms. Whitehouse."

"I'll be even naughtier if you let me, sir."

I couldn't stop the grin from forming, even if I'd tried. I kissed her smirk then thrust my tongue into her mouth, fucking her there first, needing to claim her, even as I rocked my hips and let my cock be coated in all her glossy wetness—juices that had been born from her attraction to me as well as my toying with her.

When her hands dug into my back then slid down to cup my ass, I tensed against her, aware that she'd be able to feel the rough skin, knew that she'd be able to discern the different patches where they'd taken grafts.

My breath froze in my chest, and I was unable to move for endless seconds, until she pulled her mouth from mine and whispered, "Nicholas? I want you, Professor. Please."

A deep groan escaped me, and I whispered, "You can have me."

Rearing my hips up, I grabbed hold of my cock, which was dripping with her juices, then slid the tip to her gate.

As I pushed inside, she clenched down on me and began panting again, but even though her nails dug into my sides, even though they dragged up and over to my back where I felt them bury themselves deep into the muscle, she didn't pull away, didn't try to pull back.

As I thrust into her, sinking home, she released a broken cry as she burrowed her face into my throat, her body clinging to mine as her legs cupped my hips, crossing them at the ankle so her heels dug into my ass.

I felt surrounded by her, fully encompassed, and it felt so fucking good that I wasn't sure if I'd last longer than a goddamn minute.

Her slick heat was like nothing I'd ever known before. After all the years of denial, I felt like a fucking virgin again, but I wasn't. I was an experienced lover, and there was no goddamn way that even if I was ready to burst, I'd do so without her exploding around me first.

And so, I ground my hips against hers so that each time I slid into her, I made sure to go deep enough that she felt it in her clit.

Time and again, I sank home, loving how deep I could get, how much of me she took. Then, when her pussy spasmed around my cock, a soundless cry escaping her as she flung her head back until it was rocking against the floor in silent pleasure, I let myself go.

Four years of hunger let loose inside her.

Ripped from me like the shroud she'd ripped from my life.

It was too soon, too crazy, but I couldn't stop myself from whispering in her ear, "I love you."

And when she whispered back, "I love you too," I thought my heart was going to explode with joy.

26

NICHOLAS

THE SOUND of Scottie squawking woke me up, but when he instantly settled, I knew I didn't have to move because he'd have carried on crying if he needed one of us.

The floor wasn't one of the most comfortable places to sleep, but I was certain I hadn't slept better in years because she was there.

With me.

Cuddled into my side, hugged around me until I wasn't sure where my skin ended and hers began, we were stuck together, literally, through sex sweat, and my lips curved as I remembered that particularly delicious part of fucking.

As well as the wet puddle beneath us.

Fuck, even that felt good.

Especially because I'd come inside her.

As soon as the thought crossed my mind, however, I felt like a piece of shit.

She already had a baby to take care of. I should have made sure she was protected, should have…

Her hand petted my chest, rubbing through the sparse hairs that grew there. "What's wrong?" she murmured, and I realized she'd been awake for a while.

"Nothing."

"Liar," she teased, a laugh in her voice.

"I was thinking about birth control."

"I have an IUD."

Jealousy ripped through me. "Oh."

She hummed, apparently not sensing why I'd tensed, otherwise, I doubted she'd have sounded so relaxed. I was acting like a damn caveman and I deserved to be smacked in the gut, not to be petted like a pampered pooch.

"When Mom got pregnant, I wasn't about to let that happen to me."

The breath that escaped me wasn't relieved, as I believed she might assume, but poignant with loss.

Still, even if I wanted her full and round with my child, I was well aware that she was young, and even though I wanted her tied to me in more ways than I thought were legally possible, I wasn't willing to rob her of more freedom.

As much as I'd loved Rosa, as much as I knew Phoebe loved Scottie, I also knew how all-consuming kids were. She really didn't need another baby before she hit her mid-twenties.

Even if I wanted her to have my kid.

And fuck, yeah, that was a really stupid thing to be thinking so soon, but this wasn't soon for me.

She'd been at the forefront of my thoughts for what felt like a lifetime so getting her out of them was damn near impossible.

For her to be here, in my arms, accepting of all my scars—both physical and mental—was more than I could dream of, so I needed to back the fuck off and stop being so greedy.

I kissed her temple. "Feel better?"

When she wriggled against me like a little pup, I chuckled when she slapped her hand against my belly.

"Shut up," she whined, making me laugh harder than I thought I had in years.

"Is that a yes?" I choked out.

"You know it is," she pouted, then she released a deep sigh. "I've never realized how empty an orgasm can make you feel."

I cocked a brow. "Isn't pleasure, pleasure?"

"How do you feel when you jack off in the shower?"

"I don't."

She froze. "Ever?"

"No. Well, not recently." I blew out a breath, wishing I'd kept my fucking mouth shut. "I don't like to look at my body," I admitted.

She tensed. "Oh." Her hand petted my belly, rubbing over the tissues I loathed, and yet she seemed intent on touching them all.

I clenched my eyes shut because if I didn't, I'd want to rail at her, demand she stop touching me, and I couldn't do that.

Wouldn't.

She didn't deserve my cruel words just because I was tense and on edge, uncertain and insecure.

I needed to man up.

Stat.

So, instead of being a pussy, I choked out, "Please. Don't."

"Don't, what?"

"Touch them. It makes it hard for me."

She hummed. "All the more reason *to* touch them."

Before I could argue with her, she was suddenly on top of me, straddling me, and I felt the wet kiss of her slick pussy against my belly, against the damaged flesh as she rocked into me.

On purpose.

She coated me with her slickness like the little siren I hadn't expected her to be, and when she wiggled her hips, as though she was trying to coat me with even more, I had to shake my head because fuck, I needed this.

I needed someone who didn't take life so damn seriously, and the truth was… I hadn't expected that of her.

Unless she was with Scottie, she was usually frowning. Worrying over something. And with her schedule, I couldn't blame her. I'd known med students who slept more than Phoebe did, and damn, I wanted that to change.

I wanted her lifestyle to change.

For the better.

I reached over and cupped her hips, pushing down on them so that she was grinding into my lower belly. Suddenly, her teasing turned serious as a wispy breath escaped her.

"Empty orgasms aren't always so bad, are they?" I mocked, as she rocked against me, just frigging that deliciously dirty clit against me like it was her reason for being.

She sighed. "They're not empty when you're involved."

"I watched you, every fucking time," I retorted.

"But you looked bored," she complained on a mewl, which turned high-pitched as the pleasure apparently hit her. "Sometimes, I thought you were asleep."

It stunned me that she thought that, and because I was bewildered, I didn't anticipate her sliding down, rocking into my cock, notching it to her pussy, then filling herself to overflowing with my dick once more.

"Aren't you sore?" I rasped, grabbing her hips to stop her from riding me before she was ready.

"Oh yeah," she moaned, "but it feels so fucking good."

Christ, who was I to complain?

I let her ride me, loving the jiggle of her tits, loving the way she raised her arms overhead and fumbled her hair with her fingers as though she didn't know what to do with them, as though she wanted to reach for the heavens but knew it was stupid.

When I reached between us and began rubbing her clit, she froze atop me with a startled, "Oh."

"Feel good, baby?" I asked, my voice a low rasp as I watched her slowly start to grind herself on me once more. But this time, she was scowling, like she was trying to discern the flavor profile of the pleasure she was experiencing.

It was one of the hottest fucking things I'd seen in my goddamn life.

Watching this woman coming to own her pleasure was a privilege.

I stunned the hell out of her by rearing up into a seated position, and the proximity changed our angle. She clamped down on me, making me press my face into her tits before I latched on to her nipple and tugged on it with my teeth. With each nibble I gave her, she grunted and moaned—evidently, she liked her tits played with.

Keeping one hand between us, I touched her in tandem, giving her the caresses she needed to explode around me like a light show.

When I came, it was deep and intense as her slick walls cupped me tight, held me close, like they'd never let me go, and fuck if I never wanted them to.

I'd die a happy man being this close to this woman, and hell if that wasn't the best life goal a man could ever have.

When we both fell flat on the floor again, she began giggling, but this time, she sounded punch-drunk.

"What's wrong?" I inquired hoarsely, but I was smiling. Something about her made me feel like I'd drunk a shit ton of champagne too.

"Nothing's wrong," she tittered. "I'm just thinking about how many bedrooms this place has, and how we're sleeping on the floor."

My lips curved into a grin because she wasn't wrong.

I reached for her hand, entwined my fingers with hers, then whispered, "Best night's sleep I've had in a long time. The bed doesn't matter, it's the company that does."

She fell silent at that, and I wasn't sure if I'd freaked her out or not. She seemed to appreciate my intensity, but was also taken aback by it. But tonight, she didn't say a word, just pressed her lips to my shoulder and gave me a gentle peck before nuzzling into me and falling asleep.

27

NICHOLAS

THE SUNLIGHT DAPPLED Phoebe's hair into a thousand shades of chestnut, but though she was more fascinating to me than a classical painting, I tore my attention away from her beauty, and instead demanded, "What are you doing here?"

It didn't seem like she was all that surprised to see me, because her only response was for her to cock a brow my way when she determined where I was.

Ever since we'd grown more intimate, I'd allowed technology to take a lot of the stress off my shoulders. I always knew where she was thanks to an app on my phone and hers. Hence my tracking her down to this park, but her lack of surprise…

My brow puckered as I contemplated what that meant, but she broke my concentration with her grumbled, "I want to speak with her."

It didn't take much to realize that by 'her,' Phoebe meant my she-witch of an ex, especially as we were in a damn park outside the bitch's office building.

"Why?"

Her mouth tightened, and the sun seemed to bounce off the delicious curves of her lips. She had some kind of gloss on, and gross or not, I wanted to eat it off her mouth.

Fuck, I couldn't keep my hands, mouth, or cock away from her body. She was like my very own personal drug, and I wanted to devour her.

"I saw the email."

That had me narrowing my eyes at her, all arousal shoved to the side. "Why were you looking at my laptop?"

"It pinged!" she retorted, but I saw that her color was bright on her cheeks. "You'd left it on the coffee table, and I just saw it." Then her eyes narrowed. "Anyway, this isn't something you should have hidden from me." She pointed a finger at me, jabbed it in the air. "You should have told me." Point. Point. "Why didn't you?"

I shrugged as I slid onto the seat beside her on the bench. Seamlessly, I lifted my arm and curved it around her shoulders. Though she was pissed at me, I rather enjoyed how she snuggled into my side.

"A shrug isn't an answer," she told me grumpily.

"What can I say? I didn't want to worry you."

"Worry me?" she squeaked. "This is more than a worry, Nicholas. She's threatening to tell the dean about us!"

Sighing, I reached up with my free hand and pinched the bridge of my nose. "That's why I didn't see any point in telling you."

"What do you mean?"

"Because I don't care if she does."

Her mouth firmed. "Well, I do. We've done nothing wrong." Another huff. "Just because the school is archaic—"

I laughed. "Rules exist for a reason." I dipped my head and nipped at her earlobe. "They think you devious women will corrupt us innocent professors into giving you better grades."

She rolled her eyes, but I felt her shiver at my nip. "As if. You're the corrupter here. I was innocent, just minding my own business before you came in like a wrecking ball."

"I built everything back up that I knocked down though, didn't I?" I rejoined with a smirk.

She huffed. "I guess." Then she bit at her bottom lip. "Please, Nicholas, don't joke. I'm concerned."

And those two words were my kryptonite.

I figured I'd spend the rest of my life making sure this woman wasn't concerned, which meant even though I'd been content to ignore Gina, I couldn't now.

Dammit.

I'd consider myself pussy-whipped if Phoebe wasn't just as afflicted. Although, I knew her reasoning was different than mine. Phoebe was young, had a bright life ahead of her. I knew what I felt for her and didn't expect her to understand.

"If she thinks she has power over us, she's more likely to use what she knows," was all I said, keeping my tone calm. "You sitting outside her office is the exact opposite of keeping things relaxed."

She winced. "You're right. We should go."

I snorted, squeezed her arm. "It's a beautiful afternoon. We should go for a late lunch."

"I have to study."

"You also have to eat," I countered, though she wasn't wrong. Her finals were approaching and she had two weeks left to study. My class was her last exam, which I found rather apropos.

"I know, but I can eat and study at the same time." She half-turned in her seat. "Nicholas, will you deal with this for me?"

"I can try," I reasoned. "Gina is a devious bitch."

"What is it with you two and blackmailing people?" she grumbled, but I took no offense.

Gina and I were, disconcertingly enough, cut from the same cloth.

Was it any wonder we'd been a nightmare together?

"Because we like to get our own way?"

"She's not having you back," Phoebe warned, and the fire in her eyes had my cock hardening.

"Fight her for me, would you?" I teased, loving that she bristled at the mere thought. Before she could get too riled up, I pressed my forehead to hers and stated, "I'll deal with it."

She swallowed. "I don't want you to lose your job over this." I didn't tell her that I didn't give a fuck about the job. "I can't believe she's been following us."

"Gina wants what she can't have, and what she wants, she covets."

I shrugged. "She's probably had someone following me for a long time." That Gina might be aware of my proclivities was disconcerting enough, but I figured there was one way to nip this in the bud.

Fighting fire with fire.

Humming at the thought of the evidence I'd stacked my way over the years, I knew I had enough to keep her corralled.

I was going to use it up on this, do away with the shit I'd been storing for a rainy day if Gina ever turned psycho on me again, but for Phoebe's sake, I didn't mind losing my hoard.

I reached up and cupped her chin. Letting my fingers trail along the sensitive flesh, I allowed them to trickle down her throat, dragging tender nerve endings to life.

Only when she released a stuttered breath did I ask, "Are you wet for me?"

Her eyes flared wide, but the pupils fluctuated from thick to thin as though they were unsure how to process the sudden surge of chemicals in her blood.

"Yes," she said thickly.

I tilted her head to the side with the hold I had on her jaw, and licked a line down her throat.

"How wet?"

A sigh escaped her, and I felt her sink into me a little, depending on me to prop her upright.

"Ver-ry," she hiccupped.

I hummed. "I want to taste."

That had her stiffening. "We're in a park."

Pulling away with a grin that she responded to with narrowed eyes, I began to shuck out of my light sports coat. When I placed it on her knees, she grabbed a firm hold of it, her knuckles bleeding white with the ferocity of her hold on the fabric.

"Nicholas, we can't."

My brow quirked. "Can't we?" I licked my lips. "Spread your legs slightly."

Her gaze darted from left to right, but it was a weird time of day. Neither lunch nor rush hour, and though this was the city that never slept and there was always someone around, someone watching via a camera or whatever, I didn't particularly care.

I wanted to remind Phoebe of something.

She belonged to me. Her arousal, her fears, everything. It was mine. And I protected what was mine.

I could see the tension on her face, read it as her desire to disobey, but also, she wanted me. Wanted my touch. Craved it just as badly as I needed to give it to her.

When she blew out her breath, I knew I had her. Her legs fell open slightly, not wide enough to be noticeable to anyone in particular, just a little farther apart than was polite.

I twisted in the seat and pressed my mouth to hers even as I slid my hand under the jacket. She bunched it up, making it more of a shield, and when I dragged up her skirt, shoved it out of the way, and managed to work my hand between her legs, my kiss broke off as I felt her.

Wet.

Hot.

Liquid fire against my skin.

I gritted my teeth as I pressed my forehead to hers once more. This woman was made for me. Made to burn for me.

Fuck.

"Don't stop," she whimpered, and like that, she decimated my control even more.

I'd have fucked her there if I could. Beneath the hot sun, under the blanket of blue sky that was like silk interspersed with wispy clouds, and atop the lawn that landscaped the park…

I had an image in my mind then.

There would come a day when I'd take her like that.

Outside, with nothing and no one to watch us or stop us. Where I could make her mine time and time again.

Because she pleased me, I quickly rubbed her clit, with fast flicks of my fingers that I knew would get her hot. When she clenched beside me, her forehead pushing into mine so she could contain herself, I reveled in her release. Reveled in it and loved that it was mine, just as she was.

Leaning forward, I nipped her bottom lip with my teeth and whispered, "Don't worry, Phoebe. I'll handle everything."

I wasn't about to sully the moment with talk of Gina, but I'd handle her.

The only way to bargain with the devil was to grow a pair of horns too.

28

NICHOLAS
TWO WEEKS LATER

AS I STARED at her in my classroom, I watched while she worked on her final exam, the smallest of smiles gracing her lips.

This was it.

Once this was done, we could pretty much out ourselves as a couple.

It was against the rules for faculty and students to be sexually involved, and though I knew of at least four professors who were fucking someone in their classes, it was a rule that I'd never breached before now.

Had never felt the impetus.

But my life was changing with Phoebe and Scottie in it, and for the better.

Even though, technically, we'd still keep shit on the downlow, I was going to make my move tonight.

I wanted her to stop working at *Crow,* and I wanted to hire a full-time nanny so that she could actually do what she wanted without fearing for her brother.

Although, I felt bad for calling him that. Truth was, Scottie was more like her son.

Watching her work on her final paper, I felt pride spill through me.

She was still nervous and timid around most people, but she was also getting a tad more boisterous.

I wasn't sure if it was getting away from her mother, or whether I was good for her—there was no way to tell what put that smile on her face. Hopefully, it was both things, and that was why she seemed like a load had been taken off her shoulders.

My phone buzzed, drawing my attention away from my study of her, and when I saw it was Gina, I rolled my eyes as I rocked back in my seat.

Two weeks ago, she'd threatened to tell the dean I was fucking a student and she'd been trying to blackmail me ever since.

Of course, it wasn't going to work.

Sure, I enjoyed my job, but I didn't care if I never worked another day at this college again.

Why would I?

I didn't need the money.

I did it because I loved teaching, loved this process, and after Rosa, it had given me a purpose. A reason to wake up in the morning.

Yes, it would suck to give it up, but fuck, now that I'd met Phoebe, my life could move on.

It was almost like serendipity had arranged this.

I'd come to this school in the aftermath of the wreckage of my marriage to Gina, and I'd been miserable most of that time. But I'd found a semblance of myself here, and as I'd grown, as I'd developed, it was like I'd been waiting for Phoebe to arrive.

I wasn't a man who believed in love at first sight. Marriage to Gina had been more like love at first glimpse of that ass and those tits. But Phoebe, she'd changed everything.

And she still didn't realize it.

Damn well wouldn't if I had a say in things.

Me: *Nice try, Gina. Did your boss like that little care package I sent him?*

I smirked when her reply came back almost instantly.

Gina: *What the hell are you talking about?*

Me: *You know what I'm talking about. The statements I have about you bribing my doormen to get into my home. Jackson lost his job because of you. Those pictures you sent of Phoebe me and going inside and coming out of my apartment; proof that you've pretty much been stalking me?*

Gina: *You wouldn't dare.*

Me: *Oh, I would. Well, let me correct that. I haven't sent anything to your boss YET. But I will. And let's face it. I have enough to go to the cops, and I have no compunction in doing so, except I don't think it will look good for your resume if you have a restraining order against you, will it?*

Gina: *You bastard.*

Me: *I'm only what you made me.*

Gina: *Fuck you.*

Me: *Never again, thank fuck. Your toxic cunt has burned me one too many times. You leave me and Phoebe the hell alone or I'll send EVERYTHING to your boss and to the cops at the same time. You know I can and will, and Christ, while I'm at it, I'll send it over to your mommy and daddy too. I'm sure they'd like to see my scars.*

I hadn't been happy at the prospect of revealing them to the world, but I would if it meant getting this sick and twisted weirdo off my back.

Sure, she'd been my wife and the mother of my baby, but she wasn't that anymore.

Something about us together had created a poison so deep that it had twisted us both.

Yeah, I knew it was the height of hypocrisy for me to be threatening to go to the cops over her stalking me, but fuck, I wasn't about to let Gina win.

She'd wreck my career in a heartbeat, and I could deal with that. But Phoebe had worked too damn hard to get to this point.

And the irony was that I'd never been that lenient with her grades. Even though I now saw her talent for what it was, I also knew that it didn't fit the program.

Some writers just didn't.

Some people had a gift, while others were technically perfect.

It was like a pianist. Someone could play like Beethoven, but if they didn't have the gift, it was just a random, anonymous piece of music that had no soul or heart.

Writing was like that. Technical or soul deep. There was no in between.

I wasn't sure if Phoebe would ever develop her writing, but if she did, I was under no illusion that she had the ability to make magic with her words.

Gina: *Truce?*

I stared at the screen, unsure as to whether or not I believed my she-devil of an ex.

She was definitely the kind of person who liked to lull her enemies into a false sense of security.

Me: *You'd better not be bullshitting me.*

Gina: *I'm not. I'm aiming for ADA this year. I don't need the past coming back and biting me in the ass.*

Me: *Why didn't you think of that before?*

Gina: *Because you always rolled over before.*

Her words resonated with me, and it made me wonder how she'd viewed me.

Why the hell did she want to be with me if that was how she saw me?

As a pushover.

Huh.

I stared at nothing in particular, hearing the scratching of pens—from those who liked to be purist—and the tapping of keys as my students tried to cram as much into their paper as they were able.

But as I stared, I tried to ask myself if I was a pushover, and if that was why I'd responded to Phoebe the way I had.

As I thought about it, naturally, my gaze drifted over to her. She was staring intently at her screen. Her laptop was old. So old it was a wonder it had made it into school. I only ever saw it around the times she was doing exams, so I knew she kept it at home to keep it safe.

I'd never known a woman who was more careful with her possessions, who was so careful with another's too.

Some days, I wasn't sure whether I needed to keep my housekeeper on or not. I mean, Phoebe really did do a better job than Mrs. Manifort, and only the fact that my housekeeper had been with me since college stopped me from letting her go.

The thought occurred to me that it was probably time to introduce Phoebe to my folks.

That would be fun.

Especially since they hadn't seen me in over two years.

My mouth pulled taut as I thought about how badly that Thanksgiving had gone down.

With my mother telling me I was stupid to let a woman like Gina go, and railing at me for all the things Gina had used against me in the divorce.

I'd ended up storming out of their penthouse on the Upper East Side, and I'd acted as though it were on the other side of the world rather than across town ever since.

I had no real desire to see them, to meet with them, and I gave even less of a fuck about their opinion of Phoebe—and an opinion they'd definitely have.

But she was everything I wanted, and in capital letters.

I rubbed my chin, staring down at the text box that was blinking. Gina's light was still green, and it satisfied something in me to think that she might be sweating over my response.

I wanted her to. Fuck that, I needed her to.

She'd thought me weak when all along I'd been playing her. Playing her because I'd known there was no way she'd let me go unless she was the one to break us up.

My pride and ego were at war though, but I still tapped out: *Truce.*

When the double ticks appeared and Gina didn't reply, I truly hoped that would be the last time I ever heard from her.

I certainly didn't give a shit if I never saw her again, but I'd be vigilant. She'd pulled this crap once, so there was nothing to stop her from trying to do it again.

When I looked at the clock, a second later, I called out, "You have fifteen minutes remaining."

At my words, very few people looked up, but Phoebe did, and because I was hoping she would, I shot her a smile.

Hers was gentle, a little weak, but I knew it was because she was tired, had been for the past week since finals had begun.

Honestly, everyone looked wrecked, and I was just grateful that I'd managed to get her to agree to cut down on her hours at *Crow*.

When, twenty minutes later, the hall had emptied, I flipped through the papers that had been handed in and arranged them in alphabetical order, then stared at the documents that had been emailed to me and were pending on my screen.

Technically, I had a faculty meeting to attend before I could go home, but hell if I cared. I sat back, opened up Phoebe's paper, and started reading, curious as to where she'd gone with it.

29

———

NICHOLAS

THE SCENT of lasagna filled my loft when I made it back, and as I unknotted my tie, I let the warm scent fill me with the sense of home.

Of course, it was twisted that I felt that way when I was on the brink of losing everything.

Until now, this place had been empty in more ways than one. But with Scottie and Phoebe around, it truly was turning into a haven, not just somewhere I laid my head at night.

I had too many bad memories here, but I was glad that those shitty ones were slowly being replaced, and until this afternoon, I'd fully intended on moving out and making a fresh start with Phoebe and Scottie by my side.

Normally, I'd head into the kitchen, go and see them both as she cooked, but tonight, after reading what I had, I didn't. I couldn't face her.

She knew.

That was what I read into her final essay.

She knew she was my obsession.

I dumped my attaché case by the door and shrugged out of my jacket, which clung to me uncomfortably. I felt sweaty and overheated, like no amount of air conditioning would cool me down. Leaving it hanging over the armrest of the sofa, something I never did, I headed out onto the terrace and sucked down some fresh air.

As I stared across the city, looked at the place that had been my home since birth, I recognized how out of touch I felt.

I didn't want to be here anymore.

That dream I'd had of being in France, just speaking about it with Phoebe had made it surge to life again. Scottie would thrive there, and Phoebe would be away from the rat race I didn't want her in.

But it wasn't my decision.

None of this was.

Honestly, I was astonished she was still here, period. Bewildered that I'd come back to the scents of a meal cooking, of lasagna waiting on me for our dinner when she should have been running far and wide.

Why hadn't she?

Because she needed my help? Financially?

I could deal with that.

I really could.

It would kill me if she left, but I was the master of my own fate, and there was no hiding this from her now. Not when she knew just how strange I truly was.

He's there, in the shadows. Always watching, always waiting.

Protecting me as he stalks me. Hunting me down with his cherishing stare.

His poisonous tongue bewilders, even as his caressing eyes arouse me. The toxic words overpowered by heat-filled glares and the promises of pleasure.

He's danger in male form. Peril to a female's heart. But never is he a hazard to her health. His menace is as tangible as his touch, to which this woman never wishes to be apart from…

As I looked at the tree where my faithful hound, Cara, was buried, I bowed my head as the weight of the world pressed itself onto my shoulders.

Cancer had taken those weary old bones from me, but I'd found a way to bring her back to life by burying her under a tree on my street.

I'd miss that tree when I was no longer here, but I'd miss Phoebe and Scottie more if they didn't come with me where I wanted to go. She said she never wanted to be apart from me in a final piece of the exam, which was as bemusing as it was talented.

A very personal letter to me, her stalker. From the woman whom I was stalking.

My throat felt tight as I heard her footsteps padding toward me. When the door creaked, I knew she leaned against it, and though I didn't want to know, *I had to*.

"How?" I whispered, every muscle in my back straining as I looked over the railing, staring at anything but her.

"The transcriptions—I know they're yours. Not 'Elizabeth's.' If Gina hadn't have come, I might not have realized. But you mentioned her name in them.

"Plus, those jade figurines in your office. I think you started collecting them back then. I remembered the horse and the bull specifically." She hummed then she moved, and I felt her against me. Her heat so close but not touching. "Also, Jay... I came back one day and he was waiting outside."

My cousin.

The owner of *Crow*. Her boss.

"When?" I rasped.

"Two days ago."

The fucker should have warned me.

Like she heard my unspoken words, she murmured, "I told him I knew you'd pulled strings for me. Although how you did that when I found the job offer on the college job's board, I'm not sure."

"You passed it to get to American History." I cleared my throat. "I waited until you walked past and saw it, then took it down."

"Jay said he wasn't even hiring."

Was that amusement I heard in her voice? "He owed me a favor or two," I rasped.

"I'll bet." She exhaled roughly. "Then there's the fact that I remembered you. It just took me a while. You'd been at the coffee shop most mornings I was there, and when I asked around in the VIP section a few days ago, the waitresses told me that that booth was pretty much yours. Except you hadn't been in for like five weeks."

Since she'd moved in.

When I didn't say a word, because fuck, what could I say? She sighed, and finally pressed herself into me. The warmth of her front aligning itself to my back. It felt so good, but I tensed at her touch.

I didn't want her to go, didn't want her to leave me, but God help me, if she left me now after gifting me with her warmth, it would be the death knell to my sanity.

But all of this, these revelations, meant she'd known for at least two whole days, if not longer. She'd known and hadn't left.

Still… "How can you stand to touch me?" I murmured rawly.

"Because you saved me."

"Saved you? I blackmailed you," I scoffed, bowing my head and catching sight of Cara's tree. I missed her then. Missed her so much that it felt as though if I didn't get away from all the shadows in this place, I'd be swallowed up by them.

Rosa, Cara, Gina.

And now, Phoebe.

Another shadow to add to my misery if she threw me away like the trash I was.

Like I deserved to be discarded.

"Not all knights come to their damsels squeaky clean and bright white."

My eyes flared wide at that. "You're romanticizing this," I chided her, as I'd mentally chided her during my read through of her exam essay.

"Perhaps. But I want to write romance." She shrugged. "Who better to romanticize the unromanticizable?"

"Don't joke about this," I bit off.

"I'm not."

"I'll always support you," I rasped out the words, and even though they weren't intended cruelly, I knew from the way she stiffened up at my back she mistook it for being that.

"I can support myself," she ground out, her body arching away from mine.

"I don't want you to have to," I growled. "Fuck, can't you see that? Everything I've done, it's been to keep you safe. I don't want you struggling for anything."

I twisted around so I could glare at her, and before I knew what she was doing, her hand was cupping my cheek, and her thumb was tracing the wetness from tears I hadn't known were falling.

"I don't deserve you," I whispered brokenly, my face crumpling. "I'm sick and twisted. All poisoned inside. You should go. I should let you. You need better than me, you don't need this in your life."

She met my gaze, looked straight at me, and declared, "Perhaps you don't deserve me, perhaps you are poisoned inside, but maybe you have a lifetime to make up for it. Maybe, just maybe, you have a lifetime to find the cure."

My mouth quivered before I firmed my lips. "A lifetime?"

"If you want it?" For the first time since she stepped on the balcony, she seemed hesitant.

And she hadn't been like that since the soft smile she'd graced me with while she took the exam. But the scent of lasagna in the oven belied her nervousness. Her dress—she wore a kaftan with a vintage pattern—was relaxed for a night at home.

She knew, but she wasn't running.

She knew, but she wanted to stay.

If I wanted it? *If* I wanted her?

Fuck, I wanted nothing more.

And I'd spend the rest of my goddamn life proving it.

30

NICHOLAS

MUTUAL DESTRUCTION.

I should have known it would boil down to it.

Gina was fucking stupid, too stupid for her own or my good. Still, it was done now. Her future as ADA was in rags, and mine as a professor was too.

"Nicholas, it pains me to have to say this, but—"

I raised a hand at the dean, who had the grace to look exactly as he said—pained. As a personal friend of the family, I'd expected no less. He couldn't defend the indefensible, but also, I wasn't about to regret meeting Phoebe.

I tapped my fingers against the armrest. His desk was double wide and inlaid with a kind of nacre around the rim that made me wonder what pearls would look like against Phoebe's creamy flesh.

As I pondered that thought, I asked, "How did you find out?"

I knew the answer, but wanted confirmation, of course.

"Anonymous letters with photos, Nicholas." James Masterson winced. "In a public park, Nicholas? Really?"

My lips curved as zero guilt filled me. "It was quite decadent to be sure." As he huffed, slumping into his overlarge leather desk chair, I cut a look at the picture of his wife who peered at me from the frame.

Why did people do that?

Have frames aimed outward instead of inward?

My true crime here, of course, was being discovered. I knew even the dean was banging one of the students—in his case, a history postgrad.

His wife definitely wouldn't appreciate knowing James had a thing for men.

Sometimes, it was like being back a hundred years in the past.

These *dalliances* occurred, everyone accepted it, so long as you weren't caught.

I wouldn't say anything. Indeed, saw no need to, but the hypocrisy was alarming.

"This won't affect Phoebe's graduation?"

James shook his head. "I can rely on the integrity of your grading, can't I?"

I snorted—couldn't stop myself. "If anything, I've been too harsh on her."

"Thought as much." James hummed and his fingers slipped against the rim of his desk. "She's *magna cum laude*, Nicholas. The girl deserves to graduate."

Pride blossomed inside me, even as relief followed it—James was right. Phoebe did deserve to graduate. With her hard work, dedication to her studies, and caring for Scottie too, she deserved a damn medal.

"I'm glad," was all I said however.

"Dare I ask—"

"I'm going to marry her," I interrupted before he could piss me off.

James's eyes widened. "Does your mother know?"

I bared my teeth at him. "Since when do you think I listen to mommy dearest, James?"

"True." He winced. "Dammit to hell, Nicholas. Couldn't you have waited? I'm losing a fine professor because of this idiocy."

I couldn't stop my grin. "Would you avoid Liam if you could?"

Though James's cheeks flushed, he caught my eye with a despairing glance that told me his predicament. Except he had the ties of a wife and children, who had no idea he was gay.

They wouldn't understand, of course. There was no forgiveness in the world James and I inhabited. Just as there'd be no forgiveness for me when I brought Phoebe into our society. She wasn't cut from the right cloth, was born on the wrong side of the city, and therefore, was considered worthless.

To me, however, she was everything, and Gina and my parents had better watch themselves if they thought they had a cat in hell's chance of wrecking what I had with her.

Though I'd make Gina pay for this, I felt no compunction in shaking James's hand in farewell, heading out of his office, and subsequently leaving the faculty.

It was rather freeing, in fact.

My life had changed the day Phoebe walked into it, and maybe I'd been waiting on this moment since then.

I didn't want to be a professor anymore.

I didn't need to be.

Not now.

Was it strange to be smiling the day that my ex-wife's plans to ruin my life came to fruition?

Perhaps.

But I was going to enjoy it.

Every fucking moment of it.

Neither Phoebe nor Scottie were at the loft when I returned, and I headed toward my desk, collected the packet I had inside the locked drawer, and with a whistle, headed out pretty much as soon as I made it in.

I didn't bother getting my car out of the parking garage, instead, I caught a cab to the office which pulled up outside the park where I'd fingered my woman a few weeks ago.

The city was teeming, so busy it was miserable. If anything could put a damper on my day, it was *that*.

I was, I realized, beyond tired of this place. As vibrant as it was, as alive and frenetic, I was ready for something different. Greener pastures, a change. I supposed I just had to convince Phoebe of that.

As I paid the driver, I wondered if I could get Phoebe to agree to at least visiting France. Knowing her past, she would never imagine a trip there was possible and I'd bet that once she arrived in the land of love, my romantic would fall hard and fast for it too.

Wondering how we'd go around getting a passport for Scottie, I determined we'd have to adopt him, which would mean I'd have to find her mother. It ran the risk of her worming her way back into our lives, but I was okay with that—especially since we were going to head out of the country soon after.

Still, those thoughts were for later.

When I turned to look up at Gina's office, I laughed to myself before I began the approach to the gleaming glass doors with a smile. Aware, for once, that I was actually feeling cheerful.

Her ploy might have worked, but the war hadn't been won. If anything, I'd be the winner because her career meant everything to her, and with this proof, I'd be wrecking it, as well as dampening what her parents had strived for decades to achieve.

I should have felt guilty, instead, I was delighted.

For so long, I'd believed myself a monster because of Gina. It was finally time for her to face the consequences of her actions.

Arriving on the correct floor, I couldn't help but appreciate the irony that the only reason I managed to see her boss was because of my father's name, a name that meant nothing to me, but was important in the city.

When he saw me, I smiled at him, handed him the documents, and murmured, "I'd like you to deal with a little problem I'm having."

He frowned at me. "What kind of problem?"

"I have a stalker, and I need a restraining order. I'd like you to arrange that for me."

31

PHOEBE

THAT SAME EVENING

WHEN NICHOLAS ARRIVED HOME, it registered that a thought could taste good.

Home.

Delicious.

In such a short space of time, this loft had come to represent exactly that.

Funny how life worked out, wasn't it?

A smile curved my lips as I turned away from the bowl of couscous I was preparing for dinner, and I immediately jumped when I saw he was there.

Right behind me.

Not by the front door, not in the hall.

There.

I splatted my hand to my chest, aware my heart was pounding like crazy. "Jesus, you move quietly."

Something gleamed in his eyes.

A mixture of amusement and…

Fuck.

It was predatory.

That was the only way to describe that look.

His lips twitched. "I'm light on my feet."

Deep inside, my core started to react to the inherent threat entwined around that promise.

It shouldn't have been such a turn on.

"No wonder I didn't realize you were following me around," I groused, but I wasn't really mad.

Just shocked, I guessed.

I knew he was quiet; to the point where I sometimes thought I was alone in the apartment, but for the first time, I felt like his prey.

That shouldn't have sent quicksilver sparking through my veins.

He reached up and tugged at a lock of hair that had fallen out of the topknot I'd put it in. "You look beautiful."

I hid a smile. "Flattery will get you everywhere."

"Good to know," he teased, his finger tracing the curve of my ear as he tucked the lock of hair behind it.

"I'm sweaty from cooking."

He shrugged. "Delicious."

Shivering when he moved that finger lower, along the length of my throat, I let loose a deep breath as I leaned back against the counter. Nicholas instantly stepped into me, stunning me when he rubbed his dick into my belly.

His touch was incendiary.

I was so used to him making me touch myself, to him giving me no sign of his own arousal, that it was a wonder I didn't just melt into a puddle on the kitchen floor.

His mouth hovered above mine, his breath brushing the tender flesh, and he whispered, "Are you wet for me?"

"Y-Yes," I admitted shakily.

"You like being at the center of my attention, don't you, Phoebe?"

I nodded, then groaned as he rocked his hips, grinding his cock into my softness.

He'd backed up his compliment with action—that was my idea of a gentleman.

Lips parting, I waited for him to brush them with his own, only, he didn't. He traced around the circumference with his tongue.

I couldn't stop mine from fluttering out to play, and as they coiled around the other, I let my hands lift away from the counter that had been propping me up and curved them about his waist.

As he finally thrust his tongue into me, I cried out, unable to stop myself, just as he was unable to stop himself from swallowing the sound.

He pulled back. "Scottie's in bed?"

"He is," I said on a soft sigh when one hand moved to cup my breast.

He dragged down the neckline of one of Enid's kaftans and traced his fingers over the pouting curve.

There was something reverent about his touch.

I felt like I was being worshiped.

Shawn had made me feel as if I were something to nail to the wall with how he'd jack-hammered me. But Nicholas was devout. It never ceased to make me feel special. Unique.

Until his reverence faded, and his need took over.

I shuddered at the thought.

Slowly but surely, I was coming to meet this side of him.

The side that should disturb me, but instead, made me burn with desire.

His tongue licked along my jawline, teeth nipping here and there until he reached my ear. "You like knowing that I can creep up on you, don't you? You like being my prey."

The words sent a quiver of sensation surging up my spine.

The backs of his fingers rubbed my breast. "Don't you, Phoebe?"

"Y-Yes," I said on a groan.

"You like knowing that I'm watching you."

"Yes."

"That I know where you are."

"Yes."

"At all times."

I shuddered again, sagging into him.

There was something wrong with me—there had to be. But if he didn't mind, and if I didn't mind, it wasn't harming anyone. That was my logic, anyway.

One hand crept up his chest and the other delved between us. As I palmed his cock, he grunted, but my pussy clenched down. It was so fucking tired of being empty, exhausted of that gnawing ache only he could ease.

I tugged at his hair as I forced his mouth back onto mine, and I dove into him. Not letting him tease me or taunt me anymore. I needed him. Not words. I'd had words—now, I needed more action.

With a growl, he speared his tongue into me, and I moaned as he begun dragging the skirt of my kaftan up high, not stopping until he could delve between my thighs.

When his fingers brushed my bare sex, that growl of before turned into a snarl. "Never wear panties when you're home again," he snapped, as if I'd flouted his earlier rule instead of having obeyed it.

He'd robbed me of words though.

His fingers rubbed my clit, tweaking and circling the nub before drifting down to find my slit. As he fucked a finger into me, I surged onto tiptoe and he took full advantage of the situation.

Grabbing my leg, he dug his fingers into the soft flesh of my thigh, and dragged it high, tucking my foot around his hip. As my soaked pussy collided with the front of his pants, my head fell back as he devoured me there, sucking and biting and nipping as he fucked me with that single digit.

But it wasn't enough.

It could never be enough now.

I needed his cock.

I needed it so badly.

I didn't even realize I was whimpering, "I need your cock. Please, Nicholas. Give it to me. Please, please, please."

This was what he'd done to me.

He'd made me mindless for his dick.

When he reached between us, when he freed himself, when molten heat met molten heat and his hand moved away so that he could slot the tip of his shaft to my gate, I mewled as he thrust home.

There was that word again.

Home.

And he pounded it into me, bucking into my flesh, pumping hard so that I felt every goddamn inch filling me. So that it was etched into my cunt forever.

I let my hands grip his hair, and I tugged on it, uncaring if it hurt, just needing his mouth on mine.

Always on mine.

He'd starved me of his touch, and now, I'd never be able to get enough.

My orgasm leaped up at me, taking us both aback. My cunt clamped down, clutching at his shaft, dragging his seed from him, but he didn't come. He carried me through the first wave, not stopping as he grabbed me by the nape and brought his mouth to my ear again.

"This pussy is mine."

"Yes!" I cried.

"It belongs to me. Only to me."

"Always."

"You take me so good, Phoebe. So perfectly."

"So good, so good," I whispered.

"There's no one for me but you."

"No one," I sobbed. "Only me."

"Take my dick, baby. Take it. Just like that. Just…" He paused. Groaned. *Snarled.* "Just like that."

Short, fast thrusts had me howling as another climax sent me reeling. But this time, he came too. As he filled me to overflowing, he bit my earlobe, and rasped, "Love you."

My mouth trembled as I clung to him, well aware that he'd shown me that side of himself again.

Possessive.

Hungry.

Ravaging.

My beast.

He was coming out to play more and more often. The twin sides of his nature joining forces now that he knew I was his.

"Mine," I whispered, my lips like rubber as I dragged them over his jaw.

He shuddered. "Forever."

Sighing, I collapsed into him. Knowing that he'd prop me up. That he'd hold me in place.

Sad when his cock softened and started to slip out of me, I felt the rush of our release begin to drip down my inner thigh.

He made me moan by reaching between us, tracing his fingers through the fluids, then pulling back. I opened my mouth, knowing what he'd want before he asked, but he surprised me—his hand moved to his lips, not mine. I could feel my pleasure-exhausted body strum to life at the sight.

"Delicious," he rumbled, making my bones melt as he returned for a double dip.

Jesus.

I watched him, aware my eyes were heavy-lidded, aware that my pulse was thrumming in my veins then finally, he gave me a taste.

Us.

Perfect.

Beautiful.

Weird.

Once I'd cleaned his fingers, I propped my head against his shoulder. "Where did you go? I thought you'd be home when I got back."

"Home," he said with a sigh.

I didn't comment; not when the word tasted as good as we had. Instead, I just hummed.

"I went to destroy Gina's career."

My lips curved. "A dragon vanquished?"

He ran his nose down my temple. "Vanquished and sent to hell."

Exactly where that bitch deserved to rot.

PART 3

THE BEGINNING

32

NICHOLAS
A FEW MONTHS LATER

WHEN I NOTICED she was hovering by the doorway, I cast her a glance. When I saw that she was still wearing her cap and gown, I arched a brow at her. "The waiter brought the menus."

We were in a private room in *Gilt*, one of the area's newest eateries, to celebrate her day. Years of hard work had paid off—like James had told me, she'd graduated *magna cum laude*.

The only one who'd been surprised by her results was Phoebe.

It was beyond endearing how she didn't realize that she could have done so well. In all honesty, it was a testament to her intelligence *and* her dedication. That she placed so high when she was under such external pressure merely confirmed how dutiful a student my woman was.

When it registered that she was hovering there, not entering the private room I'd booked for us, I smiled at her in silent inquiry.

Only after I gave her my full attention did she react. My smile died when she parted the sides to reveal her bare form beneath her gown.

"Where the fuck are your clothes?"

"Do you really want to know?"

Her purr had me straightening in my seat. I beckoned her forward with my hand, watching as she moved toward me, her eyes slumberous with need.

"Did you tell the waiter to leave us alone?" I rumbled.

"I didn't," she said softly, then she surprised me by drifting to her knees and slipping beneath the table.

A groan escaped me when I peered between my legs and found her there, looking up at me. Her fingers, sure and confident, started to unfasten my zipper.

The last couple months had permitted a metamorphosis. The change in her was remarkable. I hoped that I had something to do with it, in some small part, but I knew that would be diminishing the journey she'd undertaken to reach this point.

Without work, without her studies, and without her mother influencing her life, as well as having someone to share the burden of caring for a baby, she'd blossomed. Her apathy had faded along with her exhaustion, meaning that Phoebe was no longer a pushover.

She fought fire with fire.

That was clear now. Deep in her eyes, the flames burned hotly.

"Payback," she whispered, making me smirk as she reached for my dick and dragged it out between the tines.

"You loved it," I taunted, "when I fingered you at the ceremony."

"You didn't let me come."

"James called your name," I said unapologetically.

"I want your dick," she hissed, her eyes narrowing with displeasure.

Phoebe wasn't satisfied without cock now.

Hallelujah.

Her tongue peeped out and she made a show of dragging it around the tip of my dick. As she got it nice and wet, then started sucking on it, I gritted my teeth, then slouched back in my seat so I could watch her work.

She allowed saliva to drip down my shaft then made a show of slurping up each trail. As her tongue prodded the sensitive flesh along the back of it, the door opened.

My nostrils flared as I turned to the waiter who moved over to me with a placid smile.

Quickly covering her face up with the tablecloth, I returned the smile, then felt a groan take root in my throat as she started sucking hard. The pressure was intense, and her tongue made shapes on my shaft that had me wanting to arch my hips up, fuck her face like she was begging.

"Is your wife okay? She's been gone for quite a while, sir. Would you like me to have one of the waitresses check in with her in the restroom?"

Wife.

Not yet, but soon. *Soon*—it was a silent promise to myself.

"No," I rasped, "it's okay. She had to head out to the drugstore. She won't be long. I can order for us both."

The server merely shrugged. "Of course. As you wish."

When I made the order, selecting dishes I thought would take the longest, and he kept on asking goddamn questions, I wasn't sure how I didn't come.

"The chef recommends Sauvignon Blanc with the sea bass—"

"Rare or medium or well done?"

"Would you like a Rioja with that?"

Each of my answers was served with a hard suck that made me wonder how my cum wasn't already at the back of her throat.

When he finally fucked off, closing the door behind him, the moment the click of closure sounded, I dragged the tablecloth away, gripped her by the nape and started to rock my hips. There was a glint in her eye that told me that was what she wanted.

Phoebe loved being worshiped.

But she loved her limits being tested.

When I watched her fingers drift between her legs as she circled her clit, I rasped, "Get those fingers away from my cunt."

She groaned around my shaft.

But she didn't listen.

I jacked my hips up, deep enough that her eyes widened, but I pulled back a scant second before she could gag.

"Put your fingers on your thigh, Phoebe," I growled.

She bobbed her head faster around my dick—her fingers stayed put.

Humming now, slurping me up like I was a melting popsicle, I gritted my teeth as I grabbed fistfuls of her hair and fucked her face like she wanted. As I pumped my cum down her throat, she gasped and shuddered and groaned as if she were the one getting off.

But I knew her secret.

Her fingers didn't do it for her anymore.

When the fiery need stopped burning me alive, when release sent a pleasant buzz through my veins, I pulled away and dragged the chair back to give her room, snarling, "Bend over the table."

Confusion had her frowning, but, shakily, she complied. *Almost.*

She made to move around to the side, but I didn't let her. I positioned her between my thighs, tapped one of her ankles with the edge of my shoe, and encouraged her to spread her legs. Then, as I stared at her pussy, a meal in itself, much better than anything the chef here could provide, I rumbled, "Tell me why I should eat you out when you didn't listen to me."

"Because nothing tastes better than my cunt."

Her words were like a hit of heroin to my bloodstream.

Her confidence lit me up like nothing else could.

Phoebe—owning her pleasure, knowing her worth—it was almost enough to give me another erection.

I didn't make her beg; we'd already proven that she'd tamed this monster. Instead, I dove between her thighs and I gave her what she needed.

She was dripping wet, juices slick and flowing from her pussy, and I lapped them up, drowning in her like she was a banquet. When she rocked back into me, shoving her ass into my face, I grabbed a hold of my dick again and started to jack off.

As I sucked on her clit, slurping and suckling, giving her what she needed, I didn't stop until she let off soft mewls that shot straight to my cock as if I hadn't just climaxed.

I retreated, aware my face was soaked with her juices, and her delirious sob made my heart race.

"Sit down," I ordered, grabbing her hips, and hauling her onto my lap.

She tumbled onto me, and I positioned her so that her thighs were on either side of mine. Spreading my knees parted her legs and, using that to my advantage, I cupped her mound from the front, grinding my palm into her as I hooked two fingers inside her. She yelped when I used that hold as leverage to make her squirm.

The maneuver let me get my cock right where she needed it—between her legs instead of under her ass—and I slipped the tip into her from behind.

Taking note that her tiptoes barely reached the floor, I ground out, "Get your pleasure, Phoebe."

I wished I could watch her, but it was enough knowing that we were in a restaurant, that she'd just graduated, that we weren't at home, that we could be disturbed at any moment, and that she was so hungry for my dick that she couldn't wait until we made it back to the loft.

She wriggled and writhed and gave it as good as she got but only when she was sobbing, "Nicholas, please, please," did I begin to arch my hips.

"I'm not Nicholas, Ms. Whitehouse. Who am I?"

A shudder rushed through her. "Professor."

I smiled, though she couldn't see it, and supplied her with exactly what she was begging for—*me*. All of me. The side of me that only she brought out into the light.

Whatever she wanted, whatever she craved, whatever she needed, I would always find a way to give it to her.

For eternity.

I didn't stop until she was grabbing one of the napkins and shoving it into her mouth. Fucking her, owning her, giving her what she creamed over—a side of punishment with her pleasure.

I slapped her inner thighs, then began to gently spank her pussy. When her back arched, I reached up and grabbed a taut hold of one of her tits, finding a nipple and squeezing until she burst with pleasure. Cascading over me. Exploding into a million pieces, yet grounded only by my cock inside her, one hand grinding into her clit, and the grip I had on her breast.

"Mine," I rumbled in her ear as my own end arrived.

"Yours," she slurred.

"Always."

"Give me you, Professor. Give me you."

"Always."

I let my own release fly free

Who was I to deny my most promising student?

33

NICHOLAS

FIVE MONTHS LATER...

"I HAVE A GIFT FOR YOU." When she ignored me, I sighed. "Phoebe?"

She retained her focus on the stage ahead, a boring musicale my mother had insisted on attending.

"In fact, I have several."

She still ignored me.

Sulking was her favorite way of making me pay, and dammit to hell, it often worked.

In the darkened shadows of my mother's box at the opera, I leaned close to her and, straight in her ear, hissed, "Spread your legs."

I felt her immediate tension, watched as she turned her head to glower at me. "Fuck. You."

"Please do," I purred. "Are they spread?"

She gritted her teeth so hard I feared for her jaw. And when her left eyelid began to flutter, I whispered, "Do it."

She fought me, God, how she tried. But she didn't and couldn't succeed.

This was our code.

One she had to obey.

Even if she didn't want to.

It was my mastery over her body, the rules I'd inadvertently set in stone at the inception of our relationship, that had her spreading her thighs and obeying, even though she wanted to throttle me as she complied.

Her eyes promised death but I welcomed it, so long as it was at her side.

I smirked at her, aware that would infuriate her, but that was what I wanted.

Her fire.

Not her ice.

My mother was like liquid nitrogen. Capable of freezing even a woman like Phoebe, especially when she lorded it over her, using our family's name and wealth to scare her.

Take tonight.

It was the first time I'd introduced my parents to the woman who was my everything, and they'd brought us to the fucking opera.

I loathed the opera. They knew that. You didn't have to have blue goddamn blood to appreciate this shit, and yet they'd done it to frighten her. To make her realize what she was and where I came from.

My family had their private box, lived in a building that cost hundreds of thousands of dollars a year in taxes alone, and the price tag on their apartment was more than most millionaires could afford.

Each of those facts they'd rammed home very neatly. *Too neatly.* I smelled Gina in the wings.

For whatever reason, she'd always been able to get my mother on her side. Probably because my mother recognized the likeness between them.

How Gina had explained away her own dismissal, I wasn't sure, but I was content with her reputation being ruined on a professional front. Whether she turned my parents against Phoebe and me was something I frankly didn't give a damn about.

But I'd tried.

They'd never be able to say I hadn't.

I'd brought her to them with the intention of a truce, and here I was, stuck with the cold shoulder from the woman who meant more to me than life itself, while I was wailed at by a fat lady in a Viking costume.

Dear God.

My mother couldn't have tortured me more. Wagner? I hated him more than any of the other dreadful composers I'd had to endure over the years.

"Are you wet?" I whispered into her ear, finding Phoebe far more entertaining than anything else in my vicinity as per usual.

She gulped. "No. I'm furious."

I couldn't blame her, even if I did appreciate the tight longing I heard in her voice. My darling was quite accustomed to me saving her, and save her I would.

"Don't you want to know what my gifts are?" I enticed.

"No. Not unless it involves one-way tickets out of this hellhole."

I snorted. "Glad to know you hate the opera too."

"It's nothing to do with that. It's—"

"I know exactly what it is." I reached over and patted her knee. It was the last thing I wanted to do. I wanted to slip my fingers between her legs and explore her glorious pussy, claim it for my own once more, and taste her delicious cunt like it was a meal and I was a man dying of starvation.

Just the thought had my cock hardening, but I knew for a fact that she'd never come. No matter how hard I teased her, enticed her, and seduced her, my mother's rudeness had done the impossible.

Turned my woman cold.

Fuck, I loathed the creature who'd had her belly spliced open to bring me to life, and she could be damn sure that the only way I'd ever visit was if she fucking begged me to.

Even then, it had better be worth my while.

"What's my gift then?"

"Gifts," I corrected instantly, hearing the sulky sigh in her voice and knowing that was the point where Phoebe's mood turned around.

It always worked.

Just a reminder of who I was to her, her *professor*, even if I'd been cast out for my deviancy, was enough to ground her.

And didn't I just love her all the more for that?

"Okay, gifts," she whispered.

I pulled out the four items I had in my various pockets, and as she peered down in the gloom, I saw her surprise. Hell, I couldn't blame her—I'd been feeling like a walking purse since we left the loft.

"What are they?"

I passed the watch to her, then grabbed the other and placed it around my wrist, securing it before I reached for hers and did the same.

She tilted the face this way and that, and I allowed her some time to discern what she was looking at because it was damn dark in here.

When she recognized them, her mouth dropped open. "You didn't!"

My lips curved. "Would you expect anything less from me?"

She swallowed thickly, her throat visibly working before, with awe in her tone, she muttered, "Mrs. Linden's? E-Enid's?"

I nodded, and her hand snapped out to grab mine. She squeezed my fingers so tightly that it almost hurt, but I understood. She was showing me her emotion the only way she could at that moment.

I raised our joined hands, brought them to my lips, and kissed her knuckles.

"Gifts number one and two," I informed her, including the man's vintage Rolex as a gift, one I'd wear forever for her, even though she knew I didn't wear any jewelry.

I would be soon, however. At least, if I had my way.

She blinked. "Number three?"

This one was a piece of paper, and it had been fucking hard to get too. I passed over the few sheets of A4 that signified Scottie's change of status. Again, I watched as she tilted and turned it, trying to read every word. I knew the second she did because her nails dug into my thigh.

"How?"

"Money."

Her throat worked, the muscles playing in the meager light from the stage. "She sold him?"

I sighed. "Don't think of it that way. He's ours now."

"Nicholas…" Her voice wavered, but I heard the tears in it, heard the emotion, and I smiled at her before leaning over and kissing her on her trembling lips.

"You're welcome, but I didn't do it for a 'thank you,'" I informed her.

I did it for Scottie, and for us.

We were a family in everything but the eyes of the law. Well, fuck that. Now the law was on our side, and that was how it should be.

I wasn't going to allow that bitch into our lives any more than necessary. Phoebe had given her an ultimatum, a fair one, and her mother hadn't heeded it.

Well, I had, and I'd moved things to a formal, legal footing.

"I know, and that's what makes it more incredible because you did it anyway."

I grinned at her, knowing that she'd never anticipate the final gift. Especially not when my mother was shuffling at our side, silently informing me of her displeasure at our inattention to the travesty going on downstage.

With the box in my grasp, I recognized that my palms weren't even sweating as I handed that to her too. I wasn't nervous. I was beyond ready for this moment. It felt like my entire life had been leading toward tonight—to here, to now. Even if it was with Wagner serenading us in the background.

And when she opened it, her fingers feeling for the contents, every part of her was tense as though my mother, the Queen of the Damned herself, had frozen her solid.

She hadn't, of course.

Mother was closer to me than to Phoebe, by my design. The last thing I wanted when I'd seen the initial reception of my fiancée-to-be, was for the two of them to be seated beside one another.

Phoebe's mouth trembled. "Nicholas... it's too soon."

My brow furrowed. "Not soon enough," I complained, and was stunned when she laughed.

Laughed.

That wasn't in my plan.

"Well, then?" she prompted, and I blinked *and* frowned at her. "Don't you have something to ask me?"

Ah.

My grin made a swift reappearance.

"Don't you already know the question?"

"I'm sure I do," she half-purred, in a tone that had my cock leaping to attention. "But a girl likes to be asked."

And so, I did as my girl wanted.

I asked.

And she answered.

34

PHOEBE

FIVE YEARS LATER

THE HOT SUMMER sun burnished my skin, spreading warmth throughout my bones. I'd never had the time to sunbathe before. Hell, I'd never had the inclination either. Here, everything was different than New York though.

We had space to roam, space to grow. It felt endless, and when, in the evening, I stared over the vines that belonged to us, it felt like a dream.

I was in France.

More than that, I lived here now.

This was our home.

Our haven.

As I shifted against the railing, I felt the vibrator that Nicholas had insisted I insert before he left. He liked to keep tabs on me, even from afar, but it had been suspiciously still this afternoon.

Which meant he'd either been preoccupied or he was planning something.

I hoped that something involved at least three orgasms—what could I say? He'd made me greedy.

Raising my arm, I checked Mrs. Linden's Rolex, and was surprised to see that it had been quite a while since both my guys had gone out. Of course, the second that thought crossed my mind, I heard him.

"Mommy!" Scottie squealed from somewhere in the house.

My lips curved as Scottie came hurtling toward me. He barreled into my legs, cupping them tightly through one of Mrs. Linden's dresses as he hugged me like he hadn't seen me in days.

His puppy, Barbie the Barbet, a French water dog, came barreling out, knocking into him, who then knocked into me, as I used the stone balustrades to prop myself up.

"Be careful, Scottie," Nicholas growled; there as ever to catch me if I were in danger.

Though it was stupid to think I was in danger on our vineyard, he wasn't altogether wrong.

I had twins inside me now, and they messed with my equilibrium in a way that wasn't even funny. He spent most of his time keeping my clumsy ass vertical.

I wasn't even sure how he did it, and often teased him that his stalking days had been a warm-up for the torment of married life with me.

"Don't even joke about it," he'd grumbled, but though his mouth had been downturned at the corners, his eyes had sparkled.

I loved that.

Loved making him smile, even when he didn't want to.

My husband was a complicated man.

Some might say he was twisted, and the truth was, I'd agree with them. He was scarred, mentally and physically, from his first marriage, and losing his daughter had shaped him in ways that I knew made the fact I was pregnant petrifying.

For all that, I'd caught the glint of satisfaction on his face when I'd told him I was pregnant. I knew this was the final tie he needed to know I wasn't going anywhere, and I was fine with that.

Fine with him, because I loved him.

Warts and all.

Some might think me stupid, might believe I was as crazy as he was. But those 'some' had never been raised by an alcoholic mother.

Had never been dragged through CPS as a small child. Had never had to fend for themselves with an infant baby who wasn't even theirs…

My circumstances had forged me just as they'd forged my Nicholas, and that made me appreciate what he'd done.

Yes, he'd stalked me. Hunted me from the shadows, keeping me safe, protecting me from the harsh realities of life as much as he could from his position.

Hadn't he been there to find me the job I'd desperately needed when I hadn't had a clue how I was going to pay my bills? Hadn't he been there to give me shelter when the time had come for me to break free from my mother's reach?

Yes, to many, after how we'd met, what he'd done, he could be considered sick and twisted, but to me, he was perfect *because* of it.

He was my knight, tarnished for sure, but I wanted him no other way.

Scottie peered up at him from beneath a mop of curls that matched my own. "Sorry, *Papa*. I didn't mean to knock Mommy over."

We weren't sure why I was '*Mommy*' and Nicholas was '*Papa*,' but the bicultural life suited our son and we weren't about to change that, not when we wanted him to be as much American as he was French.

We were laying down roots in the Bordeaux region, and we intended for those roots to endure for him and the babies who'd yet to be born.

"Just be careful," Nicholas grumbled, even as he tucked some curls out of Scottie's face. "You need a haircut."

Scottie's face crunched into one big pucker. "No! I had one three weeks ago."

"Well, you need another one. Maybe that's why you're as clumsy as your mother, because you never know which way you're going." He huffed, then eyed Barbie who had almost as many curls as Scottie and me. "I swear, these babies had better come out with straight hair, or they'll be the death of me."

I laughed up at him, eyes twinkling with love. "Or they'll scare you straight?"

"Oh, I'm as straight as a ruler." So subtly that Scottie wouldn't notice, he rocked his hips into me. I felt his hardness and inwardly shivered as he moved his mouth to my ear and whispered, "You're a sight for sore eyes, Mrs. Maclean."

My throat felt thick. "You've only been gone since lunch."

"Too long," he groused. "I don't like leaving you."

"You were gone for three hours, Nick. Hardly a lifetime." When he grumbled some more, I murmured, "I spent most of it lying down anyway—I was finishing up my chapter."

"You didn't rush it, did you? I told you to rest."

He'd been telling me that since I'd reached the final trimester, but dammit, I was invested in the story we were crafting and, babies or no, we had a deadline.

Our publishers were eager for the next chapter in our award-winning series, and hell, I was too. I loved the way we created stories together, and it was a dream come true that someone actually wanted to read what I wrote.

We'd piggy-backed part of the plot from the book I'd written as my final assignment in Nick's class, and we'd used some of his content from 'Elizabeth's' transcriptions to create the first novel in a series critics loved.

Never in a million years had I thought we'd be doing this, especially not together, but co-authoring we were, and I was thankful every day for that.

Scottie, not happy about being cut out of the conversation, and well aware that we got lost to our plotting without prompt, tugged on my hand. "*Papa,* can we show her?"

They'd gone to buy clothes for Scottie who was running through them at a rate that made me grateful Nicholas was rich.

Very rich.

More than any of his students would have believed.

"Show me what?" I asked warily, thoughts of our main characters abandoned.

Nicholas tensed. "Later, Scottie."

Inwardly, I groaned. "What have you done now?"

"She's so beautiful, Mommy."

My eyes widened. "Who is?"

"Her name is Brownie."

"Brownie?" I tugged out of Nicholas's arms. "Show me, Scottie." I glowered at Nick over my shoulder, well aware my husband had bought something *else*.

We already had two roosters that woke me up in the morning, a coop's full of chickens that he had to collect the eggs from because they hated me, and a pissed off goat that bleated at us all the damn time.

We were turning into Animal Farm, and we weren't even supposed to be farming!

Scottie's giggles were infectious though, and as he dragged me from the tiled terrace that overlooked the neat rows of bright green vines and, in the distance, a church steeple that also acted as an irritating alarm clock, I let myself be dragged into his excitement.

He hauled me through the patio doors and into the library. It was, technically, Nicholas's study, but I found myself in there frequently—old habits died hard—and I had a sofa in there, as well as a small writing desk of my own since it was where we'd begun working together.

In the recessed bookshelves, there were the jade figurines that had been one of my initial prompts for realizing Nicholas was the one behind the journals.

My lips curved at the sight of the antiquities that he had lovingly wrapped as he brought them here, to the home we made together, away from the misery we left in New York City.

The mother who had never gone through with my ultimatum and who I hadn't heard from to this day.

The parents who preferred to believe the miserable ex over their son, and who couldn't see anything good in me after their private investigator revealed I was from Brownsville and not some swank part of Manhattan.

After I'd graduated, when I'd started making moves to earning a teaching degree and had conceded defeat by looking into hiring a nanny, Nicholas had found me sobbing in our bedroom—I didn't want someone else to raise Scottie.

Didn't want someone else to be the one who kissed his boo-boos, and I didn't want to go out into a workplace that truly wasn't where my heart was anyway.

My job would only have covered the nanny's pay and a little more, so what was the point?

When I'd told him that, he'd merely said, "I wondered when you'd come to that realization."

My robot was also my hero but he was slowly getting better, and he had a lifetime to soften up.

But, without any ties to work, after he'd proposed with his mother grumbling in the background and a fat lady hollering at us in German, a few months later, we'd come over here to get married, and we'd stayed. We hadn't gone back to the States since. And I had zero regrets about that.

Zero.

From the library-cum-study, Scottie dragged me through the foyer of the house that was way too big for just the three of us—even twins wouldn't fill up all these rooms—and took me out the front door and into what I called the backyard but what was, essentially, farmland.

When we passed the huge oak tree where I'd spread Mrs. Linden's ashes, I smiled inwardly as I always did—she'd never have imagined me in France, married and pregnant at this age, but I knew she'd be happy for me. Knew it like I could hear her whisper those words to me in the flesh.

Ten feet on, and I came face to face with a paddock that, until now, had been empty.

The horse was huge. Stocky. And old. Its brown hair was twisted with gray, and its muzzle was as well.

One thing I hated about France, something Nicholas did too, was that they ate horsemeat—on the regular.

I cut Nicholas a look, well aware that he was right behind me, and he shrugged.

Knowing that I was correct, that he'd spared this horse from the butcher, I sighed but… how could I be mad at that?

This crazy, impossible man who stalked me to keep me safe, rescued horses from the butcher, with whom I co-wrote bestselling psychological thrillers, and who was the father to my three children.

When I blew out a breath, I turned back and saw that Scottie had taken off without me, and was running around the paddock, with Barbie barking at his side as they followed the poor horse as it trundled around its new home.

I didn't have to turn around to know the exact moment he moved behind me—I felt his warmth sink into my bones.

"We're going to turn into a horse sanctuary, aren't we?" I predicted glumly.

It wasn't that I was averse to the idea of building a sanctuary, but I didn't like horses. They scared me, and I sure as hell didn't want Scottie riding them. Or Nicholas.

I'd seen him on the back of one of them when, at his mother's request, he'd played a game of polo on a trip to the Hamptons one time.

It had scared the hell out of me.

Horses were so volatile. What if he fell? What if he got hurt? Injured, or worse?

Nicholas was my rock. My everything. I couldn't deal with him getting hurt, not without it spearing me in turn.

"Maybe," he admitted, mumbling the words sheepishly. "It depends. If I turn hermit, then I'll—"

I snorted. "You'd find a way."

"True, but I couldn't just let—"

I knew that, and I loved him for it. "Of course."

I patted the hand that slipped around my belly. As I leaned into him, resting against my professor, I released a sigh when, deep inside, the buzz of the vibrator he'd triggered burst to life.

Even as good as it felt, I had to smile.

He always synced it to the same two songs.

Songs that fit us perfectly.

Tainted Love.

We'd started that way.

Tainted. Dark. Stained.

But now?

The song merged into a new one.

One that he'd added to the toy's playlist.

Ain't No Mountain High Enough.

As my body enjoyed the low throb that rumbled along my nerve endings, more than anything, I felt the meaning of those songs deep in my core.

"I love you," he breathed into my ear.

And my smile was big and beatific as I watched my son and his dog play with a horse who really didn't feel like playing, as one of his babies slept in my belly while the other danced on my bladder, as his arms wrapped around me as though I were the center of the world.

Because I knew he loved me.

Heart and soul.

Tainted, but pure for us because, to him, I was the universe.

There was no other in his line of sight. No one else in his worldview.

With that in mind, I snuggled deeper into him, and whispered back, "I love you too."

And those words barely scratched the surface of what we felt for one another, but they'd do.

Until I could show him properly later on tonight.

35

PHOEBE

FOUR YEARS LATER

"SPREAD YOUR LEGS."

I narrowed my eyes at him. "I'm not twenty-one anymore, you know."

His lips twitched. "Because you're oh, so ancient at thirty?"

His cocked brow had me wanting to reach over so I could stroke it, but I didn't because he was being mean. "It's my birthday. You're supposed to be nice to me."

"I gave you a diamond necklace. Isn't that being nice?"

At his croon, I shrugged but reached up so I could play with the expensive links on a necklace that probably required a security guard to follow me around every time I wore it—I didn't need another stalker, I already had one and he was sitting opposite me.

Cocking my brow back at him, I retorted, "Did I ask for a diamond necklace?"

That had him huffing. "You never ask for anything."

"That's because I'm content with what I have."

"If I gave you the world it still wouldn't be enough."

His impassioned words had tears clogging up my throat.

Fuck.

How did he do this to me?

How could he still, after all these years, make me melt without even really trying?

And yes, this was Nicholas *not* trying. This was him just being Nicholas. I knew because there wasn't a hint of a smile on his face or buried within the depths of his eyes. There wasn't even a hint of those lines that appeared at the corners of his mouth.

Nicholas was being serious.

If he could give me the world then he damn well would.

Inside, everything just melted, and I couldn't stop myself from getting out of my seat, rounding the table, and plunking myself in his lap.

I didn't care that we were in a restaurant.

Didn't care that it was a place that held two Michelin stars.

Nicholas didn't care either, and I loved him for that.

His smile was back now, and I heard it in his voice as he murmured, "Well, if that was what it took to get you on my knee I'd have told you that earlier."

My lips curved but I kept my face buried in his throat.

"*Monsieur*, is everything all right with *madame*?"

I could sense the server's panic, but I couldn't do anything to ease his mind except for waft a hand at him and, into Nicholas' throat, mumble, "I'm fine."

Nicholas replied in French, but even after so many years here, I hated speaking the language so I tuned him out. Terrible, I knew, but God, it was hard. Really hard. Especially when Nicholas, Scottie, Margot and Alexandra all rattled away in it like it was their mother tongue.

There was only one advantage—Nicholas spoke it to me in bed.

Yum.

"You're causing quite a stir," Nicholas said when I sensed we'd been left alone by the waiting staff.

I also sensed that that notion didn't perturb him. If anything, he was amused by it.

"These people are all robots," I retorted, only pulling back to accuse him of, "You were a robot too."

"Before you." He nodded, then his lips pursed. "And Scottie. I think Scottie did more to humanize me than you did."

"Thanks!" I retorted with a sniff, but I wasn't really peeved. It always made me want to cry when he said things like that.

Those tiny remarks were the only way in which he made it known Scottie wasn't his biological son because, to Nicholas, in every other way, Scottie was ours.

Nicholas grinned at me. "Don't pout."

"You like it when I pout," I retorted.

"Around my dick," he conceded, his tone turning gravelly, his mind drifting where I wanted it—my graduation day.

I smirked at him, knowing full well we were on the same page.

"You're lucky we're in a very public place or I'd have my hands under this incredibly sexy dress."

A dress I wouldn't fit in much longer.

That was why I was wearing the strapless black velvet number tonight. With its sweetheart neckline that cupped my breasts, and the pencil skirt that made every curve pop... I looked like sin, and Nicholas loved me in black.

Well, technically, he loved me in everything and out of everything too.

I squirmed on his lap. "Remind me why you brought me here again? I'd have been quite happy to stay at the apartment."

Sadly, the restaurants here didn't have any private rooms.

He grunted as my hip nudged his dick when I wriggled. "Don't tempt me."

"I only have to breathe to do that, don't I?" I countered, my tone sugar sweet.

When he narrowed his eyes at me, I barely stopped myself from laughing, and as I slipped my hand between us, I let the edge of my palm rub over the tent in his pants.

He was hard for me, and just like that, I was wet for him.

"Next year, do us both a favor and listen to me. No restaurants, no clothes—"

"No kids?"

At his knowing smirk, I grimaced. "Well… you know I hate being without them."

He'd bought an apartment in Paris that we used as a base for business. We stayed in the city and left the children with the nanny back home, but I hated leaving them. Hated it with every ounce of my being.

Only knowing they were happier at the house made it any better.

"You think I don't?"

God, that was true.

If I was protective of our children, Nicholas was worse. Part of me was terrified he'd worry himself into an early grave, but another part of me just accepted that this was who he was.

He worried.

Constantly.

He checked in on us.

Constantly.

We were his obsession.

There wasn't anything I could do to ease that for him, nothing I could even say. The only option open to me was to be aware of his needs, to try to help him when I could.

Nicholas was no ordinary man. No ordinary husband or father, either.

I knew most women complained about complacent husbands, but Nicholas, God, he noticed everything.

Sometimes, he made me feel like a terrible mother for not picking up on all the stuff that he 'detected,' but we were at the center of his universe—why wouldn't he see every last detail?

That wasn't to say my family didn't mean the world to me, but I just wasn't like him. I didn't see things how Nicholas did. He saw threats everywhere. He calculated risks better than an insurance assessor, and that was why I was fucking *amazed* that he hadn't spotted how tender my breasts were, how sensitive my skin was, and how I'd been feeling queasy in the afternoon for the past month.

I didn't think he was even hiding his knowledge of my pregnancy either. Now that Nicholas knew I loved him, warts and all, he was terrible at hiding things. And another child? Nope, he'd never have let that slide.

His hands fluffed at my hair before he stroked down the long curly strands bobbing around my shoulders.

"Are we eating like this?" he questioned, sounding amused again.

I knew I did that a lot. Made him laugh. It was silly but I often feared for him, fretted over what his life would have been like if I hadn't come barreling into it. It scared me because I doubted there'd be much laughter for Nicholas without us in it.

That might have been a lot of responsibility to accept, but the weight of that mantel had settled on my shoulders a long time ago. I didn't buckle under its pressure, but I did worry for him.

Of course, that was ironic, wasn't it?

Worrying over the worrier?

Talk about unnecessary.

"Just tip the server more," I countered, rocking into him again. "I'm comfortable."

He snorted. "I'm not sure you will be when my soup arrives."

I pouted again. "Next year—"

"Yes, yes," he countered. "Next year we'll eat sandwiches and chips in bed. How's that, pleb?"

Grinning up at him, I retorted, "Like you're not a pleb too." Holding up my hand, I ticked down on my fingers. "Who eats more Cheetos than me? Who craves Krispy Kremes? Who wishes there was a Seven Eleven around the corner for a slurpee—honestly, Nicholas, I never imagined you were such a sugar fiend."

He squinted at me. "You're just as bad."

"Since when?" I blustered. "I've dropped forty pounds since we moved to France."

It was his turn to pout. "And I miss every single one of them."

I blinked up at him, well aware that he meant that. He loved me chunky or slender. Loved me as I was because he loved *me*.

Fuck.

Just… fuck.

He took my breath away.

My throat was thick, all thoughts robbed from me at his words, as I managed to whisper, "You'll have a chance to grab my curves again soon."

His brows furrowed as he stared at me. His sartorial elegance highlighted by the swank environs of the expensive restaurant, his handsome features exposed in the flickering candlelight. "What? Why?"

Gulping, I reached up and laid a hand over his heart. "I'm pregnant again."

His eyes flared wide at my words. For a second, his nostrils flared too as he processed what I was saying. I could see him, the mental calculator at play as he assessed the risks and the dangers.

I half expected him to chide me for having another baby after the twins had been a nightmare to deliver and then the months of him being terrified one of them would fall to SIDS like Rosa had.

I half expected him to be angry because I was over thirty now and though the risks were pretty minimal as lots of moms had kids at this age, one risk was one too many for my professor.

But, as ever, he surprised the hell out of me.

When his mouth opened, the words that slipped from him weren't a reprimand, weren't harsh with his fear for me and the child I carried. No, they were loaded down with his emotions to be sure, but the meaning?

I'd have to be a moron to misunderstand.

"Check, please," he called out, and with that, he stood up, helped me to my feet and hustled me out of the restaurant.

My lips curved.

Someone was about to get naked.

Me.

A FEW THINGS...

The Yayoi Kasuma print that reminded Nicholas of his relationship with Phoebe can be found here: https://www.artsy.net/artwork/yayoi-kusama-endless-life-of-people

FREE BOOK!

Don't forget to grab your free e-Book!
Secrets & Lies is now free!

Meg's love life was missing a spark until she discovered her need to be dominated. When her fiancé shared the same kink, she thought all her birthdays had come at once, and then she came to learn their relationship was one big fat lie.

Gabe has loved Meg for years, watching her from afar, and always wishing he'd been the one to date her first and not his brother. When he has the chance to have Meg in his bed—even better, tied to it—it's an opportunity he can't refuse.

With disastrous consequences.

Can Gabe make Meg realize she's the one woman he's always wanted? But once secrets and lies have wormed their way into a relationship, is it impossible to establish the firm base of trust needed between lovers, and more importantly, between sub and Sir…?

This story features orgasm control in a BDSM setting.
Secrets & Lies is now free!

CONNECT WITH SERENA

For the latest updates, be sure to check out my website!
But if you'd like to hang out with me and get to know me better, then I'd love to see you in my Diva reader's group where you can find out all the gossip on new releases as and when they happen. You can join here: www.facebook.com/groups/SerenaAkeroydsDivas. Or you can always PM or email me. I love to hear from you guys: serenaakeroyd@gmail.com.

ABOUT THE AUTHOR

I'm a romance novelaholic and I won't touch a book unless I know there's a happy ending. This addiction is what made me craft stories that suit my voracious need for raunchy romance. I love twists and unexpected turns, and my novels all contain sexy guys, dark humor, and hot AF love scenes.

I write MF, menage, and reverse harem (also known as why choose romance,) in both contemporary and paranormal. Some of my stories are darker than others, but I can promise you one thing, you will always get the happy ending your heart needs!